CALL THE BLUFF

ACES HIGH, JOKERS WILD BOOK 2

O. E. TEARMANN

CALL THE BLUFF

Originally published in 2018 by Spine Press and Post

Amphibian Press
P. O. Box 190
West Peterborough NH
03468

www. amphibianpressbooks. com
www. aceshighjokerswild. com

Printed in the United States of America

ISBN: 978-1-949693-85-0

Event File 1
File Tag: Base of Operations
Timestamp: 10:00-10-30-2155

WHUMP!

The explosion sent a geyser of dust into the sky. Base Commander Aidan Headly cursed as pebbles rained down on him. He crawled out of the empty cistern pit he'd leaped into and stood, trying to wave the dust away without much success. The grit settled on him like a second skin.

Adrenaline was treating his guts like its personal skate park and taking some extra turns around his heart. But that wasn't his biggest problem right now. Hell, it didn't make top ten on his list.

He scrambled up the hill and raised his voice.

"What the hell was that? We weren't supposed to be blowing anything up today!"

Two dark faces peered out from under helmets in their own culvert, trepidation in their eyes. Aidan sighed. Dilly and Donny. Again.

The twins had turned thirteen a week ago. Maybe he should be happy that they had started begging to do vocational apprenticeship the minute they'd gotten out of bed on their birthday, but if they kept up this kind of crap they wouldn't live to fourteen.

"Sorry Aidan!" the girl called."We're trying out a new setting mechanism!" The boy beside her hollered over. "I think I know what I did wrong!"

"You better know what you did wrong," Aidan growled as he scrambled down the other side of the new site's hill toward his charges, chest still tight with the dregs of his fear. "We can't afford a blast like that again, you hear me? You guys know how dangerous drawing attention is!"

Dilly flinched. Her twin's shoulders stiffened.

"Okay, but we hit water!" Donny countered, "There's water down there, and—"

"The fuck did you two little gamma-gets do?!"

Both twins flinched as Janice Danvers climbed out of the nearest water tank, still on its side and empty so soon after the base's site change. Fire in her black eyes, the hydroelectrics specialist stalked across the dusty red earth and grabbed the collars of both teenagers' ponchos like the scruffs on a pair of puppies, shaking them in what looked like ferocity. Since the kids were barely shifting for all the show Janice put on, Aidan pushed down his instinct to step between an angry adult getting physical and a pair of kids. In the seven months since Aidan had taken his place commanding the Wildcards unit of the Democratic State Force, he'd learned to let Janice have her say with anyone pulling idiot stunts. She was a more effective scolder than him any day.

"The ever-loving frag grenade-fucking hell does 'wait till I get it damped down' mean to you two little sons of sister-fuckers, hunh?! Or how 'bout 'let me check your work 'fore we go to the next bit?!'" Janice demanded. "I said wait! You coulda' killed yourselves, you cluster-fucked CPS dumbasses! What are you, a pair of gammas? This's the middle of a relocation setup, you think I got time for you two playin' around? You wanna help me out you listen to me, you hear?!" She knocked their heads together, and Aidan noted the control the muscled woman used in doing it: just hard enough to sting, nowhere near hard enough to do the damage Janice could have dished out.

"Aw Jan—" Dilly began, but Janice cut her off.

"Ah! Don't start. You two ain't—" She glanced up, caught sight of another dark figure in the blazing sun and raised her voice. "Damian! Come over here an' deal with your family!"

Turning, the scarecrow of a man got a look at the two dust-covered teenagers. He sighed, putting a hand over his cybernetic eyes. "Dilly, Donny, what'd you do now?"

"Nothing!" Dilly defended. Striding over, Damian set a hand on each teenager's shoulder, raising a brow. His ocular implants whirred, punctuating the expression.

"*Nothing*, hunh?" He glanced with pointed attention from the crater, to the boxes of explosive material much too close for comfort, to the teens. "Funny, doesn't look like *nothing* to me."

Dilly rolled her eyes, letting out a dramatic sigh. "Fiiine. We screwed up. Sorry."

The medical officer gave his superior a wry smile. "Sorry about the monsters, Aidan. 'Go help out,' I said. I should've known better. These two are working in the garage for the rest of the week," he added darkly, letting go of Dilly long enough to straighten the wide-brimmed hat on his shaved head. Today everybody in their eighteen-man crew wore the brown ponchos and wide-brimmed hats that had earned their Force the nickname of Dusters. Inlaid with coolant, the gear kept them comfortable and made sure they weren't spotted on infrared by EagleCorp's ViperDrones. The clothes would be some protection until the base that sustained them was set up and secure again.

Aidan found himself reflexively glancing up. The readings had given them a window of a few hours before the next drone pass. Technically, they were safe for now. But blowing holes in the Dust would make them a new point of interest if the blast had been picked up by a satellite.

He forced his eyes down. If a drone was up there, it wouldn't have waited this long to drop a bomb. He knew that.

Out of the corner of his eye, he spotted Janice stealing a glance upwards.

Aidan reminded himself to take a breath, shrugging as he motioned to the crater. "They did find water, Damian. So I'd say their punishment is hauling it up and storing it for us."

Both kids groaned.

"But water hauling sucks!" Dilly whined.

Janice gave her a deadpan look. "Shoulda' thoughta that 'fore you fucked up. Get the pipes an' the lil' pump an' get over there, I ain't baby-sittin' you two no more today. Git!"

When the teens were out of earshot, Janice turned to her base mates with a sigh. "I swear those two are gonna give me a heart attack. I ain't never lettin' them assist again."

"Funny, I thought I heard that last time." Damian stated, face unreadable. "And when I heard it last time, I had thought for some reason that we made an agreement about my sibs staying away from things that go bang."

Janice gave the man a scathing look. "An' who told 'em to 'go help' an' let 'em off the leash with no moren' that? An' who's their minder around here? Cause I ain't wearin' no frilly hat an' I don't think I look much like the nanny, d'you?"

Aidan knew Janice's drawling agricultural worker's accent only grew that thick when she was rattled. Beside him, Damian opened his mouth, but Aidan spoke first.

"Guys? Relocation days suck for everybody."

Damian had the good grace to nod in acknowledgment, leaving whatever he'd planned to say unspoken.

Aidan watched the teens manhandle the temporary water pump into place, attach it to a primary cistern tank and start spooling the weighted siphon line down into the hole, where it could get to work pulling up water. The groundwater from the aquifer would be decontaminated by the systems inside the cistern, before being hooked into the base's plumbing. It'd make a good stop-gap while the main water drilling rig was being calibrated to supplement the base's water-recycling system.

We really need to get better at water recycling and depend less on ground water sources, Aidan thought with dismay. *This aquifer might be as good as Janice thought, but the aquifers are getting smaller all the time.*

"Keeping them away from explosives is probably good for everybody... they didn't screw up the well though, did they?" He glanced at the three full cistern tanks they had, squatting like deformed pineapples on wheels off to his left. The reflective condensate fins designed to catch any humidity in the air during the cool nights and turn it into supplemental water gleamed dully in the sun. The supply of water in the tanks was all the crew had until Janice, Topher and Dozer finished hooking up the systems. Was it enough? They'd come to this site for the water. If they had to drill a new well, would the water last that long?

Janice waved a hand. "Nah, we hit shale an' I didn't want the fuckin' stuff collapsin' everywhere, was the reason for the new setting mechanism. Kids set it off 'fore I was ready, is all. We'll have a new well by the end of the day."

"I'll get the kids to help me shelve and prep the med bay when they're worn out." Damian added, glancing at the module that housed his workspace, sitting on its wide wheels at an angle to the module that served as their canteen. The separate modular units that connected to make their home looked like a kid's dropped toys, each module sitting where they'd left it when they arrived.

Aidan drew in a long, slow breath, feeling the adrenaline ebb from his system. "Sounds good." He dusted himself off as best he could, picking pebbles from his hair. "Is anyone on sentry yet? My guess is that blast got us on the map for the next drone sweep, and we need to be ready."

"On it." Sarah called, setting down the crate she'd been carrying and whistling loud and sharp. On a rise, Lazarus waved a hand. Aidan blinked, then couldn't help but smile. Lazarus was kitted out in a slick poncho, the fiberoptic mesh weave mirroring the surroundings. On top of that he'd piled a couple tumbleweeds and sprinkled dusty soil over himself. If the munitions officer hadn't moved, Aidan never would have seen the guy.

"Okay great, slick tarps?" Aidan asked, counting seconds in his head. He knew the laborious process of unfolding and tying the slick tarps to their struts would take at least twenty minutes if he got a full division on it. They had an hour before the next drone flyover, but there were always watching satellites. That blast would have drawn attention.

Better be transport division with Tweak checking the connections, considering the tarps' weight and the muscles on Dozer and Topher.

"Yep!" Tweak called down from the roof of the main module. Grabbing a loose guideline meant to tie the tarp to its support struts, the tiny coder slid to the ground like something off an action vid and ran past with the line in hand, talking in bursts as she went. "All connected, software g-good, hardware up in forty. Should w-work. W-worked on l-little p-piece. We see."

"Can we move it, forty minutes is—" Aidan started to ask as Tweak looped the last line to its connecting strut, pulled out her tab and hit something. Every line snapped taut, and the carefully folded fiber-optic mesh tarps unfurled like wings. Sliding smoothly into place, the slick tarp cast dappled shade over the half-assembled base and its watching crew, protecting them from blazing sun and searching enemies. Aidan's sentence never finished.

"Goddamn." Janice murmured. "Ain't never seen it go that fast, how'd she—"

"Seconds," Tweak interrupted, trotting up with a hint of a smile. "Forty. Not minutes. Seconds." Her eyes caught the light, glinting with triumph.

"I noticed." Aidan agreed, staring up with a smile tugging at the corners of his lips.

The rest of the day was chaos. Relocation days always were. Taking a multi-section base apart into its component modular units, unfolding each module's wheeled undercarriage and hitching the things to trucks for transport to a new site, then putting it all back together was nobody's idea of fun. But neither was getting a consistent travel pattern around a base picked up by a detailed satellite reading and getting a bomb dropped on their heads. Or running out of water, for that matter.

Like every other Duster base, the Wildcards shifted sites every few months. It was a sensible safety measure. It was also a pain in the ass. Relocations ate up time and everyone's patience, starting with the nerve-wracking days before a move when hydroelectric officers went out scouting a new aquifer for their base and culminating in the heart-thumping hours of setting up under the watchful sky.

And then there was the paperwork covering a base relocation, which was nearly as bad as the move for the poor bastard who had to fill it out. Once the sun had set and he'd made sure the base was in good shape, Aidan had gotten into his office and started on his part of the job, writing up the reports he needed to file on their new position, their level of security in the new site and the procedural boxes they'd checked in the moving process. He was pretty sure it was never going to end.

"We missed you at dinner," a quiet voice remarked from the doorway, the cultured syllables warm in Aidan's ears. He grimaced at his tab. "Had to file a report on the raised danger level in this area after what the twins pulled. Then I had all the rest of this to start on. And I still have to find a good time in the calendar for a full base system shut down and defrag."

Kevin's hand squeezed his shoulder. "We traditionally do the defrag over the Winter Holiday. I'm sure Janice has it scheduled already. As for the kids, it could've been a lot worse," the soft voice murmured behind him. Kevin's thumb ran gentle circles against Aidan's jacket.

"I know," Aidan muttered without looking up from his work, "Thank God it wasn't. I just… I don't know what I'm going to do with Don and Dilly. They're trying, but…" He shook his head, finally sitting back in his seat and looking up at his boyfriend. "I know the kids think they're ready to train for the fight, but I don't want another disaster like this."

The lean logistics officer dropped down beside him, sighing. "It's hard on a lot of the kids without parents," Kevin remarked quietly. "At least they've got their brother around." Glancing at Aidan's screen, he quirked a brow. "These inventory counts are my job, you know. You don't have to do everything."

Aidan gave his boyfriend a wry smile. "You know how I get when I'm stressed. The more work the better. Otherwise I start thinking too much."

"And staying up too much. And not eating enough." Kevin added reprovingly, pushing his old-fashioned glasses up his nose. The lamp kindled highlights in his red hair as he pointedly flicked files off Aidan's main screen. The old machine struggled to keep the hologram steady and track the movement at once, and the screen blipped and shuddered under Kevin's fingers.

Aidan gave the other man a dry smile. "Look who's talking."

Kevin tipped his head, smiling thinly in acknowledgment. "Touché."

Aidan leaned back in his chair, studying Kevin's face. Behind his glasses, Kevin's eyes were downcast. His shoulders had slumped.

"What's wrong?" Aidan asked into the quiet.

Kevin pulled off his glasses, tugged out the cloth he kept in his jacket pocket and began cleaning them absently. It had taken Aidan a few months to catch on, but now he knew the signs of his boyfriend's moods. Fiddling with glasses? That was either fear or worry.

Finally, Kevin glanced up. His smile was a small, crooked thing. "Another generation of kids training up for the fight. They'll be the fourth."

Aidan nodded, catching on. "Yeah. Sucks, doesn't it?" He put his hand on Kevin's knee. Kevin sighed, fingers squeaking the cloth against the plastic of his glasses.

"Seems like our actions don't have much effect sometimes, you know?"

"They don't," Aidan replied softly. "But we have to keep trying. We can't live like this forever. And giving up isn't an option."

Kevin nodded. "I know. Only sometimes I wish..." the sentence trailed off. Replacing his glasses, the logistics officer looked at his boyfriend speculatively, then reached out to run a hand over his cheek. "I do hope you're going to get some rest now that we're settled again. If you keep staying up, you can pass yourself off as a raccoon."

Aidan laughed and caught Kevin's hand in his. "Maybe that's my master plan. Disguise myself as a raccoon and sneak into Corporation headquarters to blow the bastards up. I can be like the raccoon in that weird-ass vid you put on for everybody Friday." He drew his lips back, imitating a character's snarl from a movie that hadn't been that good when it was new and hadn't aged well. They'd laughed so hard that Sarah had fallen off the couch.

Kevin's lips quirked. "You aren't nearly vicious enough to be that character," he demurred, amused, "and I think the Corps tie their trash cans down a little tighter than that."

"Yeah." Aidan agreed with a quiet chuckle. He ran a hand gently over Kevin's hair.

"Don't worry about the kids. I'm not turning them into soldiers today."

"I'm afraid they might do it themselves. Or the world will do it to them." Kevin murmured, closing his eyes and leaning into Aidan's touch. In this light, with that expression on his face, his gene-sculpted features looked too perfect to be human. Turning his hand in Aidan's, he lifted their joined hands and kissed Aidan's knuckles. "Come to my room tonight?"

Aidan smiled softly. "In a minute. I need to finish this first."

Kevin gave a grumble of annoyance for show, leaning in for a kiss. "The price of greatness is responsibility, I suppose."

"Go to bed," Aidan muttered into the kiss. "You're being weird again."

"The word you're looking for is eloquent." Kevin rejoined with one of his sidelong smirks. Aidan watched him leave with a smile before turning back to his work.

An hour later Aidan finally allowed himself to shuck his jacket, kick off his boots, flop down onto Kevin's bed and close his eyes, letting out a long sigh.

"I hate relocation days."

Kevin's chuckle colored the quiet as the other man set aside the tab he'd been reading from and spread himself out beside Aidan, head pillowed on Aidan's shoulder. Kevin was shirtless, and his pale skin was cool where it touched Aidan's.

"Talk to Damian and get the kids assigned an actual vocation training program?" Kevin murmured, dropping an arm over Aidan's chest companionably. "You'll feel better, and they'll be better off."

Aidan grunted and gently shifted Kevin's arm away from his breasts under their binder. "We'll see."

The fingers toyed with the hem of Aidan's shirt. "Don't make Liza and I do it for you."

"Brat," Aidan muttered, rolling over to tuck his head under Kevin's chin.

"Yes sir, of course sir." Kevin smirked in the soft room lights.

Aidan yawned. "Don't call me 'sir'."

"Yes sir." Kevin repeated, a teasing note in his voice.

Aidan groaned and shoved at Kevin's shoulder. "Stop it."

"That an order?" the laughing voice breathed in his ear, warm on his skin.

"'Course it's an order," Aidan muttered, kissing Kevin's throat.

Kevin chuckled, leaning closer. "Lights out," he said aloud, and his room lights faded down to the barest orange glimmer.

Aidan smiled in the dark as Kevin's arms wrapped around him. Maybe they weren't doing a lot of good. Maybe their fragmented guerrilla force wasn't changing things yet. But they were still here. They were still fighting for an America worth living in. Nights and lives like this were worth fighting for.

"Okay guys. Let's hear it. Tommy starts, then Donny, then Dilly."

"Aw Kev, we haven't even eaten—" Donny whined, but he didn't get far.

"When I can trust you to show up and take your quiz when you say you will, then I'll stop interrogating you at inconvenient times." Kevin stated, crossing his arms and looking over the rims of his glasses at the three young people. "Until then, we do this once a week at breakfast. Go ahead Tommy."

Aidan watched absently, spooning sugar into his porridge as Kevin ran the kids through their Force education lessons.

Tommy's little chest puffed out. "CES. Citizen Excellent Standing. Two percent of the population, maybe one. Citizen Standing Number eight hundred and one to eight hundred and fifty points. They pay five percent taxes and they don't have to worry about anything ever."

Kevin chuckled. "Not exactly accurate. What kind of jobs do they have?"

"CEOs, CFOs, COO's and boards of directors. They own stuff and run stuff and make big decisions for their Corporations. Almost all of Corporations pay for the CES to get gene-mods, so they never get sick and think faster and don't care when other people feel bad."

"Except for?" Kevin prodded gently.

Tommy smiled. "Except for you!"

Kevin rolled his eyes, a smile quirking the corners of his mouth. "Thanks for the seal of approval, but I was asking about the Corporations. Which Corporation doesn't pay for their CES people to be modified?"

The little boy nodded, eyes turned upward as he recalled. "AgCo doesn't, 'cause they think it's against their religion."

"*Because* they think it's against their religion, Tommy. Watch your diction."

"Heh, *dic*tion." Lazarus smirked at his breakfast. Yvonne grinned at her cousin's wordplay. Kevin gave them both a look over the rims of his glasses.

"Must you?"

"Because they think it's against their religion," the little boy repeated obediently, "CES people can even leave the country, to make business deals." Tommy finished.

Kevin gave the little boy a smile. "Very good. Donny? Next rank down?"

Donny straightened in his seat. "CSS, Citizen Secure Standing. We think it's ten percent of the population. Citizen Standing Number seven hundred and forty to eight hundred points. They do corporate management, run plants and factories, or they've worked hard for their company and done something special and their rank's a reward. They pay ten percent in taxes, they have it good, but they can't leave the country without a CES person's approval."

Kevin nodded. "Exactly. Dilly? CAS?"

Dilly ticked off her points as if she were the one teaching. "CAS. Citizen Acceptable Standing. Sixty percent of the population. Citizen Standing Number six hundred and seventy to seven hundred and thirty nine points. Twenty-five percent tax rate. Housing restrictions; they gotta live in CAS neighborhoods. Luxury restrictions in NatBank, AgCo and Argus, because they don't want to waste resources on Low Standing people. CAS people get all the middle jobs: foreman, plumber, store manager, stuff like that. They're normal people." She tipped her head, considering. "Sometimes they get signed up for gene mods, but not a lot."

"And CPS. Donny? Do you want a second turn?"

Donny grinned. "CPS. Citizen Poor Standing. Thirty percent of the population. But sometimes people erase the middle of the P and then it's CFS, Citizen Fu—"

"Watch it." Damian warned as he spooned cereal. Donny gave him a quick, guilty smile. "Aw man, everybody says it. Fine. Citizen Standing Number five hundred and fifty to six hundred and sixty nine points. It's everybody who the Corporations don't think are any good. You end up CPS if you screw up or you're born someplace where they don't like you. Then if you have kids, they're CPS too. CPS people can't leave their spot in the Grid without approval. They pay forty-five percent in taxes, they're banned from buying luxuries by all the Corps 'cept Techo, and they gotta live in CPS housing. Which sucks."

"Except, Donny. And it's 'they've got to,' not 'they gotta'," Kevin corrected. "I know it seems silly, but the better you learn to speak now, the more Standings you can impersonate on the Grid when you grow up. And when you go on Grid, you need to remember which credentials you're carrying and stick to stores and areas which cater to that Standing. Stepping out of your Standing is extremely—"

A calorie bar landed with a splat in Aidan's porridge. Across the table Jim winced, bouncing his daughter on his knee. "Hen! No. You don't throw!"

The toddler babbled up at her father, waving her hands. The skinny man's stern expression cracked. He gave Aidan a sheepish look. "Sorry."

Aidan gave the man a chagrined smile in return. "No worries," he began, "it didn't waste more than a spoonful and the shirt's—" He trailed off as his tab pinged. Pulling it out of his pocket, he blinked. This early?

"Something going down?" Sarah asked, leaning over his shoulder for a look.

"Magnum," Aidan replied, brow furrowed. He accepted the message and took a few steps away from the tables. A holographic screen showing his sector commander's face shot into existence, surprising Aidan badly enough to make him miss a step.

"Sir?"

"Morning Headly," the older man intoned. "Checked your tab lately?"

"Not in the last few hours," Aidan admitted cautiously, "We're finishing a base relocation. Is there an issue, sir?"

"You've got a mission informational debrief with me today. In person." The man's deep voice was amused. "Can I expect to see you this week?"

Aidan winced, cursing in his head. "I'm sorry, sir. I've been caught up here, I…um. Yes, sir. I can grab a truck and be out there in a few hours, sir."

Magnum nodded. "Make it before sunset." He cut the connection on his end.

In his chest, Aidan's heart began to pound. How big did a mission have to be to require an actual call and an in-person debriefing? He'd never been called to the sector hub to get mission details before; they usually turned up on his tab and they were his problem from there. If Magnum wanted to talk about something, he saved it for their monthly meetings. Getting a personal call and a personal meeting off the routine schedule had to mean Magnum had something big in mind. The thought made Aidan's gut twist.

At the table Topher caught his eye, gave a thumbs up, and stepped away to give Dozer notice that they needed to get a truck and a route ready.

"You want company on the trip?" Kevin asked as Aidan tucked his tab back in his pocket and sat down to finish his breakfast. A hand gently brushed his knee under the table.

Aidan gave his boyfriend a smile. "Don't you have work here?"

"Spoilsport." Kevin returned with an acknowledging smile. "Come back in one piece."

"Don't burn the base down while I'm gone," Aidan replied, letting his eyes wander pointedly around the table. Most pairs of eyes turned to pin Lazarus.

The tow-headed munitions officer paused, spoon halfway to his mouth and bewildered affront on his face. "What?"

"You'll be good for an ETA of three hours if you leave at 09:30 and keep to a speed of thirty miles an hour." Dozer stepped over to add, his thick fingers running over his tab. He brought up the holographic screen, and the drone surveillance patterns superimposed themselves over the table. Heads raised, casually checking the patterns as the senior transport specialist studied them. Dozer glanced at Topher, then at the image. "How you feel about this, kid?"

Topher pushed his fedora back a little. "Um... looks good to me. Am I missing anything?"

"Nope." Dozer agreed, shutting the screen off and giving his trainee a nod. He turned his heavy face back to Aidan, smiling. "You're good."

Aidan returned the smile. "Appreciate it, Dozer."

The drive to find out just what they were getting into was long and dull. Aidan focused on his breathing and the terrain. He used a new visualization technique that his psychological wellness coaching program had been running him through to keep his mind clear, naming the colors in the landscape around him. If that worked, maybe the rest of the day would too. He could hope.

Rocks. Red. More red. Okay, don't keep using red. Umber. Burnt sienna. Roan.

Hands on the wheel, Aidan smiled. When Kevin had heard about this coping technique, he'd loved it. Aidan had started telling him a little bit about the anxiety part of his mental state, its symptoms and what he did to cope in the past two months. It'd taken some pushing from his psych program, but he'd realized that it'd be Kevin who'd see the problems most often and that his boyfriend deserved to know what was going on. Kevin didn't need to know just how far the mess in his head had taken him before, but Aidan could give him details about what the guy was going to see. As a bonus, it had gotten Aidan a fun night with his boyfriend. Being Kevin, he'd sat down with his tab once he'd heard what Aidan was trying and started bringing up tons of words Aidan had never heard of to describe colors of every shade. The conversations about words and the history of words had gone on till midnight.

Sky. Blue. Periwinkle. Aquamarine. What was the other word? Oh yeah. Ultramarine.

Something grey-blue zipped across the sky.

"Fuck!" Aidan hissed, stomping on the brakes. His truck fishtailed to a halt. Overhead, the long-range drone came back in an elliptical orbit. Fingers fumbling, Aidan slapped at the jerry-rigged touch panel Tweak had wired into the dash, activating the laser IR emitter on the roof. He forced himself to sit still and count to seven as he inhaled. A fucking random sweep drone. There would have to be one today of all days. He could only hope he'd gotten the infrared emitter on in time.

No, he could do more than that. He could breathe, and keep calm, and trust the work his people did.

The rotors buzzed overhead as the drone ran a sweep.

Fuck off. The thought burned hot in Aidan's head.

Moving fast, the drone whirred away. Aidan breathed out. Safe. He was safe.

Slowly, he set his truck back into gear and drove.

"Come in," Sector Commander Magnum invited when Aidan reached his office, his face set in its usual implacable lines. "Grab a seat, Headly."

Carefully, Aidan saluted and sat. Magnum's dark eyes held his.

"Headly, I need your honest opinion. How's your crew doing?"

"Good, sir," Aidan replied, warily watching his sector commander. "They're… they're actually doing really well. Haven't had to write anyone up in months, sir."

"I've noticed." Magnum studied his tab. "Based on your reports, your team is regularly running good missions, taking out targets, and expertly running their base. In fact..." he switched off his tab, raised his eyes and smiled. "On paper they're running even better than they did when Taylor was commanding. I've got to say, you've performed a little miracle here."

Aidan blinked in surprise at that. The base was running better on paper than when Taylor had the Wildcards? He was actually doing better than the man everybody on base remembered as a martyred hero or a lost father figure? Damn.

He shook his head. "No, sir. They're the miracle workers. I just let them do their jobs, sir."

"Well, whatever you did, they're the base they ought to be again. And that's a relief, because we need them on top of their game." Magnum straightened, studying Aidan. "I wanted to wait until after the Winter Holiday before I really put the Wildcards back to work. I'll be honest about that. But if you think they're ready, I need them on something and I need them now, Headly. I'd been planning a version of this with Taylor. When he went down and the base went sideways, I took what I had and gave the mission to Base 1320. They're known as Rolling Thunder, unit's based out of the Poudre Canyon. Exceptional unit, impressive record, highly skilled personnel." The big man's face barely moved as he spoke. "Three days ago, Rolling Thunder's base was destroyed. Their on-Grid team has gone radio silent. They're presumed dead. Best case scenario, they're in detention."

Aidan bowed his head for a moment, the one gesture everybody on every base knew. "Regards to their families, Sir."

"Respectful of you, Headly," Magnum replied. "But I didn't call you up here to give condolences. I need your team to pick up the slack. This mission's too big to drop. I think your unit's ready for something big again. Do you?"

"Sir?" Aidan asked blankly. The dark man across the desk watched him, impassive.

"Tell me, Headly. What are we fighting for?"

"The return of equality and democracy to the United States of America, sir." Aidan rattled off without a thought, brain still processing the information as he spoke. *When a team in detention is the best-case scenario, things have officially gone to shit. A mission that's too big to drop?*

What kind of mission is too big to drop?

Magnum's eyes didn't waver. "And what's that mean?"

Aidan's brain froze. "Uh...sir?"

Standing laboriously, the big man turned to study the pic holos behind his desk, keeping eyes on images of nature scenes and a few group pics rather than his subordinate as he spoke.

"It's about more than making life better for people, Headly. Though I admit that's a strong incentive. It's about survival. Either we change, or we die." The sector commander pointed at an image of what Aidan guessed the Front Range used to look like, such a startling green that it looked fake. "The Corps don't care what they're doing, to people or to the world, but if we keep going at the rate we are, this civilization's going to collapse." Magnum's resonant voice gave the words the weight of a prophecy. "It used to be a theory. Now it's a fact. We're running out of food, running out of water and nearly out of time to fix our mistakes. If we don't change things, we'll turn this country and maybe this planet into a place where our species can't survive. Other species will pull it off, but not us. Already food and water shortages are routine on Grid, never mind out here. The food we do have is so chemically altered that it's helping to bring down our lifespans. The temperature's risen between two and three degrees across the world. The population's down by twenty-one percent in the past hundred years. We're killing ourselves by inches, and we're killing our future, too. Out of the other hundred and ninety-seven countries in the world, a hundred and eighty are doing everything they can to mitigate climate change. But the United Corporations of America?" He snorted, shaking his head.

"Not a chance. And the Corps make sure to keep us too focused on short-term survival to notice the larger issues. Because if people really connected what's happening with what's coming, the Corps wouldn't stand a chance."

Slowly, Magnum paced along the wall of his office.

"What we have to do is make the issues immediate and personal. We have to make it short-term. It's the only way we'll get through to people. To do that, the Regional Commands have put together a set of data. We call it the Folder."

Turning, the big man gave a grim smile.

"You and your unit are going to be working with this packet. I want you to be familiar with the material. Review the Folder in the secondary assembly room, it's waiting for you. I won't tell you any more at this time. I want you to draw your own conclusions before we go into this further. Debrief in the morning. You eaten lately?"

Aidan shook his head. "Nothing since you called me at breakfast, sir."

The older man nodded. "Probably best. You can have barracks room 30C when you're done. Lunch will be sent in if you want it when your file review is over."

"Sir." Aidan nodded, acknowledging the order.

The secondary assembly room was airless. Carefully, Aidan keyed up the files on the unlocked tab lying in the center of the table. Something in the way Magnum had talked about him wanting food after this implied he might not. That didn't say good things for what he was about to see.

Something that would make what the Corps did personal, Magnum had said.

Something that had gotten a base bombed out.

Yeah, this was definitely going to be bad.

Breathing slowly, he looked over the list of files. They were arranged numerically. Glancing at the folder size, he blinked. A terabyte? The thing was huge.

He opened the file marked 'View First.' A list of fourteen vids unfolded from the file name.

Curious, Aidan clicked 'One.' The vid file shot up a loading bar.

Validating Proprietary Blockchain On All Media.

A heartbeat's pause.

Validated All Media. Your Information Is Secure. Playing.

"Validating blockchain?" Aidan whispered to himself. "Seriously?"

If this vid had to be unpacked from a proprietary blockchain, that meant that it had been recorded by Corporate devices on Corporate systems. Nobody could fake a proprietary blockchain, and it couldn't be edited. How had Command gotten hold of proprietary vid feeds off Corporation blockchains?

The second's blackness flicked away, the content started playing, and where it had come from was a little less important.

The camera shot was an odd one, probably from a security camera in a corner. The screen showed icons over both women, their

Citizen Standing Number and the logos that marked them as Cavanaugh-contracted burning with color. Details about their professions and their recent activities scrolled in painfully small print on one side. The woman in the bed was apparently part of a laundry staff crew, her Citizen Standing Score in the toilet. Sobs racked her body. The decent-Standing nurse in a full Cavanaugh uniform had a comforting hand on her back, murmuring something soothing.

"He'll be better off in a facility, you'll see. And we'll get you a better birth control and better screening. It'll be okay."

"I don't want fucking birth control, I want my baby!" The woman's voice was a hysterical screech.

The nurse didn't flinch. "I know honey. I know. But your baby's not going to have a good life. He's going to suffer. I mean, if you couldn't pay for the genome screening, do you think you can afford the gene-editing treatments in time? Before his brain's affected?"

The woman buried her head in her hands, sobbing helplessly. The nurse rubbed her back.

"They'll place him with an angel investor who'll pay for it. He'll be with a better-Standing family. He'll be happy. It's really better for him and for you if you sign the paperwork, okay? Trust me, I see this a lot. It'll be alright. Really, it will."

For a few minutes, all the woman did was bawl. Aidan shifted uncomfortably, feeling like a creep for watching such an intimate moment of pain like this.

Finally, the woman raised her head. "Can... can I say goodbye?"

The nurse smiled. "Of course, hon."

The nurse stepped out of the camera shot for a few minutes, leaving Aidan staring at a miserable woman. She came back with a yowling bundle.

For a long time, the woman held the baby, her head bent over the tiny bundle in her arms. Eventually she gave a shuddering sigh.

"Okay. I'll sign."

The vid cut out. Aidan clicked 'next.'

The next vid picked up on the same nurse, carrying the baby into an exam room.

"Yeah honey. I know," she was murmuring as the baby wailed. Aidan watched as the woman jotted a few records, then picked up a micro-injector and gave the newborn a shot.

The baby stopped moving.

Aidan's gut dropped as the woman methodically folded the blanket over the child's face and pulled a white keratin box from a cabinet, the kind that was designed to degrade quickly. She tucked the baby inside and dropped it down a chute in the wall marked with the words 'Bio-Hazard Waste.'

She washed her hands, tidied her work area and left the room.

Feeling the barest tremble begin in his fingers, Aidan clicked 'next.'

A sorting machine in a basement somewhere dropped sealed boxes into a refrigerated plastic crate marked in block letters: 'ABERRANT.' A set of Cavanaugh Corporation identification numbers for the Grid section and date scrolled in the corner of the recording. The bin was as big as Aidan's quarters, and it was nearly full of neatly stacked white boxes.

Aberrant.

Aidan felt as if the room was spinning as his brain put the pieces together. In the vid, workers loaded the crate into a shipping truck with an American AgCo logo.

In the next vid, a truck pulled up to an AgCo Pets factory. Not completely sure, Aidan paused the vid, skipped back to the previous clip and checked the end. This time he got the truck's serial number. He started the current vid. Same truck. Same container filled with white boxes.

He watched as the container was stacked in a holding area next to others full of huge bones still red with meat. Cow bones, Aidan assumed. Other containers held dead chickens and meaty stuff he couldn't identify. He watched as the timestamp flicked forward a day, and the container full of white keratin boxes was lifted and emptied into long cylinders. He focused on double checking the container's serial number. It still matched.

The timestamp flicked forward. The same long cylinder was being emptied of a fine, brown powder. In the corner, somebody was coughing and somebody else was yelling.

The next vid refocused on the heavy man in the corner of the meat factory. He was shaking with the force of the coughing fit that racked him, blood spattering his chin and the front of his uniform. The skinny boy beside him was round-eyed with terror, crouched protectively between the man and the shift supervisor screaming at them. The voices were tinny over the security camera, but they were clear.

"We're short on quota because of this? How many fucking breaks have you two lazy fags taken today so he can catch his breath? Fucking months you've been pulling this, you sack of CPS shit! Dragging our quotas down! Ruining our stats! We've got quotas to meet! I've got quotas to meet! You useless pointless god-forsaken fuck! You want to ruin me with your goddamn lard-ass work, yeah? You trying to ruin me?"

"Sir, if he can get a medical approval... he's coughing blood..." the boy quavered. The foreman snarled, lashed out and kicked the boy aside. Standing over the sick man, he pulled a gun.

"We're eighty pounds under our quota. You can do something useful."

The gun fired. The supervisor grinned like something rabid."Preacher said God had a plan for everybody."

Turning, he pointed the gun at the shaking boy."I want him stripped and in the rendering tank."

The boy didn't move. Stamping over, the man slammed the pistol across the boy's cheekbone.

"You do what I say, or you're going in there with him!"

"Yessir." The boy's voice was barely audible.

Aidan felt like he'd swallowed a stone.

The next vid showed the same foreman taking a late-night delivery from an EagleCorp truck. This time the keratin boxes were long. Long enough for an adult.

"Street cleaning," the driver said in a bored tone. "Boss said check it with you and take it to the biofuel production plant if it wasn't good enough."

The man grunted. "Let's see."

The driver opened the back door of the rig. Together, foreman and driver opened a crate with its lot number done in messy, dripping black spray paint.

Inside was an old man. He was emaciated, his clothes rumpled and stained. A dead dog and a couple rats had been thrown in on top of him.

The camera was at the right angle to show the skinny foreman's nose wrinkle.

"Not good enough for dog food. Take it."

Aidan was glad he hadn't eaten.

Focus. Take down truck numbers and shipping lot numbers.

The next vid began in a pristine office. Outside the window, downtown spread out in a panorama. The ArgusCo logo shone in its friendly colors on the wall. The two groups of high Standing people in their pristine office clothes sat studying holos full of data. Aidan could tell them apart at a glance: the ZonCom employees had hints of tattoos under collars, large earrings, dyed hair, even a body mod that gave one woman blue skin. Across the table, the ArgusCo men looked as if they'd been printed out as a set: all well-built, hair close cropped, eyes blank and steady.

"We can make a deal on biofuel to ZonCom at a slightly reduced rate this quarter, in exchange for a reduced ground shipping rate on our steel and metal. Agreed?"

The blue-skinned redhead glanced at her companions. Then she smiled across the table. "I think we're authorized to agree. We'd also like to pick up a lot shipment of biofuel for the cross-country trucks while we're here."

"Of course." The speaker for ArgusCo smiled like a shark and hit his tab. "The lot number is on your tab."

The woman brought up her holo-screen, a visual verification for her companions and a studied insult for the man across from her.

Aidan checked the lot number. Another match. The old man and everyone else in that truck had ended up as methane for fuel.

The next vid showed an accounting room in a National Banking office. An older man in a suit stood beside an accountant's desk.

"Williams, have you checked the monthlies on the AgCo Pets plant?"

"Yes sir," the desk jockey replied, turning in his seat. "The labor force is down and they're above quota."

The man smiled. "Glad to see that place is finally turning around. I'll recommend a pay bump for the foreman to his executive. Thank you, Williams."

Aidan watched numbly as the series of vids tracked the same lot numbers of fuel and meat meal. The bio-fuel was used to fill ZonCom trucks that carried goods across the country. The meat meal was used to make a premium dog food called 'Best in Show.' A ZonCom truck was used to take the dog food to a couple of CES and CSS level boutique stores in the Denver Tech Center.

The last vid ended with a TechoCo employee coding an ad for the new product on his shelf. The discreet holo popped up. In it, an Irish setter romped across grass, ran up to its bowl and ate enthusiastically.

"Best in Show," a woman's voice narrated in honeyed tones. "The best ingredients, for your best friend."

The vids flicked off. Aidan felt the shaking in his bones.

Columns of text scrolled by now, showing accurate figures on each Corporation: EagleCorps's detainee numbers, deaths in detention and kickbacks. There were exact numbers on the prices of goods and services for each Citizen Standing level in each Corporation. No wonder the High Standings were rich: they paid almost nothing in taxes and fees. Full details of all Corporation surveillance techniques followed. After that, there was a full report on the climate changes in the past fifty years with reference to crop yields. There was a water report detailing shortages around the country. Aidan read it all. He knew he was barely taking in a word.

When it was finished, Aidan sat stock-still in his chair and stared. Eventually, he forced his legs to move. Finding his barracks room on autopilot, he lay down on the bed and stared at the ceiling.

"So. Thoughts, Headly?"

Thoughts? Aidan stared at his commander, who stared right back. He thought his brain's system had crashed yesterday. He still felt like it hadn't completely come back online. Lack of sleep wasn't helping.

He wet his lips. His voice came out a croak. "I knew things were bad. But this is a lot."

"And what do you think people would do if they saw this?" Magnum asked.

Aidan shrugged, his mind blank. "Lose it?"

Magnum smiled grimly. "Exactly." The big man shoved a cup across the desk. "Drink some coffee, Headly. Did you eat?"

Aidan shook his head. "No sir."

"And I imagine you didn't eat yesterday. Do that once we're done. That's an order."

Loosely steepling his fingers, he studied Aidan.

"Tweak seems to be taking orders these days," he remarked obliquely, dark eyes patient. "Is that right?"

Despite himself, Aidan laughed. Changing gears was a relief.

"I don't give her an order if I can help it, sir. Suggestions work better."

"But she is on board with our mission and generally falling into line, am I right?" the sector commander asked patiently.

Aidan considered a moment before nodding thoughtfully. "For the most part, sir. She's been doing coding that funds our unit and a couple others with cash redirects from one of NatBank's holdings, and doing a lot of things that make life easier on base. She's working really good with Grid-related missions, coding things for the teams making the runs. I wouldn't trust her to make mission decisions on her own yet, but… she's doing pretty good."

Magnum smiled quietly. "How good would you say Tweak's coding skills are?"

"The best," Aidan replied reflexively. Based on what he'd seen since she arrived, he doubted there was a better freelance human coder in the Western Region. Maybe not a better coder, period.

His commander nodded. "That's what I thought. Based on our plans and the abilities we've observed, myself and the other Sector Commanders have decided to ask you to pick up where Rolling Thunder left off. We'll give you everything they had, and everything the missions before attempted."

"Missions before, sir?" Aidan asked, feeling his chest slowly constrict.

Magnum tapped his desk's surface thoughtfully with two fingers as he spoke.

"We should have made this happen twenty years ago, but the attempts made at that time failed. Several similar missions have done the same over the years. We've gotten closer every time. We've tried this with six lone operatives on Grid; each one was found and taken out. We've learned what doesn't work through trial and error. Rolling Thunder has been the best attempt so far. But with the benefit of hindsight, we see a chance of getting it right this time. I'm asking you to make, gain approval on, and execute a mission plan." Magnum's heavy brows rose. "Unless you'd prefer to refuse?"

Aidan swallowed hard. Refusing a mission this big. That'd go in his record. That was setting himself up to lose his base. Besides, there was no way in hell he was letting what he'd seen yesterday keep going on without trying to do something. He forced the words out.

"No, sir. I don't want to refuse. But if I can speak freely, can I know what the mission is?"

Magnum smiled. "We're requiring your unit to code a virus with the Folder as the payload file. We require these specs: complete copy fidelity, fault tolerant and redundant. Self-replicating. Able to breach all Corporate firewalls up to the CSS security level. We want to take advantage of the Winter Holiday Shopping Season to help cover your team's actions. The Commanders require that this goes out before New Years'."

Aidan blinked. "Sir... there's no way in...." He wet his lips. "The Grids're... I know the sensory overload's through the roof on Grid during the Winter Holiday Season. Our people don't do great with the grid-buzz. I know it's crazy hyped up this time of year in there, but even in the middle of that the Corps will spot a file like this and kill it in seconds, no matter where we upload it. Won't they?"

"Not if it's coded properly," Magnum replied calmly, dark eyes holding Aidan's. "And not if it's delivered directly through the Social Feed, to every profile in the system."

Aidan's chair squeaked as he jerked.

"Um. Sorry, sir, but... I thought you said you want us to put a file into every Social Feed profile in the US."

"Is there a problem, Headly?" Magnum asked, his patient smile never wavering.

Aidan's brain spun. He had heard what he thought he heard. Holy shit.

"N-no, sir. I just...um. That's a...very large mission, sir."

"For a very talented base. I think it's a good fit. Faced with verified proof that the worst Corporate crimes aren't urban legends after all, the population's going to have a personal reason to fight back.

Especially the lower Standings, since they're fighting for their lives in a very real way here." Magnum's chair groaned as he leaned forward. "The population's systems will authenticate the Corporations' dirty laundry with the Corps' own tools. It's taken twenty-four months to put together the evidence in this file. Every word is backed up with sources. Incontrovertible evidence. Documents. Pics. Details. All linked to them and encrypted with their software in a way they can't deny. And that's why we need the population to see it."

For the first time since he'd met the man, Aidan saw real fear in Commander Magnum's eyes. It was hidden down deep, but it was there. He wished he hadn't seen it as his Commander spoke.

"Frankly, Headly, we can't afford to scrap this work and start over in a few years. We need this win and we need it now. The Force needs this win. The country needs us to start winning. You follow me?"

Staring into his black eyes, Aidan nodded. "I follow, sir."

The big man nodded. "Then you'd better get to work. Consult on anything you need here at Sector before you leave. And go eat, Headly." The Sector Commander nodded slowly. "Dismissed."

Aidan saluted and got the hell out. He walked to the canteen in a daze.

Infiltrate the Social Feeds with a viral file that would make it to every user?

Holy shit.

Would that be possible, even for Tweak? Was that possible for *anyone*? After all, other bases had failed. Several, Magnum had said. Aidan wasn't surprised. He knew for a fact that TechoCo had the Social Feed locked down tighter than some banks. Nothing in the seven filtered streams of the Feed they provided themselves and the other six Corporations got by them. It was hard enough staying under the radar with simple conversations, and if you started talking in a way your Corporation didn't approve of on the Net you might as well write yourself off.

How many times had Command picked a base to try this insane stunt? How many operatives had died trying this?

And now it was his unit's turn to go up against that monster of a system and try to deliver a terabyte-sized file that would set the country on fire.

"This is nuts," he whispered, "this is fucking nuts…"

Aidan had no idea what he ate for breakfast.

By the time he reached his own base it was late. He'd spent most of the day trying to figure things out at Sector, and he still hadn't come up with a way to tell the crew what he'd gotten them into.

"Look out!"

A splatter of bathtub-hot, dirty water rained down from the ceiling as Aidan opened the base entry door, along with some of Janice's foulest cursing. Metal squealed, and the sheet of water shut off abruptly.

"I'll fucking kill the little pissants! I'll fucking sell their asses to the organ market and make the rest into motherfucking dog food!" Janice's head appeared upside down through an open ceiling tile. "Aw, fuck a donkey with a dong, sorry Aidan! You okay?"

Aidan blinked up at Janice, adding soaked to the bone to freaked out and tired on his state-of-mind list. Great.

"What happened up there?"

Janice rolled her eyes. "Dilly and Donny was helpin' Dozer clean, an' Donny dropped a coupla' cleanin' rags in the sink. They went down the drain, an' guess where they ended up in the water reclamation system? Cloggin' up all the overhead pipes where the pressure's low.

Have it fixed in a couple hours... Damn, you look like somethin' took a chunk outta you."

"Yeah. Something did," Aidan muttered. He sighed and pushed sopping hair out of his eyes. "We'll have a briefing after duty tomorrow."

Janice watched him walk away with worried eyes. Then she shook her head and got back to fighting with pipes.

Aidan scrubbed with washing powder in a stall of the men's showers until the scent of reclamation water no longer clung to his skin. He used as little water as he could to rinse off, watching it sluice over the long scars on his legs and spiral down the drain. Too bad he couldn't wash off the fear with the grime. Pulling his clothes out of the wash-dry unit in his stall, he fought his way into them.

For the first time that day, he stood still and let everything set in. The ache inside his chest pressed like a vice. He hadn't slept the night before on account of it. He knew from experience that he'd never get to sleep like this and using pills to knock himself out was a bad idea. He'd watched people go down that road before, and it didn't end anywhere he wanted to be.

He knew he ought to sit down and talk this over with Omi. Get his head on straight. But just for a little while, he wanted to stop thinking of what he'd seen.

Okay, no pills and no talking.

Well, I do have one other option these days.

Finally, Aidan got his feet to move.

"It's open!" Kevin's voice called through the thin plastic of his door. Aidan slid it to one side, giving it a shove when the panel stuck on its track.

"When did you get in?" Kevin asked, glancing up from his reading with a smile. "Did you eat at Sector? You missed dinner here, I'm afraid."

Aidan shook his head. "I'm not hungry. Can I stay for a bit?"

Sitting up, Kevin gestured to the bed in one of those unconsciously graceful gestures Aidan loved to watch.

"Feel free. You look done in, by the way."

With what felt like all the energy he had left Aidan crossed the room, unlaced his boots and flopped on the bed. He met his boyfriend's inquiring eyes with something like a smile.

"Been home about half an hour. Just got out of the showers. Janice doused me with reclamation water when I got in the door."

Kevin cringed. "Oh dear... Damian's remanded the kids to helping in the kitchen under Andrea's eye for the foreseeable future, if that helps at all."

Slowly, his smile faded as he watched Aidan's face. Reaching over, he tapped his tab, then put a hand on Aidan's knee. Soft music began to play.

"Unless it was raw sewage, you seem just a touch overly upset by it. Janice isn't concerned about damage to the systems, if that's what you're worrying about. It really wasn't as catastrophic as it seemed."

"I'm not worried about the pipes," Aidan replied. "I'm worried about the mission Magnum gave us."

In the background, an artist with an earnest voice was singing something about carrying on when you felt lost, soothing and uplifting at the same time.

He wished he could snag seconds like these and live inside them.

"What's playing?" he asked quietly. Kevin stroked his hair with absent fingers. "This? It's 'Carry On', one of the last pre-dissolution bands that was worth anything did it. They called themselves 'Fun' oddly enough. I've always liked it for bad days."

"Yeah." Aidan agreed, his voice odd in his own ears.

For a moment they sat in silence. Aidan listened to the music. *Carry on*, the singers chorused. The words of the song poked pinpricks into his numbness.

"So, this mission?" Kevin asked softly.

Aidan sighed and pulled up the mission files he'd been given on his tab, handing it to his boyfriend.

Kevin adjusted his glasses, studying the screen. "What is it? If it's more new ID entries I can take the hard copy in, have them uploaded to one of the NatBank computers we can access and be back in the afternoon." He glanced up. "But you look like this is something bigger than that..."

Aidan closed his eyes. "Read it?" he murmured.

Kevin's hand stroked his hair. "That bad?"

Aidan allowed himself to lie back on the bed, weariness pressing down on him. "Pretty much."

Eyes closed, Aidan heard Kevin draw in a breath a little while later. "Good God above." Kevin's voice had an awed note.

"Yeah." Aidan agreed quietly.

"And they think we can pull this off?"

"Yeah," Aidan agreed, his voice cracking on the whisper.

"What's in these vids?" Kevin asked softly.

Aidan closed his eyes, opened them again quickly. He didn't want to see the things those words brought up in the dark behind his eyelids.

"We'll watch them together tomorrow. I've got a base-wide debriefing set. I'm going to have Billie take the kids until we're done."

Kevin glanced at him. "Billie? Really?"

Aidan nodded. "This stuff is a brain fuck. I don't want her or the little guys seeing it."

Kevin nodded, his face taking on that distant look. "I see."

There was the rustle of sheets, and Kevin's body traced his. Long fingers stroked his hair.

"Well, sufficient to the day is the evil thereof."

"What's that mean?" Aidan asked quietly, feeling the pressure in his chest beginning to ease.

"In less exalted terms, it means we'll worry about it tomorrow." Aidan nodded. "Yeah. Um. Kev?"

"Mm?"

"Can I stay here tonight? I've got to get some sleep, but... I'm having some trouble."

Warm arms wrapped around him.

"You don't need to ask, Aidan."

"Thanks." Aidan whispered against his skin. "Help me figure out how to tell everybody about this in the morning?"

"Of course."

The vid screen was already loud when Aidan and Kevin stepped in the next evening, some crazy drone-racing tournament thing on the screen. Sprawled on the couch and the floor, the crew had segregated itself into two teams and was taking turns to groan and cheer for their favorite. Alice's latest knitting project uncoiled like a deformed snake across one arm of the couch. On a desk chair in the back of the room, Tweak sat and watched with what looked like mild amusement. It was hard to tell with her.

"Hey guys, when's halftime?" Aidan called into the racket. Sarah glanced up, spotted him and grinned. Snatching the controller, she waved it, pausing the program.

"What's up?"

Aidan tried for a smile. "I want to get that debrief out of the way. We got assigned a pretty big mission. Billie? Can you take the kids?"

With a quick smile, the teenager gathered Tommy, the twins, and Henrietta.

"We, as in all of us?" Lazarus asked once the children were gone. Aidan shrugged. "At this point, no idea. Maybe. But we're all going to want to see this stuff. I'm not going to say anything, I want you guys to get your own perspectives first. But heads up, this stuff's a brain fuck. Seriously. If anybody wants to give it a miss, now's the time to head out."

Nobody moved.

"Now that you've got us in suspense, you going to let us see?" Damian asked patiently. That brought a grim smile to Aidan's lips. Taking a seat beside Kevin, he brought the Folder's table of contents up on his tab and sent it to the main vid screen. That done, he braced himself. Kevin's arm laid itself gently across his shoulders.

This time, he watched the faces of his crew as the vids played. He saw the shock first. Yvonne's jaw dropped open. Topher stood up for a better look, craning over Alice, which got him inadvertently stabbed with one of her knitting needles. Quiet curses hissed around the room. Kevin's arm tensed against him.

By the halfway point, Andrea had tears tracking down her face, and so did Liza. Blake had scooted down the couch to sit beside the personnel officer, gently rubbing the younger woman's back and murmuring something meaningless and comforting. Dozer's fists were white-knuckled on his knees. At his feet, a stone-faced Sarah sat with her shaking wife. Yvonne would occasionally bury her face against Sarah's collarbone before forcing her eyes back to the screen. Blank-faced, Lazarus rhythmically flicked a folding knife open and closed as he watched.

Behind the couch, Tweak was pacing, eyes glued to the screen. The squeak of her boots was a monotonous counterpoint to the sounds on the vids.

The look on Kevin's face could have frozen nitrogen.

"Holy Christ fuck me sideways on Sunday." Janice whispered when the texts flicked on to replace the vids.

"Nobody's going to believe any of this," Damian stated, his voice flat.

"Nobody can fake proprietary blockchains and everybody knows it. And there's unbelievable amounts of proof. This thing's a terabyte." Aidan replied quietly.

Studying the page floating in the air, Janice's eyes narrowed. "Okay, that's serious an' all. Now what're we doin' with it?"

"Dropping it into the user profile of every client on the Social Feeds before New Years'. In a form the Corps can't delete," Aidan stated simply, numb with the words he was speaking.

The room exploded. Everyone talked at once, drowning one another out. Aidan stood, took a couple of deep breaths and waited for the noise to die down.

One by one, the crew saw their commander standing quietly and shut up. When the room was quiet again, Aidan spoke.

"It's a big job. Hell, it's insane. It's already killed a couple other bases. But it's our job now." He drew another slow breath, let it out. "So, help me out here guys. How are we going to do this?"

The crew glanced at one another for a heartbeat.

In the silence, Tweak's boots squeaked. Walking to the front of the room, she studied the holographic screen, tapping one foot slowly.

"Lotsa work."

"Yeah." Aidan agreed. Tweak turned to stare at him. She glanced around the room. Then she gave Aidan a knife-sharp grin.

"This's gonna end them."

Aidan returned the smile. "It's a start."

The talk in the room revved up again. This time, it went on for hours.

Late in the night, Aidan rolled over in Kevin's bed. A moment's panic shot through him when he found a cold hollow in the sheets.

Sitting up, he looked around the room, instinctively pulling the sheet up to cover his chest as he did.

Kevin sat against the far wall in his boxers, knees drawn up, his tab reflected blue from his glasses. The screen had been set to its lowest brightness, giving a ghostly luminescence to Kevin's pale skin.

Aidan blinked sleep out of his eyes. "Kev?"

Kevin's head rose slowly. Pulling his 'buds from his ears, he gave Aidan a lopsided smile.

"Did I wake you? Sorry about that."

"What're you doing up?" Aidan asked quietly.

Kevin shrugged. "Oh, you know. Trying to soothe the savage beast."

"Hunh?" Aidan asked blearily. Kevin gave a breath of laughter. Standing, he set his tab and glasses on the bedside table and curled up against Aidan again. The orange night-cycle lights were just enough to make him out by.

"It's my turn to have trouble sleeping, that's all. Go back to sleep." He kissed Aidan's temple. "I'm fine."

"Yeah, but you're up..."

"Just trying to stop thinking, that's all. Nothing you need to worry about." Kevin's words were light, but there was a brittle note in his voice. Aidan pulled him a little closer.

"What's up?"

Kevin was quiet for so long that Aidan thought he might have drifted off. When he spoke, every word was said with effort.

"It's idiotic and I know it, but... my parents ended the Aberrant Progeny Policy. There really *were* angel investors and placement for aberrant babies—I—I mean, for special needs kids. I keep thinking that if—if I'd stayed, I could have stopped...that."

Aidan rested his head against Kevin's chest. "Kev. You would've been dead if you'd stayed in Cavanaugh. They would've killed you."

Kevin sighed. "I know. But I still... I don't know. The old White Knight Complex kicking in again, I suppose."

Aidan heard the strain in Kevin's voice as he changed the subject.

"When we pull this off, we are going to throw the mother of all parties."

Aidan gave his man a lopsided smile. "So, I guess you think we can do this?"

Kevin smiled grimly. "Between myself, Tweak, Jim and Yvonne on the technicalities and everyone else at our backs, I think we can give it a damn good try. A few of us had friends in Rolling Thunder, especially in the mission team that was captured. Johnny Red was an amazing tech, and Candace was a logistics colleague I admired. If nothing else, we can do this for them." His sensitive mouth set in a thin line. "We're all tired of losing friends to the bastards. It's time we made them pay for what they take. Besides..." Kevin sighed, trailing off.

"Yeah?" Aidan asked quietly.

Kevin slowly waved a hand, encompassing the situation in a vague circling gesture.

"The kind of fighting we've been doing isn't getting us any closer to our goals. Decry the Corporations, send out docs and pics as fast as TechoCo can take them down in the Social Feed, embarrass and expose Corporate cronies. Smuggle refugees, survive, repeat. That's all we do, and the poor saps on the Grid are caught in the crossfire. We might change a few people's lives, but we're not addressing the causes of their suffering." Kevin's grey eyes glittered, voice growing tight as he spoke. "It feels as if we aren't doing anything *effective*, and that terrifies me. I want to do something, *change* something. This could really change the way people think. If we can pull this off... how phenomenal would that be?"

Aidan stared at him for a long, long moment. "You think we can? A lot of people couldn't before us."

"I think we have to try." Kevin replied in a murmur.

Aidan nodded against his chest. He let out a long, slow breath.

"Okay. In the morning we give it a try. Right now, get some sleep."

Event File 4

File Tag: Mission Statement

Timestamp: 08:00-11-8-2155

"So, you think this'll work?"

"No f-fucking clue." Tweak snapped. "But I already spent a week coding them. If you got a better idea, you do it. Have fun."

Jim glanced up from the device between his fingers to blink at her. Kevin repressed the urge to take the brat to task for a response like that.

Beside her friend, Billie glanced away. "We think they might work. It's a start anyway," she murmured, fingers fiddling with the hem of her shirt. "I wired the casings. They're touch sensitive. Press them and they'll start transmitting code. There're twelve viruses on each transmitter. If a system's vulnerable a green star's gonna show up in the left-hand corner of the screen. That means one of our viruses got in and we can let it start slaving other machines in the TechoCo setup. It'll get to a comp we can use sooner or later, one that's got authentications that'll get us onto the Social Feed as an admin. Then we can upload the Folder direct, without using our rig at all. If it can't find a way in, it'll buzz three times."

Kevin took one of the little black boxes carefully, studying it before passing it to Yvonne.

"Why not just—" Jim mimed typing, "—hack in and do it that way? Probably safer than us walking from place to place seeing if something's unlocked."

Tweak's glare skewered him. "Safer? You even *read* the specs, *genius?* Bases tried this four t-times before. Four. Twenty y-years ag-go. 'L-leven years ago. Six y-years ago. R-rolling Thunder. Those bases. Tried. To. Hack. The Social Feed. With something big. On their rigs. All. Those bases. Got bombed. All. Of them. Are dead." She crossed her arms, one foot tapping. "You don't. Screw. With Techo systems. Head on. You do. You die. That simple. I d-don't know if this'll w-work. B-but for now, we try it. Then we'll know."

The little beast was at it again, speaking to them as if they were all gibbering idiots. Kevin loathed and despised that trait of hers.

The problem was, the little beast was right. Kevin had read the mission packet Aidan had brought home from Sector, and bases who'd tried variations on this sort of attack through direct hacking had been traced. They had died.

Swallowing his pride, he gave Tweak a nod. "Well, thanks for the hard work. We'll put the idea through its paces."

Tweak stared at him for a long moment, weighing his words. Then she shrugged.

"Start with cafes. Easy marks."

They took Tweak's advice the next day, setting off at dawn and slipping onto the Grid in time to blend with the lunchtime crowd.

"I still say this is nuts."

Kevin shot Jim a smirk as they walked. Keeping his voice low and trusting the noise of the crowded street to camouflage their conversation, he allowed himself a little humor. "We have to do something insane on a regular basis, don't you know? Otherwise our reputation will be ruined."

Jim smirked as TechoCo contracted employees eddied around them. That was what the vids always got wrong, Kevin mused as he stepped through a holographic ad of a dancing woman wearing nothing but a Santa hat. Films made a novice mistake on clandestine work. You didn't go to an out of the way place for the purposes of holding cloak-and-dagger conversations. You went to the loudest bar around, sat in a back corner and let the inanities of the world drown out the intelligence.

The Denver Tech Center provided more than enough noise to hide a conversation with, no doubt about that. The ad campaigns for the Winter Holiday Shopping Season were already in full swing, and the Tech Center was the place people came for the gifts they couldn't get anywhere else. Each Corporation's proprietary shopping area conformed to its policies, with Sixteenth Street and The Pearl up in the Boulder Complex being some of the few integrated ventures. In TechoCo's case, that policy seemed to be 'if you can afford it, you can have it.' There were all the usual shops for food, toiletries and amenities, but there were also streets for body-mods of all sorts. Streets where holographs showed sex acts poured overly-rehearsed screams of passion into the afternoon. Down there, tired people looked at you with eyes that made their poses seem artificial. Kevin averted his eyes from those streets.

Today they walked the streets of the Tech Center under the guises and DNA signatures of two CAS level TechoCo employees they'd coded into existence. Their falsified credentials had gotten them through the employees' doors into the gated complex, bypassing the long Visitor's line where Citizen cards were read and anyone whose Corporation didn't approve of what TechoCo sold in its proprietary retail areas was turned away, their attempt at entry logged.

Moving down the round promenade with its fifty subsidiary streets, the two Dusters hunted accessible public consoles that might be exploited for delivering the Folder. It was bedlam. In addition to the usual ad holos, speakers played music on every corner, blending discordantly with the noises of ads and people. Every building and fixture sported a holographic decoration: fluttering faeries, chuckling elves that appeared in the corner of a viewer's eye. Reindeer walking the streets. Bedecked trees concealing lampposts. Wrapped presents hiding utility boxes.

It was supposed to be festive. Judging by the number of people wearing glasses designed to block the holos or walking as if they were in a storm, it managed to be a sensory burden and not much else

Catching Jim's eye, Kevin nodded discreetly at a Kitty Cafe. The other man nodded, wincing as a green and red-clad image of an elf popped into existence and offered him a present. Kevin walked through the ad.

Slipping inside, they wound their way between the other patrons and the handful of cats wandering free around the cozy room, paid a ridiculous amount for their net access and their undersized drinks and found seats. Kevin would have liked something more to drink, but the sign by the register reading '*Today, Small Drinks Only for Our Customers Of CAS Standing And Below. Water Shortage in Effect. Sorry for The Inconvenience*' made that a moot point.

A kitten hopped up into Jim's lap, and he smiled down at it. Kevin signed into the console. The layer of printed epithelial cells covering his own skin gave an oddly muted effect to the touch of the keys against his fingertips. Since wearing the coded Synth hid his own DNA and removed the threat that a particularly keen security guard would scan his genome and get curious about a man with CAS standing credentials and CES standing genetics, it was a small price to pay.

"Too bad Hen can't see this place." Kevin remarked as he typed, bringing up a Social Feed and casually browsing the Top Stories Today. Dross as usual, save for a story that made him sigh. The water allowance had been reduced by half in AgCo, TechoCo and National Banking's Citizen Poor Standing neighborhoods. Barely citing the snow pack on the mountains that provided the entire city with water, the idiot article focused on the political infighting between the Corporations imposing water restrictions and the Corporations who refused to 'jeopardize employee quality of life.' That line made Kevin want to curse.

Of course, the whole thing glossed over the fact that the snow pack sustaining the city was down by seventy-five percent for the fifth year in a row. Denver was dying by inches, and the Corps were intent on keeping it too distracted to notice.

Jim chuckled, pulling Kevin's attention away from the article and down to the kitten curling up to sleep in his lap. "Yeah, Hen'd love it," the other man agreed, oblivious to Kevin's darker train of thought. "One of these days I should get her a cat or something. Couple of years maybe." Jim's smile softened, the way it always did when his daughter came up.

Kevin caught his subordinate's eye for a moment, quirking his lips slightly as the anger in his gut cooled. He always enjoyed doing a run with Jim. He was the brains of the logistics division and Yvonne provided the impetus with her boundless energy, but it was Jim who held them together with his calm efficiency.

As he typed, Kevin gently pressed his elbow against his side. The code broadcaster in his pocket gave a soft buzz of initiation as it set to work trying to pry open a crack that a deliverable folder could be squeezed through.

He killed some time flitting through the Social under his John Smythe persona, repressing a sigh when his code broadcaster buzzed three times in succession against his flank. Another failure. This was the seventh cafe they'd tested and found well and truly secured against files sent over the Net. Plugging something in wasn't an option: TechoCo had learned not to put accessible ports on their public terminals decades ago.

This was turning into something of a frustrating run.

A cat rubbed against his legs, and Kevin bent to pet the creature. It was a shame the base couldn't afford to feed extra mouths. Having an animal around would be a liability they couldn't afford, not with their limited resources. But it would have been nice for the kids.

An ad flashed into existence between them, the eight-foot tall polar bear with a Santa hat leaning down over them both. Jim jumped. The kitten in his lap catapulted to the floor and scrambled away.

"Fifty percent off all merchandise. Come in today. Show how much you care." The bear holo rumbled, flashing the logo of a jewelry and wearables store between its paws.

"Oh for godssakes." The barista stepped out from her station and pulled a tab from a rack on the wall. She hit the screen, and the polar bear vanished.

She shot the two men an apologetic smile. "Sorry folks. That ad's emitter is fritzing, it keeps getting its direction wrong and projecting in here. We talked to the chain about it."

"No worries," Kevin assured with a smile. He caught Jim's eye, leaned back and stretched. "Well, I've finished. Feel like walking?"

"I got nothing going on," Jim agreed, the code phrase meaning he hadn't gotten through either.

A flock of image-only ads assaulted them as they stepped out of the café, washing them in a riot of color and false cheer. Kevin caught Jim's eye and rolled his a little, making the dark man smirk.

"This is getting incredibly old." Kevin muttered.

"You're telling me. When the ads start showing up in stores, I'm officially done," Jim replied in the same quiet undertone.

Kevin glanced up the hyper-colored street beneath its billowing shade cloth awning, and back at his subordinate. "Let's take a break, shall we? We need new vids and something for Topher. He turns twenty-one next week. I've got some ideas about that, and I'd like to get him a bottle of something especially nice to accompany the festivities."

"So, he's not sticking with that thing about Muslims not drinking when he hits twenty-one?" Jim asked as they wove through the crowds, Jim closing his eyes as they passed through a pop-up holo advertising the newest tab.

"Asked him about that actually," Kevin replied lightly as he sidestepped a chattering group of teenagers, "According to him that's not such a big deal in Lebanon. Given that he put himself in the med bay a few years back observing Ramadan, I don't think his piety's in doubt."

"Oh, I remember that," Jim laughed, rolling his eyes. "Hundred and eighteen outside and he won't drink water. Crazy."

"Religion's never made all that much sense," Kevin agreed wryly, "his or mine. Of course, I'm probably going to hell for saying it." He crossed himself and adopted a saintly expression. Jim rolled his eyes, shaking his head as he smiled. "Okay yeah, let's look."

They stepped down a side street devoted to indulgences. Boxes of fine cigars stood in one stall, marred with the glaring red sticker reading *'Warning: Cavanaugh Corporation Employees Not Permitted This Purchase. One Year in Detention and Sixty Point Drop in Citizen Standing.'* Beside them, bottles of what said it was coffee liqueur stood gleaming darkly, their prices well into the Citizen Secure Standing range. Given the roya blight that had killed most coffee trees before the geneticists could render the plant immune, Kevin doubted the stuff had even a passing acquaintanceship with actual coffee.

He studied bottles and considered. Topher had talked about being allowed sips of arak at family parties before his family had come to the US. That would be a nice touch.

"Jim let's check the international section. I think I've got an idea."

They purchased eight bottles of imported arak at prices Kevin was glad he wasn't actually paying, courtesy of the carefully edited cards they carried which fooled systems into believing they'd received money. The tariffs on international goods were through the roof in the Tech Center, but the grin these would bring to Topher's face would make it worth the effort.

And Topher wasn't the only one who had a birthday coming up either. Aidan's birthday was in two weeks. That had been in the back of Kevin's mind since he'd checked the date: November 20th.

His mind flicked away to safer territory; after all, there was Christmas at the end of the next month to consider.

"Speaking of coming events, what do you think the new folks will think of our Christmas festivities?" Kevin asked. As Jim packed the bottles into his padded backpack, Kevin idly studied an adult boutique across the street. The name, Sub Rosa, surprised him with its level of sophistication.

"That we're nuts," Jim replied blithely. "I—" An ad showing a sugar plum fairy asking if he'd like to purchase music appeared in front of Jim's nose, and he nearly dropped the bottle. He grunted and swiped his hand left, dismissing the thing.

Kevin gave a quiet bark of laughter. "Well at least we're consistent. We don't have a lot more carrying capacity, but if we see anything special the event is just around the corner. We should start hunting about. We don't want to be down here too long with this level of sensory bombardment."

"You're telling me," Jim remarked, quiet but heartfelt. "Remember who ended up in his room for two days not talking the last time."

"I remember," Kevin agreed quietly. He did, too. It was hard enough for unaccustomed brains to handle the sensory overload on an average Grid day, but the level of advertising and the social-engineering tricks played during the Winter Holiday made an average run into a gauntlet for those born off-Grid. After Jim's bad time three years ago, Kevin had run some mission statistics and written a proposal for a base regulation to send only Grid-born personnel out on Winter Break runs, restricting those runs to emergency-only. More than one Dust-born operative had gotten killed through sloppy actions brought on by the distraction or lost track of time and blown a mission. Of course, everyone on Grid was distracted by the constant bombardment as well, which was what made the Winter Holiday a nice period of downtime for Dusters. But Sector had picked the restriction proposal up, and then Regional had adopted it. Last year it had become a national thing, so apparently everyone agreed that it was better to avoid the Grid all together during the Winter Holiday Shopping Season.

Of course, some of them wouldn't have the luxury of staying off-Grid this year. Not with the Folder to deliver. Kevin absently made a mental note to check with Damian and try to figure out some sort of mindfulness routine that would help their people fight the sensory overload they'd have to endure as he watched the store across the street. The ad holo wrapping around the Sub Rosa building flowed through a series of images, holding his eyes. A red rose held between perfect white teeth. Two silhouettes of indeterminate gender, just about to kiss. Fingers trailing through rose petals.

November 20th.

Kevin knew exactly what gift would make Aidan happiest. What he hadn't decided was whether he had the courage to cross the street and get it.

If only his legs didn't feel like lead. If only this was easy. If only he could shrug off the fears that had once kept him safe the way he'd slip out of a slick poncho. But human psychology was never that simple.

Children in Kevin's class had been reminded again and again that they were as close to the peak of human perfection as possible. Human perfection had been the aim of everything he'd been taught outside the home. Every medical and technological tool at Cavanaugh Corporation's disposal was used to uplift the human race. That was their public line.

But when perfect became a possibility, imperfect became criminal. A fit person shouldn't have aberrant urges. Immoral and unnatural behavior was aberrant. Aberrant behavior was to be rooted out and destroyed in order to protect the future. How many ways had the Corporation found to try to drill that into his head?

His parents had tried to soften the blow. They'd given him shields of Socrates and Shakespeare, Styx and Ignatius de Loyola to hold up against the battering indoctrination. But they'd only been able to do so much.

Cavanaugh's concept of human perfection was utter garbage and Kevin knew it. Cavanaugh's corporate policies were a sick stew of hubris, exceptionalism and marketing, using people's fear of being seen as less than worthy to sell them endless prescriptions and procedures. Any deviation was a reason to write people off and throw them away.

He'd seen the dead children being turned into dog food in the vids from the Folder. The Corporation had no right to speak about moral behavior. Their own immorality knew no bounds.

And yet there were still times like this, when he felt the shame of failing to live up to the standards that had been set for him soiling his thoughts. He still stood here, feeling as if the word 'aberrant' was written on him in letters of black slime.

He was aberrant. He always would be.

"Kev?" Jim asked behind him. Kevin gave an abbreviated 'nothing's wrong' wave of the hand, the software of his mind trying to process.

"Okay then," Jim remarked quietly; accepting, as usual, that his officer had these silent spells of thought now and again. One of these days he should mention how much he appreciated that, Kevin thought distantly.

He slipped his hand into the inner pocket, fingers brushing over the plastic baggie he'd been carrying since he'd begun thinking over Aidan's birthday present. He drew a long, slow breath in and let it go.

"Mind poking around on your own for a moment? I've got something I want to buy across the street."

Jim shot a look across the street, blinked several times. Then he caught Kevin's eye and nodded. "I got this."

Kevin gave him a smile. "Thanks."

Squaring his shoulders, he crossed the sidewalk.

The electronic bong of the bell over the door nearly made Kevin flinch. He hadn't wanted to hide from the casual gazes of others this much since his first run as a logistics specialist.

He forced his breathing into a steadier rhythm as he stepped inside. The establishment was surprisingly clean: white walls, accents of dark wood, red carpet. Something inside Kevin had expected sticky floors and grime. He'd expected physical filth because he'd associated this act with being dirty, he told himself, and that was another piece of psychological refuse he could toss out.

As he moved, he activated a security-check program on the tab in his pocket with a series of taps on the case. A casual glance at the screen a few minutes later gave him the layout of the security systems. Nothing to worry about. Good.

The man at the desk was clean-cut and patient-eyed, speaking softly to a customer when Kevin came within hearing range.

"...Sorry sir, but AgCo doesn't approve of the practice associated with your purchase. It's banned in your contract."

"Wha?" The skinny man muttered, blinking watery eyes. The store attendant surfed his voice over the customer's with practiced ease, hiding behind formality.

"Your Corporation's Mission Statement is to feed the masses and serve the Lord as a Christian Corporation. To protect your immortal soul, your Corporation has listed this purchase as outside the bounds of Christian morality. I'm sorry for the inconvenience."

Kevin heard the tell-tale note in the voice that gave away the reading of a script projected on the man's cornea via an implant. A casual glance at the store attendant and the glint of green in his brown eyes confirmed it.

"Oh shit…" the customer groaned, covering his face with a hand for a moment. Raising his eyes, he took a step back. His eyes were wide. "You ain't gonna have to report me, are you?"

"I'm afraid so, sir," the attendant replied quietly, "It's TechoCo's policy to work synergistically with all Corporations in accordance with their stated policies. I'm sorry for the inconvenience. Have a nice day."

The man gulped and scuttled for the door. Kevin spared him a moment's compassion as he studied collections of cock rings and flavored lube. Poor bugger was really in trouble now, breaking a clause in his Citizen Contract. American AgCo was a harsh master too.

Come to think of it, how had someone from AgCo gotten into a TechoCo proprietary area? They were usually banned.

After a moment's consideration, he shrugged the thought off. It could have been any number of things, none of them his problem today.

He waited until the store had lost the sense of tension before casually strolling to the desk himself.

"Afternoon. I'd like to place an order," he stated, holding out his Citizen Card. Seeing the TechoCo logo on it, the attendant visibly relaxed. He met Kevin's eyes with a quick, genuine smile of relief.

"Of course, sir. Just let me run this."

The man took Kevin's card. He could feel his pulses pounding in his wrists, pounding down in his gut. Breathe. In for a count of five. Out for a count of five. Repeat.

The card reader binged green, and the attendant handed the card back with a bright smile.

"What can we get for you today?"

"I'd like to place a bespoke order for a personal toy with a DNA lock. Mind if I see your printing options?"

"Right this way sir," the young man agreed, putting his hand under the table to press what Kevin knew was the button to call another employee from the back. According to his check, the security button was on the other end of the counter.

The printing room he was led to was another tastefully appointed space, the printer a slick dome totally unlike their clunky monster. The printer back on base looked like an overfed mechanical scorpion on treads.

The attendant walked through possibilities and Kevin made his choices in a shockingly brief span of time.

"Now if I can get the DNA sample sir?"

The attendant held out his hand, smiling. Putting on a polite smile in turn, Kevin slipped the plastic baggie out of his pocket and held out the blonde hairs. If Aidan had any record on the Grid whatsoever this would be impossible. Lucky for them he'd been born in the Dust.

The 3-D printer whirred and ran. Fifteen minutes later, Kevin's serviceman held out the neat black box. "Thank you for your business. If you and your girlfriend enjoy the product, please write us a review?"

"I'll do that," Kevin agreed politely, taking the box and tucking it under his arm with a smile.

Stepping outside, Kevin drew a long breath as his heart soared. He'd done it. He'd actually done it. Hell yes.

A spring in his step, he crossed the sidewalk, eyes scanning for Jim's lanky form among the liquor bottles.

He spotted the tall black man a few meters down the promenade, walking up to the man who'd been in Sub Rosa getting a telling off. The man wore a tray around his neck and a hat projecting a holo ad at least as tall again as he was:

'Ask Me for a Sample! Best American Rye. Brought to You
by Nodding Wheat Distillery, an American AgCo Brand.'

Now the fact that he was in here made sense. Kevin was glad to clear up that little mystery. Disparities always made him edgy on Grid runs.

"Hey, I'll try one," Jim remarked easily as Kevin drew level with him.

The harried man turned, eyes haunted. He looked Jim up and down, and his face folded into a leer that dropped Kevin's gut into his boots.

"I don' serve monkeys," the AgCo employee drawled. The drink he had been holding out was dumped on Jim's hand, soaking his sleeve.

"Fuck!" Jim snapped his hand back, shaking it off. Kevin glanced at him for a moment, made his assessment, stepped in and snagged the man's collar in one hand.

"Listen to me, you little plebe," he stated, every syllable cutting like a knife, "I just recorded your behavior. You will apologize to my colleague and you'll do it now, otherwise I'll turn in an inter-Corporation CSS level complaint which will drop your Citizen Standing Number so low that you'll need to beg the rats at the city dump for table scraps. Are we clear?"

The man yelped, the glasses of amber on his tray painting his shirt in fragrant splashes as he was yanked forward.

"What the... aw fuck seriously?"

"Do I sound like I'm making a joke?" Kevin asked, tightening his grip a calculated fraction. The little rat in his hand swallowed hard.

"Sorry sir. I never had no good upbringing, God bless."

"Whatever," Jim grumbled, wiping his hand on his pants.

Kevin let the sample-vendor go with exaggerated distaste, dusting his hands off. "Mind your manners in future."

He turned away.

Behind him, he heard the AgCo employee hawk and spit.

"Gene-tampered blood-muddying degenerate children of Lilith," the little man grumbled.

A lance of rage ran through Kevin's gut. He forced it down. No point in running the risk on giving this man more than a piece of his mind unless it was truly warranted.

The man's mutter continued behind him as they walked. "Running with a goddamn nig—"

That did it. Kevin glanced at Jim for the look of the thing.

"We have an anti-defamation and defense of brand clause in our contract, right?"

"Right," Jim agreed warily, "but—"

"Thought so."

Kevin turned, stepped back and delivered a very neat undercut to the man's gut, fast and hard. The man's sample tray spilled as he dropped to his knees. Kevin stepped neatly out of range as the man vomited his lunch. He glanced at Jim and smirked, massaging his aching hand.

"And now I'll need a wash," he added as he turned away, pitching his voice carefully to ensure the man heard the comment as they walked.

Half a block later, the rush began to wear off. Kevin was quite glad that TechoCo had anti-defamation clauses in their agreements with other Corporations that allowed physical responses for anyone provoked. At the moment, he knew cameras would already have run the events through the system and approved his calculated action. If they hadn't, he'd already have been stopped by a Peacekeeper.

He had calculated, but he had gambled too. That had been a stupid move on his part.

But damn it, if he didn't stand up where he could, what was this fight worth? Besides, that little cretin had needed a lesson in manners. Children of Lilith indeed. And what he'd called Jim had been far worse.

He caught Jim watching him out of the corner of his eye. "What?" he asked, forcing himself into more casual body language. Jim held his eyes for a moment beyond what was comfortable.

"You scare me sometimes man. Thanks, but still."

"Yes well." Kevin shrugged. "He's a plebe. He'll think twice about that sort of garbage the next time. My good deed for the day."

Jim shrugged, glancing down. Then he blinked, shoulders stiffening.

"Fuck..."

"What?" Kevin asked sharply, hearing the fear in the soft word.

Moving a little closer to Kevin in the crowd, Jim pulled out his tab and placed it in his left hand, covering his move with an act of showing Kevin something on the physical screen.

Kevin sucked in an involuntary breath, brain kicking into high gear. The Synth on Jim's left hand was peeling away in strips.

"The alcohol?" Jim asked quietly.

Kevin nodded. "Think so."

"Shit."

"Hands in your pockets," Kevin muttered. "Don't let a camera catch an image. Come on."

Eyes scanning, Kevin hunted for the biggest crowd available. They needed somewhere to get lost.

Two blocks down, a holo sign flashed in eye-searing yellow over a sidewalk thronged with people:

Water Allocation and Assignment Station. Please Wait Your Turn Calmly.

Kevin nudged Jim and sidestepped his way into the back of the line. Perfect.

For the next half hour, they stood waiting. People fidgeted. People complained. People played games on tabs. People shuffled their feet.

"Least it isn't fricking hot." Jim muttered. Kevin nodded absently.

Such a large group of people standing together triggered every sensor on the block, and ads popped up every second or so, their jingles and messages blending into a discordant clamor.

In his head, Kevin kept a running clock on their Synth. It could last for six hours in middling temperatures. They'd put it on four and a half hours ago.

They were running out of time. But there was nowhere else crowded enough to confuse the cameras. Once they were in a crowd rather than a line, people going in many directions at once, Jim could slide on his riding gauntlets without an informer or a camera catching a glimpse of the peeling synth.

"All right! Next fifty, inside!" a Peacekeeper bawled beside the door. They crowded forward with the rest of the throng. Jim shifted to avoid being touched by the fat man behind him or the girl in front of him as the crowd clustered with the two hundred people already in the space, the general scrum filtering into lines that led to fifteen clerks at deal-table desks in the echoing meeting hall. At least there weren't any ads.

"Next."

Kevin could hear the clerks giving out applications for water increases, handing out approvals and denials based on...what? Probably how much the people could pay. Possibly extenuating circumstances.

Around the walls, Peacekeepers stood watching carefully, but Kevin knew their habits. They were watching for antisocial behavior. Quiet action would fly under the radar.

One of the men in crowd beside them leaned on a silver-tipped cane, his outdated bionic leg creaking. He glowered at everyone in sight. A young woman bounced a crying baby on her hip and chewed on her lip. Far, far ahead, the officials behind their desks simply did their work, voices never changing tone.

"Jim," Kevin murmured under the base rumble of the crowd, "kneel down and dig out your riding gloves. They're fairly stylish; wear them around. I'll make sure you're not trampled."

"Yeah." Jim agreed tightly. Going down to one knee, he dug in his backpack.

Kevin idly watched a man argue with a clerk.

"What do you mean I'm not approved?!"

The official's voice was too low to come across as anything but 'mumble mumble.' The man behind the table didn't look up from his console.

The man in front of the table threw up his hands. "Paperwork?! My kids haven't had water for three days, asshole!"

'Mumble MUMBLE mumble.'

"How much?! You bastard! You've got a job, and if you don't do it, I'm gonna—"

The man was too angry to realize that he was in a slowly widening circle of empty floor. He was too angry to notice the Peacekeepers closing in until they grabbed him.

There was the smack of metal on flesh. The sizzle of electricity. A high yelp.

Kevin looked away, his gut burning. Water for his kids. That was all the man had wanted. Water for his children.

And there was nothing Kevin could do to help him. If he said anything to stop this small crime, he wouldn't be around to help end the systemic injustices.

He knew how the equation of the situation balanced. He still hated it.

Clenching his fists, he stood still as the man was dragged away. Those around him met his eyes with glances of blank fear.

And that was the bloody infuriating part of it all. If everyone in this room stood up and said 'no' together, the Peacekeepers wouldn't stand a chance. But no one was standing up if they ran the risk of being the one who was shot down for it. No one who'd been on their knees as long as these people found the idea of standing up easy to contemplate.

Jim stood and nodded. Tight-lipped, Kevin returned the nod. "I'll make an appointment and come back later. Too crowded in here," he remarked for anyone listening.

Turning, they pushed their way to the exit.

It was a long, quiet ride back to the secure room where they'd stashed their extra Synth in the refrigerator. Kevin took the risk of disabling the room's wall screen, giving them some peace. He put a 'bud in one ear, chose a song on his player and focused on scrubbing the day's dead Synth off his hands in the room's basin. He didn't intend to be rude to his base mate, but he needed the music to get him through the moment.

He used a scrubbing pad as he would at home rather than wasting precious water, filling his mind with the simple task and the music.

Don Henley was right. The dice were loaded. The good guys had lost.

Jim's voice was quiet when he spoke.

"You haven't said anything in a while. You doing good?"

Methodically, Kevin set aside the cleaning pad.

"Just thinking. Out, damned spot, that sort of thing."

"Hunh?" Jim muttered. Kevin smiled bitterly, the moan of bluesy notes in his ear.

"Did I ever tell you about Lady Macbeth?"

"This another history thing?" Jim asked, his voice accompanied by the flop of his body hitting one of the beds.

Kevin nodded absently. "Yes."

"You gotta tell me right now? I'm beat."

Kevin breathed a laugh. "Sorry." He rinsed his hands clean.

"The gridbuzz getting you down?"

"Yeah. Feel like my brain's full of static," Jim's weary voice replied behind him. "How you stay chill I still don't get."

Kevin shrugged. "Oh, it gets under my skin eventually. But I did start VR education at two years old. A little more than a decade of VR and AR educational programs wired my brain for the stimuli."

Jim grunted. "Lucky."

Kevin didn't respond to that. The man wouldn't call it 'lucky' if he'd seen the child Kevin had been coming home sobbing with exhaustion.

But that was in the past. He had more important things to focus on now.

"Well. We can make a few more tries in another neighborhood tomorrow, before we head home. Tweak said this code broadcaster was only her opening volley." He forced himself to raise his head. "We'll make this work."

"How's the hand?" Jim asked.

Kevin made a fist and grimaced. "Aching like the devil. I think I must have hit one of his ribs."

"Nice going," Jim observed dryly.

The bed creaked as the man stood. Jim's hands took his, feeling along each finger as he spoke.

"No breaks. Doesn't feel like a sprain or anything. Still, want me to get the kit out and check?"

"No thanks. My nanites will take care of it," Kevin replied quietly. Jim raised his eyes, measuring.

"So, you know I hate that garbage about blood muddying as much as you do. But hitting the guy?"

Kevin looked away. "Stupid of me. I know."

"Yeah, it was," Jim agreed, his tone level.

Kevin shrugged. "What he called you was untenable."

Jim cocked a brow. "He called you a Child of Lilith and you didn't crack."

Kevin shrugged. "Yes, well. He can call me what he likes. To put it bluntly, my genetic situation is an issue in some places and an unfair advantage in others. What he called you... well, it's kicking a man when he's down. I don't stand for that."

Jim gave him a cockeyed look. "To put it bluntly is right. And here I thought you were good with words."

Kevin dropped his eyes. "Sorry. It did come out rather badly."

The taller man smiled wryly. "Eh. If you think about it, he's on us both for the same thing: genetics. Which is rich coming from anybody out of AgCo. They changed the genes in every food species there is, then they talk about 'defying god' when it's the human genome getting some work. Go around calling themselves unsullied. My ass. I guess it'd get to me too if I wasn't used to it."

"You shouldn't be used to it," Kevin muttered irritably, "and then on top of it...on top of it, people like that little rat take my faith and turn it into one more whip across everyone's backs. It makes me livid."

Jim gave him a cockeyed look. "Thought you were some kind of Catholic. They're Protestants. Not really your faith."

"Jesuit, true. But getting sect-specific is a waste of time. It's still Christianity."

"Christianity's been a stick to hit folks with a long time, man. You know more history than me."

Kevin sighed. "You have a point. All the same... it shouldn't be like this."

Jim let go of his hand. "Way of the world, man. And by the way, gene-mod boy, you're all good. I bet you won't even notice this in an hour."

"Probably not," Kevin agreed quietly, flexing his aching hand.

Crossing to his chosen bed again, Jim pulled up a book to read on his screen. Kevin stared at his fingers, flexing them slowly.

Way of the world.

The way of the world was to force you into unacceptable choices. Accept evil in exchange for safety. Decry it and become a target. Stand up and sacrifice your chance to do future good. Keep quiet and sacrifice another person's life.

The world presented these choices every damn day. And he had to keep making them.

"You're still thinking about that guy, aren't you?"

"Hmm?" Kevin glanced up.

Jim spoke without looking at him. "The guy in the water line. You still thinking about him?"

Kevin gave him a gallows smile. "How did you guess?"

Jim snorted. "Man, I know you."

"Fair point." Kevin dropped onto his bed, closing his eyes. "Jim?"

"Yeah?" Jim asked.

"Something's got to change. I'm...I'm getting tired of feeling like I've got blood on my hands, you know?"

Jim sighed, turning his head to stare at the ceiling. "Yeah man. I know."

After the miserable run they'd had, Kevin welcomed even the mountain of paperwork waiting for him at home. Yvonne was rotten at administrative work and he'd allowed her to let her clearances lapse, so the stuff always piled up when he and Jim went on runs together. It wasn't his favorite way to keep his mind occupied, but it served the purpose.

When the day's work was done, he tucked the data stick sitting on his desk into his pocket and headed down the hall. Now he could allow himself a much better way to clear his head.

Aidan wasn't in his office when Kevin checked, so he followed logic and ended up outside Aidan's room, knocking quietly.

"Aidan?"

Silence.

He shoved his tab deeper into his back pocket and slid Aidan's door open, slipping inside and quietly closing the door behind him. As the lights sensed his presence and flicked on, he glanced around.

"You'd think a convict slept in here," he muttered under his breath, eyes wandering around Aidan's sterile quarters.

He took a few moments to pick up Aidan's clothes and throw them in the hamper, check his store of testosterone and make a mental note to get more, and aimlessly tidy a few things. Then he dropped onto the bed and allowed himself to close his eyes, content to wait. The quiet was blissful.

The next time he was on Grid, he decided, he was going to scrounge up something nice to make Aidan's room look less like a monk's cell. Either that or he could bring up the idea of sharing his room...but no. It was too soon for that.

It had been so long since he'd had a boyfriend to think about pleasing that the idea still made him a little giddy. And Aidan's standards were a lot lower than Peter's had been. So many small acts brought a smile to his face.

Kevin couldn't help grinning as he lay, waiting for the sound of the door opening. The Folder might not be delivered yet, but at least tonight he could make Aidan smile.

There was a soft ping of Aidan's tab turning itself on. A voice spoke in the silence, high and feminine. "Hello, Aidan... you are not Aidan."

Kevin shot up on the bed, scrambling to readjust his glasses and feeling his heart lurch. He gulped in a breath of air. "What the..."

The shimmering, holographic image of a young woman with eyes like two aquamarines smiled down, giving the appearance of standing beside the bed.

"Greetings. I apologize for startling you. Usually it is Aidan who occupies this room at this time. Has something happened to him?"

Kevin drew a long breath. "Um... no. No, he's just running a touch late. I take it you're his..." he trailed off, studying the hologram. "Query for program function," he stated, enunciating each word in case the mic pickup on Aidan's tab was subpar.

The program image smiled a little more widely, her head tilting ever so slightly to one side. "I am Omi. Program function: psychological wellness coach program for Aidan Headly."

Kevin blinked. "Psychological wellness? Details of program," he requested, studying the design. Visually it was a fair piece of work, but nothing impressive. The speech patterns were surprisingly good, though. Somebody's freelance side project? Aidan's perhaps?

"Completed program or work in progress?" he added thoughtfully. Where had he seen the program's face before? It resembled something he'd seen not long ago.

"I am complete," the program said, a hint of laughter in her voice. The coder had done an amazing job with inflection and tonality. "I was designed to facilitate healthy coping skills and promote mental health for Aidan Headly. Designed and coded on Base 1491 by Jackson Perez. Query for your relationship to Aidan?"

Kevin blinked. "Er..."

For a moment, he bit his lip. What would Aidan want him to say? The program, from all appearances, was AI: what he 'taught' it was going to be devilishly difficult to code out. If he changed its parameters with new information...

The hologram blinked in and out of visibility, a visual reminder that he needed to make a response. He swallowed.

"Boyfriend. Er, significant other."

Omi smiled again. "You are Kevin McIllian. I have heard a great deal about you. It is a pleasure to make your acquaintance."

"Mutual, I'm sure," Kevin managed, watching the program. "Switch off?" he requested hopefully, wanting to avoid giving the thing input that might make it stop acting as Aidan would want. The program smiled at him, but it remained visible.

Head cocked, Kevin studied it. Aidan had said he had a program that gave him anti-anxiety tips, but he'd never said it was so advanced. And as for why it looked so familiar....

He snapped his fingers. "Omi! Of course! Is your image based on Naomi Headly?" he asked, glancing at the sketch tacked to the wall. Kevin had only heard a handful of things about his boyfriend's little sister, but he did know the girl was a bit sassy. And she was important enough to Aidan that his expression softened whenever he mentioned her. Yes, the face in the sketch was the same.

Omi laughed. "It is. I was modeled on the image of Naomi Headly before the destruction of Base 1440."

The door to the room slid open. Aidan walked in, absently tapping at his secondary tab.

"Hello, Aidan," Omi said, turning to him. "You are late."

"Sorry," Aidan muttered without looking up. "Had to break up a bitching session between Janice and Blake again, they're still pissy with each other over the price on what Janice's been requisitioning for all the tests and drilling she's doing. The battery on your tab was acting up. Remind me to ask Kev to get new batteries and piping on his list for the next run."

"Reminder recorded."

Kevin cleared his throat. "Er...right. That piping could be tricky," he murmured, his voice quiet.

Aidan's head jerked up. He blinked at Kevin, glanced at Omi, turned his eyes back to his boyfriend. Kevin could see his throat move as he swallowed.

"Omi, uh. Thanks. That's all tonight."

"Of course." Omi smiled, nodded, and the hologram switched off.

"Uh. Hey." Aidan flipped off the secondary tab and awkwardly slid it onto the top of his little dresser. "Um. Been waiting long?"

"Only long enough to trade identities with your program." Kevin shrugged, smiling softly as he stood. "Impressive AI work," he added as an afterthought, wishing it didn't *sound* so much like an afterthought and a cover.

Aidan winced, rubbing self-consciously at the back of his neck. "Yeah...uh... you said you had a new vid for tonight?"

Kevin nodded, but his eyes strayed to the blank tab again. A full AI program, coded to look like Aidan's sister. That was something to contend with.

"I may have accidentally changed some parameters on the program," he managed eventually. "I don't think I did too much damage..."

Aidan gave a jerky shrug. "You, um…probably didn't change anything important."

For a moment, he stood as if he didn't know where he should be, blue eyes wide and woebegone. Kevin wished he hadn't pressed.

Aidan cleared his throat. "Vid? What'd you get?"

"Oh." Kevin scrambled to pull the data stick from his pocket. "It's a Tortuga Isle flick, they just finished filming it before they had to bug out this time or, so I heard. It's a retelling of Romeo and Juliet and I think it'll make you laugh; they've really thumbed their nose at the Morality Laws this time. It's a gem, but there are some scenes that might make it better for a private viewing. I thought perhaps we could use my wall screen and—"

Both their tabs went off like sonic bombs with the drone-proximity   alert.

"Shit." Aidan hissed as the lights snapped off, leaving them in blackness. Kevin reached for Aidan's hand.

"No sense trying to get to the canteen. We'll sound like a herd of buffalo stumbling around in the dark."

"Yeah." Aidan whispered. "Here. Bed's right here." Kevin let the other man guide him across the room. He put his arm around Aidan's shoulders, squeezing his hand. Aidan's fingers had begun to tremble.

"Hey. What advice has your program given you for handling this?"

"Breathing exercises." Aidan whispered. "That and a visualization thing. Sounds stupid but it kinda helps."

"Tell me about it?"

"I'm supposed to visualize floating up in clouds. I told you it sounded stupid."

Kevin squeezed his shoulder. "It's only stupid if there are fluffy wings and a harp involved."

Aidan gave a snort of a laugh. Kevin smirked.

"So," he asked as quietly as he could, "why'd you choose the name Omi for the program?"

"Didn't." Aidan whispered, turning his head and resting it against Kevin's shoulder. "My sister Naomi couldn't say her whole name when she was little. She called herself Omi. Nickname stuck. I figure if the program looks like her...yeah."

"I see." Kevin trailed off. The expectant darkness pressed in around them. He couldn't hear the drone's rotors. That was a good sign.

Five minutes crept by.

"You must really miss your sister," Kevin breathed, pulling Aidan a little closer against him.

Aidan sighed in the dark. "Kev... can we just not talk about it? Please? It's no big deal."

Silence filled the room. The darkness pressed in.

"You know," Kevin murmured before he could think about it too much, "there's an awful lot we just don't talk about."

Aidan crossed his arms over his chest, shoulders hunching beneath Kevin's hands. "I'm sorry. I just... I'm used to... It's hard...to talk about things. Okay? I'm sorry."

Kevin put a hand over Aidan's crossed arms, silent for a moment.

Maybe he shouldn't push this.

Instead of speaking, he reached up and stroked Aidan's fine, straight hair gently, fingers slow and soothing. He'd been reading articles on helping people cope with anxiety, and most of them agreed that simply letting the person know they weren't alone was a help.

In the dark and the danger, Kevin didn't mind that reminder himself.

Aidan took several deep breaths. After a long, long moment, he whispered, "I do miss her. She's... she got me through a lot of shit. She was really the only one on my home base who accepted what I was. Who I was, I mean."

"When did you lose her?" Kevin asked softly.

"A little over three years ago." Aidan shifted closer to Kevin. "She's fine, we just aren't in touch. Our base got hit. Bad. We were taken to different bases to recuperate. And we just…haven't been able to reconnect since." He took a breath as if he wanted to say more, but let it go without speaking.

Kevin blinked in surprise. "Can't you send her a Greynet message? You should be able to look her up…"

Aidan shook his head against Kevin's shoulder. "I tried a while back. System has her down as Mission Communication Only. She's been an on-Grid asset for two years now, records say. Deep cover." Kevin nodded, then realized Aidan wouldn't see the gesture.

"Ah. That is tricky."

Drawing a breath, he chose his words with care. "You know…I'm glad you've got such a helpful program, but if your primary tab's ever out of battery again, you can knock on my door for more than vids and…" he cleared his throat, "the usual," he managed finally, pressed to find a delicate way to phrase it. He'd be damned if he'd call the nights they spent together by a derogatory term, but there were so few options which were complimentary. Why a language as beautiful and complex as English had to be so barren of words worth using for intimate relations he'd never understand.

Aidan shifted uncomfortably. "I know. It's not… Omi isn't…it's just… I don't want to bug you with little shit. And it's all little shit I talk to her about. Nothing important, really."

Kevin sat quiet for a moment, embarrassed on the other man's part and frustrated by the embarrassment. When he couldn't take it any longer, he carefully wrapped his arms around his boyfriend, resting his chin on Aidan's shoulder.

"Aidan? Life *is* little shit. It's all the little, unimportant things we say to each other. I rather expected that we would share those things...didn't you?"

Aidan sighed in the dark. "It's not… I just… I'm working on it, okay? I'm just not...used to having someone, you know?"

Kevin nodded, letting Aidan feel the gesture. "I know. It's still new for me, too, but...well." He shrugged, smiling nervously. "I'm here, all right? And not just for the vid or for the night."

"Yeah." Aidan turned his head, nuzzling Kevin gently. "Thanks."

Kevin smiled in the blackness. "Any time." he murmured.

For a time, they simply sat, holding onto one another.

Finally, the lights flickered on.

"Vid in my room?" Kevin asked, kissing the top of Aidan's bright head. Aidan nodded against Kevin's shoulder. He took a breath and raised his face, smiling weakly. "Yeah. Sounds good."

Kevin smiled. "Come on then."

They settled against pillows propped up on Kevin's bed, lounging as Kevin sent the file to his wall screen and watched the load bar crawl towards completion. That was always the problem with indie films: the screen took forever to validate files without TechoCo metadata, even after the tinkering Peter had done years ago.

Finally, the credits began to roll. Kevin shifted, snuggling down against Aidan. "All right, comedy time. Get ready to laugh." Aidan leaned over and lay his head on Kevin's shoulder by way of agreement, settling in comfortably.

The movie opened traditionally enough. As the lines of Shakespeare's most overdone play rolled by, he picked out the rewritten sections. Kevin started to smile in anticipation, though he took the time to shoot a glance at Aidan. "Tell me you're getting this?"

Aidan's sapphire eyes were blank as he glanced up at Kevin. "Not nearly as much as you are, probably. Civil blood sounds like a tragedy. Isn't this one some big love story?"

Kevin sat up a little straighter. "Wait, you do know the plotline of the original play, don't you?" Reaching over, he paused the film. "The rewrite won't be as much fun if you don't know the issues the new film rectifies. You have got the gist, right?"

Aidan smiled, shaking his head. "They don't teach stone age fiction in Duster education programs, Kev."

"Stone age my ass!" Kevin exclaimed, genuinely appalled this time. "How do you get a sense of human nature without literature? That's why it's part of an education."

"You live with people and deal with their shit," the blonde man retorted, words carrying a note that told Kevin he'd been a touch too patronizing. He sighed.

"Fair point, sorry. Anyway, the original play. Want to hear the backstory?"

Aidan shrugged. "Sure."

"It's one of those infuriating ones where you simultaneously love the characters and want to shake them," Kevin began a little too quickly, glad to have the new subject. "To synopsize, there were two feuding families, the Capulets and the Montagues, right? A child from each house falls in love, and trials and tribulations ensue—it being a play, of course they do—but the story ends with both of the young people dead, mostly through lack of intelligence or forethought. I used to insist on reading only the first half because the ending irritated me so much. Anyway, Tortuga Bay just put out this version on the Greynet and from what I hear they fixed the main problem in the best possible way."

Aidan nodded, considering. "Okay, cool. Turn it back on and I guess we'll see."

With a nod Kevin settled back, arm around Aidan's shoulders.

A few moments later, Aidan glanced at him. "Okay, you're grinning. Am I missing stuff?"

Kevin chuckled. "Listen really closely when Sampson—he's in purple—says the next line, and then think about it a second."

On screen, one man teasingly shoved the other, their period costumes giving themselves away as CGI in the sudden movements.

"Therefore, I will push Montague's men from the wall, and thrust his maids to the wall!"

Kevin snorted. Aidan blinked. After a moment, his eyes widened. "They... they're making dirty jokes?"

"Yep. Dick jokes of every persuasion, actually." Kevin agreed with relish. "At least half of Shakespeare is really just dick jokes. What we've been hearing so far are mostly the traditional lines with a few rewrites in the prologue, but after this from what I hear the rewrite goes off canon and... yes!" he crowed as Mercutio and Benvolio kissed behind a wall while the other characters bickered. "I heard they rewrote the whole thing!"

Aidan stared in amazement. "I... how the hell did you find this? I'm amazed the Corps didn't burn every copy outside ZonCom and Techo turf."

"They would if they ever saw it," Kevin quipped. He paused the movie and turned to Aidan with a grin. "Tortuga Isle is a tiny indie company that shoots their stuff in secret and uses the Greynet to disseminate it as widely as possible. I met one of their distributors a few years ago and I've been getting their work for the base ever since." Kevin gestured at the screen, eyes dancing behind his glasses. "Like it so far?"

"It's incredible," Aidan breathed, staring at the screen. "I didn't... I had no idea people were making things like this that weren't Corporation restricted."

"It all depends on where you look." Kevin quipped, hitting play. On screen, Mercutio caught Juliet's hand and grinned winningly.

"Come now, desist this sighing. Only a little ring will free thee Giving liberty unto thine eyes; Explore other avenues. Two little rings, and then! Freedom for your heart is won!"

"And for you sir?" Juliet asked nervously, and the actor playing Mercutio swept a hand pointedly downwards.

"With a filly in the stable, why, no one will say ought if the stallion's let out his pen!"

Kevin burst out laughing. It took Aidan a moment longer, but Kevin knew he'd cottoned on when he started to chuckle, shaking his head.

"Wow.... that's awful."

"I know," Kevin agreed with a wicked grin. And the movie only got better from there. Instead of star-crossed love, pining and mistaken death, Mercutio married Juliet and their good friends Benvolio and Romeo took journeymen's lodgings in the house next door. Every night Benvolio and Romeo traded places to spend their evenings with their respective darlings, with hilarious results.

The lines didn't scan, the slang wasn't period, and the dialogue wasn't in proper sonnet form. But it was wonderful. Lines like 'and now lady, I take my leave, ere cock crow another cock must find most pleasant coop' made Kevin laugh so hard that his stomach hurt. Near escapes and daring rooftop chases—including one without Benvolio's pants—and the absolute baffling of the authorities washed away the fear that had come earlier in the evening.

When the vid switched off, Aidan shook his head, grinning. "That was totally gamma. In a good way, but yeah."

"I know." Kevin agreed, grinning. "I have got to show this to Blake some time."

Aidan shook his head, still chuckling. "Shit, don't, it'll give him ideas. He's kind of a walking cliché already."

"I know." Kevin agreed with relish. He pressed the back of his hand to his brow. "But how could I deny The Original Queen his chance to perform his *theatrics*?"

"Queen?"

Kevin waved a hand airily. "A man who isn't afraid to be *utterly fabulous*," he replied, imitating his mentor's speech habits.

"Hunh?"

They blinked at one another for a bewildered moment. Kevin gave a surprised little chuckle. "Didn't you know anybody gay as a kid? I thought you would on a base."

Aidan shrugged. "There was one guy, older than me. Didn't know him real well. Dad made him get a transfer."

Kevin made a face. "Ugh. All right, explanation: it's a joke about gay men who wear their preferences on their sleeve the way Blake does. Effeminate and regal, right? Hence, queens."

Aidan snorted, snuggling against him. "Okay, Queen of Hearts." Kevin rolled his eyes and tugged his boyfriend's hair gently. "Don't you start."

Aidan chuckled. "Okay, okay. He's got being a 'queen' and you've got poetry."

"Indeed, I do." Kevin tipped his head and repeated a line from the vid. "My such a long arrow, young Cupid, and you do shoot so trim. Pray, let me provide the quiver?"

That set them both off laughing all over again.

To his surprise, Aidan's smile faltered after a moment, an emotion like a cloud crossing his expression.

"What?" Kevin asked gently.

Aidan shrugged. "Nothing. Just thinking."

Kevin tipped his glasses down his nose and gave Aidan a look over the rims. "Yes, and you're allowed to say what you're thinking."

Aidan smiled crookedly. "I wish we could do that... I mean..." He shook his head.

"Well we practically do." Kevin chuckled. "Dodge the assholes and kiss behind their backs, beat them at their own game."

Aidan shook his head again. "No, I mean...with us. And...um. You being my quiver. I mean...you know."

Kevin studied his face, his grin fading. Aidan looked down, crossing his arms reflexively over his chest. He looked like a slightly scruffy Saint Jude, his face soulful and his blonde hair softly gleaming as he grieved over all the lost causes in the world. Kevin wanted so much to soothe away that expression.

For a flash of a moment he was tempted to get the box hidden under his bed out now rather than waiting for Aidan's birthday. He restrained himself.

"I know," he agreed eventually, reaching over to push Aidan's hair back from his eyes. "We make do, I think." He leaned in for a soft kiss, the arm around Aidan's shoulders pulling him closer.

"Yeah. We do," Aidan agreed, looking up with a crooked smile. Sometimes he looked so much like a character stepped from a sacred painting, forlorn and gorgeous. He leaned forward to kiss Kevin again, and Kevin returned the kiss with interest.

"You want to sleep here tonight?" Kevin asked softly, hoping the answer would be yes.

Aidan gave him another crooked quirk of the lips. "Can't. I need to finish up some paperwork and check up on the drone proximities before I hit the sack."

Kevin sighed. "We are time's subjects, and time bids be gone," he rejoined wryly. "That's another play for another night I guess."

"You should get on finding it, give me that education," Aidan replied with a chuckle. He kissed Kevin again and moved to get off the bed. "See you tomorrow."

"See you. Sleep a little bit at least." Kevin replied quietly. He watched Aidan cross the room, tensed as he put his hand on the door. *Say something, you coward*, he ordered himself.

"Aidan?" he asked. Aidan looked back over his shoulder, hair catching gold highlights from the hall. Standing, Kevin crossed the space and took Aidan's hand for a moment, thumb running over his knuckles.

"Er... don't worry about things, all right?" He leaned in for a last, soft kiss. "Making do is an awful lot of fun so far."

"I'll try," Aidan promised, his smile a little stronger. "Thanks."

He slipped out without another word.

"Shit on a biscuit," Tweak hissed. "What just... fuck! F-fuck this shit!" she snarled, dropping her tab in disgust.

Aidan looked up from his breakfast, blinking. He really needed more caffeine before he started dealing with Tweak.

"What's up with you?" Sarah asked, starting to reach out towards the girl in the same comforting hand-on-shoulder gesture she used with everyone else. She remembered to stop herself in time, which was a really good thing.

Tweak turned and dropped her tab in the recycling bin in one sharp gesture. "Another one. Hit f-f-firewall. Fried. Fucking fried."

"Uh Tweak, kiddos," Jim remarked quietly as his daughter chuckled and chewed away at a calorie bar.

Tweak rolled her eyes with a mutter and gulped her coffee, glaring at the table. "Kevin. New tab. B-better p-p-processor. Fast."

"Does her highness require any other royal needs be met?" Kevin asked dryly. Tweak gave him a poisonous glare, but she only shook her head. Irritably, she poured another cup of coffee and downed it.

"Don't you ever eat?" Billie asked in her half-whisper of a voice, and Aidan watched Tweak's face soften.

"'S-still c-coffee time. Shuddup."

"It's seven, slug," Billie retorted softly, taking a calorie bar. She broke it in half and held part of it out. "And it's a bad day to miss meals, you're working."

"Not working. F-fucking up," Tweak muttered, one bandaged arm reaching out to take the calorie bar. She chewed absently, fingers tapping the table, then stood and stamped out of the room.

"Whoa. Who came in her cheerios?" Janice muttered.

Lazarus held up his hands in mock-defense. "Don't look at me, she's not my type."

In her seat, Billie's shoulders hunched.

"Guys, give her a break. She's been stuck on this problem two weeks now," Andrea added, catching everyone who'd been joking in that gently reproachful look that always worked. Aidan was getting more and more impressed with the way the cheerful cook could get through to everybody by pulling that mom-is-disappointed look.

Janice shrugged, which for her was an acknowledgment. "S'pose gettin' stuck's no fun for nobody." She glanced at Aidan. "You want I should go check in, see how the kid's doin'?"

Aidan considered the idea. Janice was about as good as he was at getting through to Tweak, for some reason. But it was his job as Commander. Keeping his people on target was part of what he was here for.

"I think she's got a handle on it," he replied, yawning through his next sentence, "I'll check in with her later."

"Commander, you gotta quit letting Kev keep you up," Sarah sing-songed, grinning like a pet cat on CES level cream.

Kevin rolled his eyes. "He was doing paperwork, for your information. Do try not to project your own relentless libido on others for once?"

The crow-haired munitions specialist smirked. "Paperwork. Riiiight."

Kevin gave one of his theatrical sighs. "I hate you occasionally, you know that?"

Aidan stopped himself from shaking his head. If he didn't know better, he'd clock most of his crew's ages at fourteen from the way they talked.

"I'm gonna load the dishwasher, okay Mom?" Tommy asked, slipping from his seat at the table. Andrea glanced at him, then at his empty plate, before giving her son a smile. "Okay hon, thanks."

Nodding, the boy went around the table collecting plates and dirty cutlery. Arms full, he tottered across the room.

Breakfast was never a long meal on the base, not with the workload they had. Aidan had intended to head to his office and get into short-term mission briefs immediately, making sure he understood what other bases in the area were doing so that he could keep any of his plans from interfering with any of theirs. But first he had a hacker to check on.

He had nearly reached the door to the tech room when he registered the sound of the voices.

"—make sure you had a snack for later," Tommy's high voice was saying. There was a long pause. Aidan's stomach filled itself with ice.

Shit. A little kid like Tommy around somebody as volatile as Tweak. *Shit.*

He sped his steps, but the words that came next caught him before he reached the door.

"T-thanks," Tweak chirped, her voice shockingly gentle. Aidan blinked. Tweak was actually being nice to the kid?

"You look scared," Tommy's voice matched Tweak's: tentative, a little nervous, soft.

Tweak sighed in the coding room. "Yeah. This isn't w-w-working s-so good. I g-gotta g-get it r-r-r-r..."

"When my mom got sick and lost her voice she typed everything on her tab. You want to type stuff?" Tommy's voice asked. A few seconds later, Aidan heard Tommy give a small laugh. "Yeah but you're awesome. You won't get us found. You're good."

Aidan took the chance and stepped to the door. Inside, Tweak and Tommy were watching each other with expressions so similar it was almost funny. Both looked hopeful, and both looked scared stiff. Tweak's hand clutched a calorie bar, fingers crinkling the wrapping.

Aidan glanced at Tweak's main screen. The words gleamed in the hologram.

"I have to find a better way to do this. I can't use the main computers for the base. If I get this wrong and they trace it back to us, they'd know where we are. I don't want to get you guys found."

Tweak's expression shifted, a smile softening her face more than Aidan had believed possible. For a second, she looked like the kid she was.

"T-thanks."

The floor creaked under Aidan's feet. Tweak sat up with a jolt. Tommy glanced up, mildly interested as usual.

"Hi Aidan."

"Hey Tommy," Aidan managed a smile. "I'm going to talk to Tweak about mission stuff okay? I think your mom's looking for you."

"Kay." Tommy agreed. He gave Tweak a last quick smile. "The bar's chocolate, those are the good ones. The peanut butter ones are gross."

"T-thanks," Tweak repeated, her lips quirking in a tiny smile.

Aidan watched until the little boy had ambled down the hall before leaning against the door, crossing his arms over his chest. "He's a sweet kid, hunh?"

"Yeah," Tweak agreed stiffly. Setting the calorie bar to one side, she turned back to her tab and started to type. "Whatcha need?" she asked as her fingers worked, eyes fixed on the hologram.

Aidan shrugged. "I was going to ask you that. I'm good with where you've gotten on this thing, but maybe you aren't?"

Tweak's sigh was loud in the cramped quiet. She flicked another window into existence, typed furiously for a moment, then hit the key that projected the text in the right direction for Aidan to read where he stood.

"Look,"

he read,

I can't use the main coding rig for this, because if I fuck up at all TechoCo will be able to track our Greynet IP back here, and then we'll get a bomb dropped on our heads. The code broadcasters failed. I'm trying to use unregistered tabs. They run on a mesh-net, tracking won't happen. But the little pieces of shit can't run the defenses that are worth shit against the kind of anti-threat viruses that stick to your OS if you so much as touch the firewalls. They're unregistered but they're useless. The code broadcasters were useless. I need another option.

Aidan nodded carefully, sorting the jargon Tweak was slinging and considering. "Can you try sending code broadcasters in with the Logistics guys again? Maybe try another kind of code?"

Tweak gave him a look that implied he needed his brain upgraded. Her fingers danced.

"What, you think after the twenty attacks I packed onto the last broadcasters didn't work, another ONE will?"

Aidan held her eyes. "Tweak, I'm not good at this stuff. You know that. Instead of telling me off how about you talk to me about this?"

Tweak glared at him, eyes narrowing into black slits. Aidan stared back blankly. Finally, Tweak jerked her hands into motion.

"I can't do what I need to with the tools I have, okay? I. Can't. Do. It."

Aidan took three long, slow breaths.

"Maybe you're aiming at the wrong thing. Have you tried aiming at something besides the firewalls? The coder on a base I used to be on would get into the Corporation's Feed as a regular user and just read up on people. That's a place to start."

Tweak cocked her head. "Y-you mean go phishing? Phishing s-sucks."

"Could you get into TechoCo's Social Feed as a normal reader?" Aidan asked patiently.

"Yeah? Then what?" Tweak asked, crossing her arms as if to imitate him.

Aidan didn't let himself react. "Tweak, don't play stupid. It isn't helping you or me. If you can't hack the tech, hack the people. They're easier."

"S-s-sucks." Tweak snapped, eyes flicking down to her boots. Aidan studied her lowered face. Had he ever seen Tweak turn down trying to make something happen? Not a chance. So, what the hell was going on?

Was she having issues with him telling her what to do again? No, that wasn't it. She'd been frustrated with the project, but if Tweak thought you were bossing her around, she didn't get sullen. She told you off.

So, what the hell was all this about? Why was she shutting down?

Then it clicked.

"Kind of feels like we're acting like the Corps, doesn't it?" He asked quietly, studying her. "Getting into people's personal feeds and screwing with them to get what we want."

Tweak's shoulders hunched. Bingo.

"Doesn't f-f-feel like it. Is it."

Aidan blinked. "Um..."

Tweak rolled her eyes. "What they used to have me doing. TechoCo. What, you think when they ar-r-r—" she swallowed hard. "—arrest you they just s-sit you in a b-box? I w-was one of the ones they used to t-tear d-d-down an-n-nybody they d-didn't l-l-like. They had me d-doing phishing. Hacking p-people. G-getting in and m-m-messing with p-people the C-C-Corp had a problem w-with. S-stealing files. Planting stuff. R-r-r-rewriting r-records. Framing people. M-messed with people in other c-countries too. S-s-s-sucks." Tweak whispered the last word. She let out a long sigh. "I h-hate g-getting into people's l-lives and stuff. Feels like s-shit. Wanna hit the Corps. Not people. Not an-n-nymore."

Aidan nodded as the pieces fit together in his head. No wonder she had an issue with this. "Yeah. I know it sucks. But right now, we can't get at the big guys without going through a couple little guys along the way. That's why it's a war."

Tweak's head shot up, eyes hot. "Fuck that."

"No. Seriously, Tweak. Don't assume you know what I'm going to say. Listen to me, okay?" Aidan stated carefully. He waited a beat, letting the girl settle before he spoke.

"It sucks. It does. But we're not doing this to get something for ourselves. It's like medicine, that's what somebody told me once. Like a doctor treating injuries. Sometimes you do have to hurt somebody, but you're going to make their life a whole lot better in the end. The little bit of pain makes that worth it. And right now, you can't think about 'everyday people' and 'the Corps', because it's not that easy. Everyday people work *for* the Corps. They don't get a choice. You know that."

Tweak gave a slow, grudging nod. "Yeah. I know. But I don't w-wanna s-s-screw people over. G-get them in t-trouble c-c-cause I h-hacked them. I'm n-n-not l-like that no more."

You were like that when you hacked Kevin's credentials to order luxury goods, Aidan thought as he studied the girl. *You are like that when you hack banks for us and siphon off cash. When you falsify records for us. For everything we do, somewhere there's some tech who's going to get shouted at, have their Citizen Standing Score dropped, get fired for incompetence at work. There's always a price. Someone always pays it.*

But you only think about it when you look at a face and see a person. You really don't think you're hurting anybody when you do the stuff we ask you to do.

You're lucky, Tweak. But the fact that you can be this smart and still not be able to put two and two together is a little bit terrifying.

He kept those thoughts to himself when he spoke.

"They used to make you do coding that hurt people. So, you know exactly how they work it, right?"

Warily, Tweak nodded. "Y-yeah?"

"Then you can turn that around. You can think up a way that gets you in without hurting anybody you don't want to," Aidan replied, letting a note of sternness into his voice. "You figure out what we need to do, and we'll figure out how, okay?"

Tweak glanced away. "Yeah…" she swallowed. "S-sorry. B-being a b-b-bitch."

Aidan's lips quirked. "A little bit, yeah."

Tweak glanced up at him, half-smiling. Aidan returned the smile.

Stepping out of the code-room door, he almost ran into Billie. He grabbed the pot she was holding reflexively when she jumped, and realized that was a stupid move once the heat seared his fingers. He yelped.

"The coffee's hot!" Billie exclaimed, yanking the pot back just as instinctively as Aidan had yanked his hands away. The statement was so ridiculously obvious that it got Aidan to stop shaking his stinging hands and give her a chagrined smile. "I think I got that."

The high squeak behind them turned Aidan's head. Tweak was leaned against the door, a bandaged hand over her mouth, shaking with laughter. Billie grinned sheepishly.

"Want?" she asked, holding up the coffee pot and a cup.

"Yeah. Want," Tweak agreed with laughter in her voice, "C'mon. Help?"

"Sure," Billie agreed, stepping past Aidan into the coding room.

Watching the door over his shoulder, Aidan headed for his own office and his own work. There was plenty of that.

"Ain't seen you for nine hours," a voice drawled from the hall, making Aidan start out of his mission-report induced brain freeze. He sat up straight. Janice gave him a lazy smile from her leaning post against his door. She tipped her chin in the direction of the other end of the hall. "Was startin' t'wonder if Tweak'd killed you yet. I was comin' down t'see if that was goin' okay. She got it in there?"

Aidan rubbed a hand across his eyes. Tweak and her work. Right. He tried to kick his brain back into gear. Did Tweak have this whole thing? Probably not yet. But at least she wasn't banging her head on something impossible any longer.

Turning in his chair, he gave his hydroelectrics specialist a smile. "She's getting it."

Eyes on the coding door, Janice nodded slowly. "Kay. Got somethin' of my own for you then."

"Yeah?" Aidan asked, his gut tightening. Deadpan, Janice tipped her head in the direction of his spare chair. "I'm gonna wanna sit down."

Aidan's hands clenched. He forced them to relax, giving her the nod. Janice settled in her chair with elaborate ease. "Y'know I said this aquifer was a good one 'fore we moved to this site?" she asked, casual as only somebody who was working at it could be.

"Yeah?" Aidan asked.

Janice picked at her nails. "I'm startin' to think it might be bettern' good. Startin' to see signs that—"

The thump of boots on pre-fab floor panels brought both Dusters to their feet before Janice had finished her sentence.

"I got it I got it I got it I got it!" Tweak practically skidded into Aidan's office. Bouncing on the balls of her feet, she planted her fists on her hips and grinned like a coyote. "I got an idea."

Janice smirked. "Well praise the Lord an' post it on the Feeds."

Shooting her a dry look, Tweak flipped her off.

<u>Event File 7</u>
<u>File Tag: Occasion of Note</u>
<u>Timestamp: 07:00-11-13-2155</u>

"That's quite the elegant solution."

"What's el-l…talk English." Tweak's high voice snapped. Kevin repressed a sigh, but he caught Aidan's eye and forced himself to give the coder a smile.

"I mean it's a nice work around. Good job."

Tweak gave him a glare that very clearly stated 'don't patronize me, asshole.' He was never going to win with her.

Sighing, he glanced around at his logistics team and his Commander, then back to the shaky flow chart that Tweak had drawn up.

"So, let me make sure we've got this right." Reaching past Kevin, Yvonne traced the flow chart with one finger.

"You went phishing and found a bunch of the guys who code and write copy for Techo. You think we can hack one of them and use their credentials to write in the system directly?"

"Y-yeah," Tweak agreed, bobbing her head. "If w-w-we get in on a w-work tab w-with authenticated c-credentials, this'll be lots easier."

"Okay cool." Yvonne traced her finger in a circle around the box. "So you're thinking, we find a guy who takes his work tab home with him and...what? Steal it?"

"Not steal," Tweak snapped with scorn on her tongue. "Borrow. N-not at their home. N-not unless we get d-desperate. Too many s-security systems to w-worry about. It's better in p-public. We find a guy who stops for a d-drink after w-work. Lunchtime c-coffee. Something. Bag under his chair. Distract. B-b-b-borrow. We d-don't steal it. M-minute he knows it's s-stolen he'll cancel its authentication. G-get it straight."

"Okay, borrow," Yvonne agreed easily, the insult sliding right off. "Then we throw on some kind of keylog bug."

"B-better if he uses an ex-ex-external k-k-keyboard. Insert a m-modified input chip w-with a l-logger," Tweak put in. "Find one of the n-nerdy guys who's worried about his wrists. The chip d-doesn't show in p-processing so b-bad as a b-b-bug. Logger sends keystrokes t-to me here. We got his password."

Kevin nodded slowly. So far so good, he thought, but that meant someone would be making more than one trip into one of TechoCo's employee relaxation areas, and probably a high-Standing one too. Followed by a great deal of indiscreet people-watching. After that, what would need to be one or two very discreet thefts in one of the private employee areas for the corporation that came a close second on the Most Vigilant ranking.

Joy.

"So, we do our thing, you get the key logs and get this guy's passwords." Jim added carefully. "Then it looks like you...what, steal the machine?"

"Nope." Tweak shook her head. "Seriously, forget theft. Sneak in. D-distract the t-target. Use their r-r-registered computer, their password, send out a b-blast. Put it back. N-nobody knows how we g-got in."

"Okay..." Yvonne nodded slowly. "Why can't we do more of this online? This is getting to be a lot of physical runs and some big risks. I mean, keeping this guy distracted while somebody walks off with his tab and then brings it back isn't going to be easy."

Tweak let out a long, loud sigh. "Seriously. Does nobody read the b-background intel? Online's. How. They find us. *Genius.* One wrong step. One wrong move, they t-track us we die. Even on the G-greynet. Other b-bases tried it that way, they died. Techo's p-proprietary systems are protected with AI r-running on quantum c-computers. C-can't beat that. You guys sneak in. You use their em-emp-employee comps. We're safe. We keep using our comps. With these guys. We're dead. Get it?"

Yvonne's eyes widened. "Okay, I get it."

"Anyway," Jim continued in a 'let's play nice' tone, "we get into the bar, we... I don't know, drug the guy and pretend to be buddies taking him home, chat him up, something. That still needs figuring. I mean, we could have somebody invite him home for the night...'course the two hot ones in Logistics are taken—"

"Damn straight." Yvonne agreed pointedly. "And Sarah doesn't share. You want to share, Aidan?"

"Don't be crass. And for your information, a TechoCo home is the last bloody place we want to end up," Kevin snapped, each word clipped. "They have terrifying security and surveillance systems in place on all their domiciles." Yvonne rolled her eyes as he continued, "So, once we're on the fellow's work tab, we can use the machine to attach the Folder to a Social Feed update or something of the sort. It pops up on everybody's profile in the US."

"Yep."

Tapping her screen, Tweak brought up an image of a web-work covering the continent. "Social engineers got all this. Posts. Biometrics. Cornea tracking. They got logs on who every p-person pays most attention to when they p-post, what they p-pay attention to. They got algorithms they use. You get in, you can use it. One guy c-clicks when it comes from his g-grandma, another guy when it comes from his b-buddy. Looks organic. The folder. I'll build mirrors, s-stick them on some Greynet s-sites. End of a day. Everybody got a copy. It gets deleted? It gets shared again." Sitting back, Tweak crossed her arms, a small smile tugging at her lips.

"And that's it?" Aidan asked.

"That's it," Tweak agreed, dark eyes sparkling, "Whatcha think?"

I think there's about ten thousand ways this could go to hell, Kevin thought. But he chose his words with more care. "There's a lot of room for error and bad luck in a plan this convoluted. We're going to need to discuss contingencies..."

"You think it's bad, you got a better idea, CES?" Tweak snapped, whipping around in her chair to glare at him.

He held her eyes. "No, I don't have a better idea, and I did not say that it was a bad plan. I said that it was a convoluted plan. A complicated one. It is my job to spot the discrepancies in a plan before they get someone killed, Tweak. That's why I'm here."

The teenager sat coiled for a moment longer. Relaxed.

"Yeah, okay," she muttered, looking away. Kevin didn't allow himself to show a sign of relief. Not so many months ago the little coder would have lashed out in a tirade when she was criticized. For that matter, she would have said 'you guys die,' not 'we die.' Maybe Aidan was right. Maybe the kid was changing.

Beside him, Yvonne put on the 'hell with it' smirk she wore just before she did something inadvisable.

"Well I say we go for it. I'll do the bugging run, I like flipping the douchebags the bird."

Kevin looked at her over the rims of his glasses. Time to deflate that attitude before it got out of hand. If you didn't rein Yvonne in, she'd run at a new problem like a kid offered candy.

"Flipping them the bird is exactly what we don't need." Yvonne gave him an impatient look. "Kev, you're no fun anymore. I can—"

"You can end up dead if you treat this like a game. Or worse," Kevin finished pointedly, "but the details we can work out in due time." Glancing back at Aidan, he nodded. "I can make the logistics happen, if you want to send the general plan in for approval. It won't be easy, but it's doable."

Slowly, Aidan nodded, eyes meeting each of his crew's in turn. "If you guys are sure, I'll send the preliminary plan in."

"Sure." Tweak stated categorically, holding his gaze. Yvonne gave him a wide grin. "We got this."

Aidan's blue eyes met Kevin's again, and he saw the fear his boyfriend was working so hard to hide.

Smiling, he nodded. "I'll make sure."

Aidan nodded. "Okay then."

Feeling the tension in the room, Kevin spoke. "And on a lighter note, isn't it time we signed off? I've still got to pin down Dozer and the rest of you have lyrics to memorize."

Jim rolled his eyes. "I still can't believe you talked us into this."

Kevin smirked, leaning back and crossing his arms. "You did help me buy the alcohol for it."

"Yeah, but nobody told me I had to sing," the specialist grumbled good-naturedly.

"You g-guys talking 'bout the party again, I'm out," Tweak stated, standing sharply. In a clatter of boots, she was gone.

Yvonne's pranking grin nearly split her face as she leaned in. "Laz and I got it all ready, everything's a go, only Dozer's left to talk to 'cause every time we look he's with Topher, and he never reads his messages."

"You pranked him so many times that he sends yours to spam." Jim interjected. Yvonne shrugged, not contrite in the slightest.

"I'll catch up with him tonight," Kevin replied with his own smile, "I think if I wait in the canteen that should work. I still need to find a poem to put the grace note on the evening, but everything else is set. You got Andrea what she needed for the cake?"

"Yeah, I did a trade three days ago."

Aidan glanced between them. "Wait...I didn't approve any extra runs three days ago."

Yvonne flapped a hand. "I just did something quick when I was checking in with Base 1432 for coolant precursor, no big."

Kevin caught the concern on Aidan's face and made a mental note to address it later, in private.

"I'll see if I can pin down Dozer tonight."

He did it by stepping out of a hidden corner of the canteen by the washing machines as the older man passed.

"Psst! Dozer. Step over here a moment."

Smiling warily, the bigger man stepped in. "Okay, what gives? Sarah tried this twice yesterday, Yvonne too."

"Topher's birthday is on the twelfth, right?" Kevin asked, eyes dancing. "Well, you know how he talked about family parties in his childhood, drinking arak and singing and all that? The kid's turning twenty-one, so Jim and I dug a few bottles of arak up, Yvonne got the supplies for a traditional cake and I found the words to a few Lebanese—well, I think they're Lebanese, I'm almost sure—anyway, a few drinking songs. If we all learn them, we could make a great night out of it. Everyone else has a copy of the lyrics, may I give you one?"

Dozer blinked at Kevin. Slowly, a chuckle rumbled through his barrel of a chest.

"You want all of us dumbasses to learn a new language in less'n a week? You'd have better luck moonin' the Corps, man."

Kevin sighed in his most expressive manner. "You don't have to learn the language Dozer, just pronounce the syllables. I've got recordings of everything for you to listen to. Besides, it really can't be that difficult; they're drinking songs."

"Have you heard the boy cuss? Damn near impossible to pick apart," Dozer replied with another chuckle.

"Yes, well, you say that about me when I get angry as well. That might say something about you rather more than it does about the men you're indicting," Kevin rejoined with a sly smile. "You aren't saying you're too intimidated to give it even a try, are you?"

Dozer propped his fists on his hips, eyeing the slimmer man. "Just saying you better know what you're doin'. Toph's like a son t'me, you know."

"I'm eminently aware of what I'm doing, for your information." Kevin cocked his head. "And as a surrogate father, don't you want to get the kid drunk and make him grin?"

"'Course I do," Dozer replied levelly, "only I'm imaginin' the cringe when we fuck up the songs is all."

Kevin smirked. "I repeat, they're drinking songs. I think the appellation implies low levels of skill."

Dozer shrugged. "If you're goin' to get high and mighty wordy on me, guess I got no choice. When's the party?"

"After duty on the day, of course, it's on a Friday so we can do this properly. We'll call it a vid night and when he gets in, we'll surprise him with a couple bottles, a cake and a lot of bad Arabic." Kevin finished with relish. He brought up the file on his tab, pointing it out. "There, I've sent this folder to you." With a half-salute and a last quick grin, he stepped out of the shadows.

Two days later, Kevin was off duty and engrossed in poetry from another country, laid out in the warm shade of the compound roof and digging through all the files he could find. It was banned literature of course, technically labeled 'Islamic extremist propaganda,' but being banned had certainly never stopped Kevin from reading something before.

Pulling up a new page, he ran a finger across the holographic words, watching as they translated themselves. He smiled as he read.

A shadow fell across his screen. He started, shutting it down reflexively before he glanced up. With a relieved little smile, he brought it back up. "Hello stranger. I'm looking for something to use as a little grace note at the end of Topher's party; just have to choose the right poem. Want to take a look?"

Aidan chuckled as he dropped down behind his boyfriend, his chin on Kevin's shoulder. "Am I going to understand a word of it?"

"Eventually, once the translator finishes the page." Kevin murmured, studying the words. "Damn. Another love poem. I'm looking for something about bravery, but all I seem to be getting is love poems."

Aidan laughed softly and pressed a soft kiss to the back of Kevin's neck. "Too bad. That why you're reading outside?"

"Mm." Kevin agreed, turning his head to smile softly up at Aidan. "Topher tends to come in and have a chat fairly often when I'm in my quarters. Besides, I rather like being outdoors when it's cool enough. Amelioration for the claustrophobia inside." He glanced down at his screen. "I found one here that I rather like. Want to see it?"

"If it's been translated," Aidan agreed amicably, fingers playing with Kevin's hair. The gesture sent small, electric frissons running down Kevin's neck.

"If it was in Arabic, I couldn't read it either. They taught me German and Japanese, Mandarin, French and Spanish, but I didn't get this one." he demurred lightly as he brought up the poem. He propped the tab so that they could read together.

When love beckons to you follow him,

Though his ways are hard and steep.
And when his wings enfold you yield to him,
Though the sword hidden among his pinions may wound you.
And when he speaks to you believe in him,
Though his voice may shatter your dreams as the north wind
lays waste the garden.
For even as love crowns you so shall he crucify you.
Even as he is for your growth so is he for your pruning.
Even as he ascends to your height and caresses your tenderest
branches that quiver in the sun,
So shall he descend to your roots and shake them in their
clinging to the earth.
Like sheaves of corn he gathers you unto himself.
He threshes you to make you naked.
He sifts you to free you from your husks.
He grinds you to whiteness.
He kneads you until you are pliant;
And then he assigns you to his sacred fire, that you may become
sacred bread for God's sacred feast.
All these things shall love do unto you that you may know the
secrets of your heart, and in that knowledge become a fragment
of Life's heart.

"Very zen, isn't it?" Kevin asked quietly. "Kahlil Gibran. He's starting to be a new favorite of mine."

"Scroll back up a second?" Aidan asked, and Kevin obliged.

"Not sure I get it," Aidan added quietly when his second reading was complete. "But it's very you."

Kevin glanced back up, searching Aidan's sun-tanned face as the warm breeze ruffled their hair. He gave a small smile. "Shall I take that as a compliment?"

Aidan kissed Kevin's cheek. "That a love poem is very you? Yeah, that's a compliment."

"Fair enough," Kevin murmured, taking comfort in Aidan's weight and his warmth.

"Learned your drinking songs yet?" he asked as an afterthought. "I've never heard you sing before. Looking forward to it."

Aidan choked on his next breath. He must have inhaled dust; he pulled away to cough.

"Yeah… uh. Not exactly a singer," he admitted eventually, "Naomi used to say I could break glass just trying to find a note. And that was before I started on T."

Kevin gave a sigh, rolling over and lacing his fingers behind his head to look up at Aidan. "Some time I'm going to have to meet this elusive sister and give her a telling off for all the damage she's done to your ego, you know?" The breeze played with his hair, and he casually batted it back out of his eyes. "Besides, as a group we sound like a bunch of alley cats in heat; nobody will notice how bad your voice is in the process of bawling out their own terrible renditions."

"I'll play conductor," Aidan insisted. He leaned down to kiss Kevin gently. "Rhythm I actually have."

"Well I already knew that," Kevin murmured against Aidan's lips, low enough to keep it between them. "You've demonstrated it very conclusively in bed."

Aidan snorted a chuckle, touching their noses together. "So, I win. Conductor."

"I cede the point," Kevin agreed with a smile.

It took Kevin the rest of the week and much of his off-duty time, but by the time he was taking inventory in the motor pool on the twelfth everything was in place. Dozer tossed a ruined rag in the bin and ducked his head under their newest truck. "More rags too."

"Those we can print." Kevin mused, jotting it down on his inventory list. "I think we have the fabric precursor, I'll check and have the girls pick it up on the Monday inter-base run if we're out. Anything else?"

"Think that's it." Dozer remarked, leaning further under the chassis. "Hey kid!" he added, raising his voice, "we're not breaking the black box on that thing and getting it reprogrammed tonight. Let's call it an early night, get showers; new vids're in anyway an' I wanna vote this time on what we watch."

"Be there in a sec," Topher called back, hauling on the wrench he was using to try and loosen the bolts on the black box. "'Nother one of your half hour seconds, or a real one?" Dozer asked, bending creakily to get his subordinate's attention.

Kevin dropped to one knee to peer under the truck. "He has a point, we need all hands on deck to out-vote the girls and their heinous vid choices. Come on!"

"Look who's talking about shitty vids!" Topher retorted, putting more pressure on the wrench.

"You oughta knock off early when it's your birthday. Vids an' a drink, c'mon," Dozer cajoled.

Topher rolled his eyes. "I can get this loose in ten minutes, Doze. Birthdays come every year man."

Dozer sighed, then did what he usually did when Topher didn't listen: he simply reached under the vehicle, grabbed the bottom of the kid's wheeled work board and pulled him out from under the truck. "Yeah well, this one's here. An' you're off work, 'cause I want off work an' if you're in here, I gotta be here to keep you from screwin' up. So, you're off work, yeah?"

Topher groaned, but he sat up, reaching for a rag to wipe grease off his hands. "Okay, okay. Fine. Jeez."

Not long later, the two specialists were reasonably clean and ready to join their crew. The vid room was already packed by the time they arrived, and Dozer coughed to hide his smile as they entered. Other people weren't bothering to hide much of anything.

Dozer flopped down, and Topher grabbed a seat nearby. That was the cue Kevin had set for himself. He stood up in front of the media center, placing the backpack that had been slung over his shoulder carefully at his feet. He cleared his throat theatrically.

"Down in front!" Sarah called, and Kevin flipped her off without bothering to look in her direction.

"So, as all of you know, our junior transport specialist is officially old enough to make all the stupid decisions he likes."

Laughter ran around the room, and a couple people leaned in to punch Topher lightly in the arm or slap his back. He rolled his eyes, grinning.

"To mark the occasion," Kevin continued, "we decided to give a nod to the country who gave us such a prodigy. So, without further ado—" He opened the satchel and extracted the first of the bottles with a flourish. "Let's drink to Lebanon, shall we?"

Topher blinked at the bottles, then at Kevin. "Holy crap. I should have lied about my age earlier!"

Laughter broke out again, and Jim reached over to punch the kid lightly in the arm.

Grinning, Kevin passed out the bottles; there was plenty of the strong anise-tasting arak to get them all nicely drunk. He took his first good mouthful, bracing himself for the intensity of the first sip as he watched his comrades inspect the new liquor. You could tell who'd had anise seed before and who hadn't by the expressions.

Damian finished his first sip, coughed and drew in a gasp. "Damn, I'm not sure if I should drink this stuff or light it on fire."

"Chickenshit," Janice remarked, grabbing the bottle, taking a swig, then coughing hard as the fiery distilled spirits hit her throat. Turning, she looked Topher up and down. "You grew up on this stuff? Shit boy, you're tougher'n you look!"

"Man, Janice; he's not a boy anymore," Kevin corrected, toasting Topher with his bottle before passing it to Aidan.

Topher just laughed and took another swig, coughing a little himself. "Not exactly this. I mean, this is hella strong."

"No shit," Aidan muttered through the coughs brought on by his own swallow.

"Well, balance it out with this!" Andrea announced from the hall. Grinning, she and Billie guided the serving platter held by Tommy, Dilly and Donny into the room. On the plate a wide slab of cake glistened with frosting, the number 21 written on it in brilliant red. Someone had printed a toy truck to sit in the center. Kevin couldn't hold back the grin that spread across his face as the cook and her assistants held their burden for all to see. The room filled with whoops and cheers. Topher shook his head. "You guys are total gammas," he managed through his laughter, eyes bright.

Andrea's brown eyes danced as she cut a slice, put it on a plate Billie held out and served it to Topher. "Make a wish and take a bite. You know how this goes."

"Yeah, okay." Topher made a show of closing his eyes, mouthing a few words silently. Then he took his ceremonial bite of cake.

Kevin passed around plates and waited until everyone was well supplied with cake and drink. Timing it for a lull in the conversation, he stood with a carefully calculated flourish.

"And now for something even more traditional!" he announced, turning on his music app. He and Yvonne had spent two hours removing the voice frequencies from the song in order to create their own karaoke track, and it really hadn't turned out too badly. Around Topher, his base-mates wolf-whistled and started in on their best attempts at the song.

"Leh bet t'asser tanoura
leh bet t'asser tanoura
btelha treyoune al chabaaab
Heeeeeeeeeeey!"

Topher nearly choked on his next sip, his eyes gone wide. "Oh. My. God."

The next raucous verse began, filled with horrible pronunciations, forgotten lyrics and laughter.

In a vacant corner, Tweak watched the crowd around the boy, though she managed a small smile whenever anyone glanced her way. Kevin noted it, but he wasn't letting anything kill the mood tonight. If she wanted to leave, she had every right.

Topher cursed vehemently through his laughter as the song ended.

"Man, you guys murdered that!"

Yvonne ruffled his hair. "You're the only one who knows, kid."

"Have a couple more drinks and you won't know either," Sarah added, pecking the junior specialist's cheek.

Topher grinned, hefting his bottle. "Happy birthday to me, then!"

At two in the morning, Damian gently lifted Topher's head and frowned. "Aidan? I think this is one drunk kid."

"Le la le la le..." Topher giggled, glassy-eyed.

"He's going to get a great lesson on hangovers tomorrow," Damian sighed. "I'll write him in the medical bay roster tonight, I might as well."

Aidan gave a laugh, leaning hard against Kevin, who held him up with a grin of his own. He'd never seen his boyfriend drunk before, but if he was any judge Aidan was well past tipsy.

"'S what twenty-one is for!" Aidan announced to the room in general, waving his free hand and grinning from ear to ear. That smile might be eighty percent alcohol, but it was good to see regardless.

"Might need to get the commander on the roster, too," Yvonne snickered, throwing an arm around her wife's waist. "He's drunk."

"Look who's talking!" Sarah giggled as Yvonne ran a very insistent hand over her breasts. "Looking for something, hon? This maybe?" She pulled the taller woman in for a long kiss. Yvonne hummed happily against her wife's lips. "Mmmmhmm."

"Okay Maureen." Kevin called over, pulling the joke from a movie Aidan had found and everyone had fallen in love with.

Yvonne gave him a goofy grin. "Ouoooooot tonight!" she wailed off key.

Kevin covered his ears. "Wrong note *and* wrong character, dear girl."

"Kissing? We're doing kissing now?" Aidan muttered with a grin, his words slurred. He made a stumbling turn and kissed Kevin hard, hands holding tight to his boyfriend's jacket collar. Kevin swallowed an amazed squeak, shocked at Aidan's boldness. Aidan, kissing in public? He really must be drunk. But Kevin wasn't about to complain.

"That's it!" Liza's laughing voice shouted, "*Everybody* get a room!"

"Finally, an order from her I don't feel obliged to disagree with," Kevin murmured into Aidan's hair. Taking Aidan's shoulders, he guided him down the hall. Aidan stumbled beside Kevin, still wearing that infectious grin. Kevin couldn't help but smile in turn.

"That song is going to be stuck in my head for a week." he murmured laughingly as they slipped together into his room.

"Sing somethin' else and you'll forget that one," Aidan mumbled, chuckling to himself. "I mean, you know like a million. Do one of the bugs ones."

"I think you mean the Beatles."

Kevin let Aidan flop down on the bed, knelt and pulled off the other man's boots before he undid his own. He set his glasses aside and snuggled down beside Aidan.

The lights gleamed through a lovely fog of inebriation and nearsightedness. Kevin smiled lazily, taking in Aidan's face. Seen like this, he seemed to have a halo.

Aidan half-opened his eyes, his messy pageboy-cut hair fanned out around his face. "What?"

Kevin smoothed his hair back. "You look like a saint in this light."

Aidan chuckled, reaching up to cup Kevin's cheek in his palm, thumb stroking his cheekbone.

"You oughta let Damian do your eyes. Your sight's all kinds of messed up."

"No, really. Saint Jude. Patron saint of lost causes." Kevin leaned in, kissing Aidan's throat. He breathed the words of a song into Aidan's ear.

"Hey Jude, don't make it bad,

just take a sad song and make it better..."

Aidan laughed, rolling clumsily into his arms.

"You're drunk."

"I'm drunk? Pot and kettle." Kevin tapped Aidan's nose. "For your information, I'm tipsy. You're drunk."

Aidan closed his eyes, a grin on his lips. "Okay," he managed, tripping over the words. "I'm drunk."

He snuggled down against Kevin, resting his head on Kevin's chest. "Mm. I love you."

Kevin's breath caught in his chest.

I love you. Aidan had just said that. He'd really said it.

He forced himself to give a laugh, though it sounded tinny in his own ears.

"I…" He swallowed hard, forcing the words out. "I think I love you too. But given that you're drunk, I doubt you'll remember."

Aidan chuckled and pulled him back in for another kiss. "Shuddup an' kiss me."

"With pleasure," Kevin agreed, rolling them so that Aidan was on top of him and kissing him long and softly. He made a point of keeping the kisses easy, asking nothing from a man as drunk as Aidan was.

Eventually, Aidan closed his eyes and lay draped bonelessly, his breathing slow with sleep. Leaning tipsily on the edge of sleep himself, Kevin let himself bask in this moment: the warmth, the contentment, the feeling of Aidan's chest rising and falling against his. Smiling softly, he slid his hand under Aidan's shirt and unzipped his binder. Aidan would sleep more easily with that pressure off his chest.

Pulling the covers over them both, he let his eyes fall closed.

Aidan had actually said those words. *I love you.*

Said them while drunk.

But he'd said them.

Aidan woke slowly in the morning, refusing to open his eyes.

His head throbbed. His mouth was dry. Kevin was warm against him.

He really, really didn't want to move. If he didn't move for a moment, he could pretend he wasn't a base commander, that they weren't constantly at war with the Corps, that he didn't have to leave the comfort of Kevin's bed.

Of course, life didn't put up with that for long. One by one, his damn body made its demands. His bladder was uncomfortably full. The mesh of his binder was itching. His breasts ached. His head too.

With a quiet groan he rolled out of bed, peeled his shirt and binder off and pulled on one of Kevin's biggest knit sweaters before shuffling down the hall to the bathroom, glad no one else was awake so early on their one day off.

"Commander," Janice muttered sleepily in passing, headed for the women's hygiene room. A rattling bottle was shoved into his hand as she passed. "Figured you for another one who couldn't hold a drink."

It took Aidan way too long to realize what she'd given him. He blinked blearily after her. "Uh... thanks."

He dropped the bottle into his pocket and slipped into the bathroom to pee and scrub his face. It helped a little. Not enough.

Glancing in the mirror, he felt his brow furrow. Why the hell did Kevin own a sweater with a giant pair of lips and a tongue sticking out? It was one of Alice's knitting projects. Another Wildcards in-joke?

He shook his head. He'd figure it out later; he was too tired now.

Janice's voice caught him as he closed the door of the men's room. "Was startin' to think you fell in."

Aidan looked up groggily at the sound of Janice's voice. She smiled wryly at him. "Ain't easy for me to get ahold of you, you know that?"

"Been a busy week. Anything wrong?" he asked, rubbing at his face.

"Nope. Somethin' right, actually." Janice tipped her head. "Take one of those pills I gave you an' come sit down for coffee. I wanna talk to you for a minute now you're payin' attention."

"Can it wait?" Aidan asked, hearing the hopelessness in his own voice. Janice gave him a cockeyed look, her smile widening into a smirk.

"Christ on a cruise missile, you're worsen' the kids. Take a pill an' c'mon."

Aidan sighed, dug the bottle out of his pocket, stuck one of the pills under his tongue and slouched after his hydroelectrics specialist.

"They should've made you a commander," he muttered as they stepped into the canteen.

"I ain't got the patience, don't even want t'be an officer," Janice replied with a chuckle, "don't put up with whinin' an' bullshit long enough to be any good at the job. Give me rock, work an' water thanks."

Janice must have been up a while; the coffee pot was already full and sitting on the table. The older woman pulled a cup and pushed it across the table. The liquid scalded his tongue.

"Been tryin' to get you for a couple days now." The woman's voice was quiet in the morning hush, but Aidan's head rang with it all the same. What the hell did they *put* in arak?

He forced a smile. "Well, you've got me. What's up?"

Janice sipped her coffee, savoring it. Aidan had no idea why; the stuff tasted like battery acid.

"You remember I was sayin' this was a real good aquifer? Maybe bettern' good?"

Aidan dredged his memory. "Sort of?"

Janice set her cup down. "I wasn't kiddin'."

Aidan gulped another mouthful of coffee and pushed down his irritation. Janice always had a point to make when she said something, and it usually mattered. You had to let her lay it out in her own time. If he dared to ask her to get to the point he'd regret it for a week, but damn did he want to.

Janice brought her tab out with care, flipping it on and bringing up the screen. A web of blue displayed itself against a brown background.

"See this?"

"Yeah?" Aidan asked, squinting.

"This's what under our feet." Janice stated quietly. "An' it's got connections to another four spaced around this hogback for about ten miles. I been gettin' the idea this was around, but I was never sure. Just did an electrical resistivity reading. Now I am."

The air crystallized around Janice's words.

"How...how much water is that?" he asked, the words brittle on his tongue. If he moved too fast, spoke too loudly, this moment would shatter.

"Enough for 'bout a hundred years." Janice stated, voice very quiet. "Enough to get Taylor's ol' Ten Year Plan off the ground, if we can land some seeds an' the sprouting hormone they need an' put an irrigation system together. If a miracle happens an' we can land unpatented seeds that're gonna sprout without GA soaks an' ain't gonna be sterile after the first generation, we can get our own food supply goin'. Get off dependin' on Grid runs, 's long as we got enough slicktarp to hide us an' enough supplies."

"Holy shit," Aidan muttered, his voice matching hers.

"Yeah," Janice agreed. Glancing down, she took Aidan's mug, refilled it, pushed it back to him. "Pretty damn fine, hunh?"

Aidan nodded, staring at his mug. He watched the oil float on the black surface, mind blank.

There was quiet in the canteen. Aidan could hear his heart beating.

"So what d'you think?" Janice asked. Aidan swallowed too much coffee. His throat burned.

"Honestly...I think I'm hungover and half awake. Give me a day to think about this, okay?"

Across the table Janice smirked, tipping her head. "Fair 'nough. You're gonna want to take another of those pills when you get back to bed."

Numbly, Aidan nodded.

Back in Kevin's room he dropped the bottle on the nightstand and crawled back under the blankets. Warm arms wrapped around him and Kevin made a small, sleepy noise into his hair as he spooned them together. The word 'Saturday' was buried somewhere in it. Aidan hummed quietly in agreement, not entirely certain what Kevin had said.

Enough water for decades. Enough water to start a farm.

The thought followed him into sleep.

A few hours later, Kevin raised his head, smiling a sleepy, squinting smile.

"Morning."

"Hey," Aidan muttered, eyes barely open.

Leaning over, Kevin stretched. "You got painkillers?" He brushed his lips over Aidan's brow. "Oh, thank you. I could worship at your feet right now."

"Worship quietly," Aidan mumbled with a wince, even Kevin's soft voice like a nail in his eye socket. Janice had been right. He did need another dose.

Whatever was in arak had to be banned by at least one of the Corporations.

Kevin's chuckle mixed with the rustle of bedclothes. "Get this under your tongue," he murmured, tracing Aidan's lips with the pill in his fingers. "You'll feel better in a minute."

Aidan opened his mouth and let Kevin place the tablet under his tongue. Kevin nuzzled his head down against Aidan's collarbone as he waited for the pill to work and let time drift.

Water. They had enough water for the rest of their lives.

But only if they stayed here.

In one place.

Which was suicidal.

Should he say something to Kevin?

What if Janice was wrong? Scratch that, she knew her stuff.

He'd say something when they were more awake. It was their day off. They had time.

"Better?" Kevin asked somewhere around twenty minutes later.

"Mmm," Aidan grunted quietly in agreement. He pulled away a little and propped himself on his elbows in order to look down into Kevin's face. Enough water for life and this guy in his bed. Life was getting pretty damn good.

Gently, he brushed sleep-mussed red hair off Kevin's forehead. "Thanks."

Kevin chuckled dryly. "Don't thank me; you got the pills...my love."

Aidan's heart stopped.

Kevin glanced up with a nervous smile. He gave an awkward half-shrug. "You did say it first, after all. Last night. Though you were drunk, so you have an escape clause… if you want it."

Aidan stared at him for a pocketful of breaths, feeling his heart race. He had said he loved Kevin? Fucking hell, he had, hadn't he? Right before he fell asleep. He'd said he loved the man.

His brain kicked into overdrive. This was a bad idea. He had an out. He'd been drinking. He could say it was something stupid brought on by drinking and leave it there, keep them both safe. It'd be easier. Love was too…

What? Too dangerous?

Hell, they lived dangerous every day.

Too easy to lose. Better not to get used to it.

But he had been getting used to Kevin. In his bed. In his life. Kevin was the first relationship he'd had that he could see himself continuing, if he didn't screw it up. Kevin was the first guy who he had undressed in front of after starting the hormones. The guy who had stolen him three new binders with zippers, the man who treated making sure he was stocked with testosterone as casually as making sure they had milk powder. This was the guy who'd accepted his boundaries and made him feel handsome, even in this fucking mess of a body. The guy who made him feel as if he was filled with champagne when they kissed, even more so when they had sex. Maybe…

Maybe that was what love was.

He drew a breath so deep it hurt.

"No, I… think I might have meant it."

Kevin studied his face a long, long time. Then he leaned up and gently brushed his lips over Aidan's. "Say it again?"

"I meant it?" Aidan muttered, confused. He pulled away again to meet Kevin's gaze.

"I… I'm not alone on that… am I?"

Kevin chuckled, rolling his eyes.

"You just wrecked a moment worthy of a romance vid, you do know that?" Reaching up, he stroked Aidan's hair. "And to answer your question, you're not alone. I love you."

"Why?"

Aidan hadn't meant to ask the question. He knew he shouldn't have. The word had slipped out before he could stop it. He knew he wasn't fall-in-love material. He was a depressive mess, stuck in the middle of transition, always so caught up with his work, and physically... and how many times had Omi and Kevin both told him to stop thinking like that?

He chuckled self-consciously. "Sorry... hangovers make me ruin moments, I guess."

Kevin levered himself up on one elbow, bringing them nose to nose. "Hangovers make you honest. As does drunkenness. It has its merits. You want to know why I love you? I could ask you the same question." He kissed the tip of Aidan's nose. "I'll tell you my reasons if you tell me yours."

"Sap," Aidan teased, hoping his fear was hidden behind the humor.

"Yes, I'm a sap. Is that a reason?" Kevin asked, one copper brow arched.

Aidan took a couple breaths. It took him forever to collect his thoughts, but he eventually muttered, "I... I love you because you... you see me the way I really am. You always know the right things to say, and I—even when we're naked, I don't have dysphoria with you. Instead of freaking out when I told you my past, you—you researched the hell out of it. You're chill. You're a huge nerd, but it's cute. And you're the best kisser I've ever met."

Kevin's soft grey eyes held his for a heartbeat. He managed a smile. When he spoke, his voice was strained. "Honesty's...harder than it looks, isn't it?"

He drew a breath. "I... I love you because being with you is like standing in the eye of a tornado. The world's insane, but... you're quiet.

You listen. And that quiet is such a gift." The redhead murmured the words as if they might cut his mouth, his eyes fixed on Aidan's. "With you I don't feel the usual pressure to be something, to do something, and for a little while... I'm at peace. That's something I haven't had in a long time, and it shows during the day. It's helping me become the person I want to be, not the snide bastard I usually am."

He glanced away, swallowing hard. "This is trite, but there's a place inside me that's been empty a long time and...when I'm with you...I'm whole again."

Aidan's breath caught in his chest. He had no idea what he had done to deserve this kind of love. But here he was. Here they were.

After a long moment, he kissed Kevin softly and muttered, "You're not allowed to watch any more romance vids."

Kevin burst out laughing. "You bloody hypocritical jerk!" He tousled Aidan's hair. "You sounded just as sappy, don't deny it!"

"I didn't sound exactly like a vid script," Aidan protested with a laugh.

"All right, all right, I said it was trite," Kevin grumbled good-naturedly. "See if I bare my soul to you again."

"Can I add the stupid poetry to the list of reasons why I love you, or is it too late?" Aidan smiled gently and brushed red hair off Kevin's forehead.

"I'll accept it as an addendum, Aidan my love." Kevin murmured softly. "Though I will take issue with the 'stupid' comment. Poetry is the epitome of a more civilized age."

"So civilized that no one ever figured out what it meant," Aidan chuckled, basking in the thrill of Kevin calling him 'my love' again.

"Not a lot of civilization around these days. We live in barbaric times," Kevin replied quietly, his eyes sliding away from Aidan's, growing shadowed. Then he glanced back, the shadows gone. "Hey, have I showed you Star Wars yet? If you want to talk about stupid lines that's the perfect example. I'll look positively staid and conventional by comparison."

Aidan chuckled softly and kissed Kevin's nose. "That's impressive. Prove it."

Event File 9
File Tag: Research and Development
Timestamp: 10:00-11-16-2155

"Alright Headly, I got the word. National Command has issued approval on the new preliminary plan. I want a full write up when you've got concrete details."

Aidan's gut lurched. Great, they'd gotten approval for their plan to put the Folder out there. Now they actually had to put the thing into action. The absolutely gamma, batshit crazy thing.

"Thank you, sir."

Magnum gave him a cockeyed look. "So, do we have a time frame yet?"

Aidan swallowed. "Working on it, sir. We think we can find a window when Officer McIllian can be away for the time period he needs in under two weeks. After that Tweak estimates three weeks' worth of reconnaissance and prep work. We're on schedule to finish before New Years' is what I can tell you."

Magnum nodded, watching him. Aidan hoped the man couldn't see how much he hated the idea he was presenting. Tweak had found that most of the coders they were targeting spent their leisure time in the same recreation pavilion. But the intel they had gotten so far on the area was garbage. All they knew was the location of the restrooms and a few parts of the electrical setup, but they had no idea what sort of security the place had. Kevin would have to go in there alone to vet their candidates on the ground and take the first steps on the plan. He felt like he was sending Kevin in blindfolded.

"Good," Magnum agreed eventually, "I don't want your people on Grid any longer than they need to be. The place is a madhouse right now. We lost too many operatives during last year's Season. McIllian handles the Grid perfectly, so no worries there."

"Yes sir. Officer Coson and Officer McIllian are putting together a mental exercise routine for the team that will go on-Grid. It'll help them handle the overstimulation."

Magnum blinked. "Huh. That's a new one. Nice work."

"Thank you, sir."

Aidan's face felt as if it had frozen in the blank expression he hid behind under his commander's eyes.

"Scared, Headly?"

Aidan really hated those kinds of questions. He shrugged. "Be stupid not to be a little freaked, sir. But we're doing it."

Magnum laughed. "Good answer. Walk me through the plan again, and then we'll get on what you and Danvers sent in."

It took half an hour to run through everything and explain it to the sector commander's satisfaction. Finally, Magnum sat back, his chair creaking.

"Sounds like you've covered all the bases, Headly. Now. You wanted to make a proposal?"

"Yes sir." Aidan pulled out his tab and brought up his screen, displaying the work Janice had done and the visuals she had put together.

"Specialist Danvers has found an aquifer with enough water to keep a base for seventy years, and she thinks there's enough to support small-scale agricultural planting as well. These are her figures, we'd like to submit them to Regional for checking—"

"But considering Danvers runs the hydroelectric specialist training program for the entire Region, you don't really think that's necessary," Magnum added, eyes on Aidan. He drew a slow breath.

"True, sir. I'd bet on Janice's work any day. Still, she wanted everybody to get a look at it. Because we're asking for approval to become a sedentary base if it is."

Magnum blinked. "Well I'll be. You want to stay put by the water and start that farm Taylor came up with. Don't you?"

"Um... yes sir."

"No *'um's*, Headly. Either you want to, or you don't."

Aidan nodded. "Yes sir. I want to give it a try, when we get the supplies."

Commander Magnum ran a hand over his bushy mustache. His eyes were searching. Aidan felt his heart begin to pound.

Finally, Magnum sighed.

"I can't approve it, Headly."

Aidan's heart sank.

"Sir, we could—"

"All end up dead," Magnum cut in, surfing his voice over Aidan's. "I'm sorry Headly, I can't approve a sedentary base at that location. It's too dangerous given the current situation. I'm not losing one of my best bases because they want to grow carrots."

So that was it. No farm. Nothing to show for all the hoping.

Aidan nodded, feeling his good-soldier mask slide into place. "Of course sir. Thank you, sir."

Magnum eyed him steadily. Then his lips twitched in the tiniest of smiles.

"Now let me show you what I can approve."

Magnum tapped at his tab. Windows popped into existence, changing as Magnum moved blocks of figures. Aidan wasn't particularly good at reading things backwards, so he settled for waiting quietly to hear what his commander had in mind. He realized his fingers were scratching against the fabric of his pants and forced his hands to relax.

Magnum studied his work for what felt like an eternity. Then he nodded. "What I can approve for you is two more mobile water reservoirs, a moving schedule that cycles you back to that location every three months, and a project recommendation. Tell Danvers to look into the file I just sent your tab."

Aidan glanced down. The image on his tab showed—he blinked—what looked like a box on wheeled legs. Plants waved green fronds from its top. The next image showed schematics.

"A base in the Vermont Region came up with these," Magnum stated, humor coloring his voice. "They're re-purposed stockbots, designed to handle broken terrain. They can move at a speed of forty miles per hour, solar-powered. The covers designed for them allow travel without harm to the produce. Design schematics and 3-D print plans for your printer model are in that packet. I'll give you approval to source and put together eight of these growing beds and enough slick-tarp to cover them. The supplying will be your problem, but that's never stopped Base 1407 before."

Aidan glanced up, barely able to suppress a grin. "Sir, thank you, I-I mean..."

Magnum gave him another cockeyed look. "Don't thank me, Headly, I just landed a whole pile of work on you. But if you want it, it's yours. The Folder's top priority, we're clear on that?"

"Yes sir." Aidan agreed automatically. Magnum's heavy head nodded. "All right then. When that's complete, feel free to work on this. And if things work out with the Folder, you may get that sedentary base sooner than you think. Dismissed."

"Bullshit!"

"You callin' me a liar, boy?"

"We've got how much?"

Janice rolled her eyes and pointed at the screen she'd hung over the table, showing the crew. "Ain't you never learned to read? It's on the map. We got enough water for ninety-seven years at our current use rate. Seventy years if we go with the water usage I worked out for the Ten-Year Plan way back when."

"Was Sector notified?" Liza asked, eyes wide with hope she wouldn't allow herself yet.

Janice nodded. Aidan stepped away from where he'd been standing beside the specialist and took his seat. This was Janice's show now.

He'd let her know the minute he'd gotten in from Sector what Magnum had given them, and they'd decided to announce it at dinner. The reaction was everything Janice could have wanted, but the hydroelectrics specialist was playing it engineering-straight and as pessimistic as she could. It was kind of funny to watch her work on her glare.

"No sense getting' everyone excited 'til I check the quality on all of it," Janice continued, "an' then we gotta get pipes an' shit...sorry Jim, an' stuff for the irrigation. An' then we gotta get seeds an' the GA soak that'll make 'em sprout, which is a mess I don' even want to think about considerin' how tight Ag locks them things down. I ain't tellin' you guys get your hopes up. I'm tellin' you we got somethin' to work with, savvy? Don' go—aw, fuck, don' hug me! Jesus." Janice grumbled as Dilly and Donny jumped out of their seats with cheers and swamped the specialist in a dual bear hug. She shoved gently at them. "Don' start huggin' me, I ain't done nothin' yet."

"Bullshit," Lazarus repeated with the biggest grin Aidan had seen on his face since he'd been posted to the base, "you knew you were going to hit the jackpot this time, didn't you? That's why you got pissy before the move! And that's why you took forever checking your readings before you moved us here! You knew!"

"Yeah I knew," Janice drawled, "an' I didn't say nothin' 'cause I knew you dumbasses would start actin' like we was all set an' sittin' pretty. Well, we ain't. All we got's approval for a plan on paper. I ain't got piping or filters. We ain't got these stockbots yet, we ain't got seeds an' we ain't gonna get 'em soon. I don't know what's in this water beyond the first chamber I checked: could be brine, could be heavy metals, could be anything. So, all of you cool your tits. We ain't hit it big yet."

Her searchlight glare swept the room, and the commentary trailed off into sheepish quiet.

When everyone had settled, Janice allowed herself a small, grim smile.

"But we ain't doin' so bad neither. So now you know what's goin' on, keep an ear out for stuff we can use on this. That's all I'm sayin'."

For a moment the room was quiet. Then Tommy's voice piped up. "So, can we serve dinner now? I'm hungry."

Chuckles broke the quiet. Aidan caught Andrea's eye. "Dinner'd be good."

Dinner was better than usual: some of Tweak's work was letting them reroute shipments and get hold of food that hadn't been freeze-dried for six months without getting anyone shot. It showed.

"So, what'd the girls say when you showed them?" Kevin asked, eyes dancing as he cut away at something that actually resembled chicken. "Were they thrilled?"

Aidan glanced up from his quinoa. "The girls?"

Kevin blinked. "Yes, Sarah and Yve said they'd probably see you at Sector. They're out on a run to get printing precursors and making some trades for older-model parts with some Fringe contacts. Didn't you see them?"

Aidan shook his head. "No, but I was kind of busy in Magnum's office. What's their return ETA?"

Kevin dug out his tab, dinner set aside. His body grew taut as he studied it. Aidan felt his chest tighten.

"What?"

Kevin looked up, eyes blank as two silver coins. "I've got nothing from them, and their ETA was three hours ago. Their base tracking signal reads 'offline.'

Lazarus's head snapped up. "Where were they supposed to be?"

"Sanctuary Station," Kevin replied, brow furrowed, "at least, that's what they filed. They've been there dozens of times, it's an approved group, but the trackers..."

"Fuck." Lazarus stood. "Kev, c'mon let's go."

Kevin stood as well, but he reached across the table to put a hand on the other man's shoulder. "Laz, think for a moment. Sunset's in half an hour. We can't go hunting for them in the dark when we have nothing to track them with. I'll get a sweep plan put together, we'll go at five in the morning and—"

"Fuck that!" Lazarus snapped, "Dude, if the girls are in trouble—"

"Then you'll be lost in the dark and they'll still be in trouble." Kevin retorted, words clipped.

Aidan glanced around the table, taking in the tension. He stood.

"Guys, let's take this to my office. Finish dinner everybody."

Quietly, he closed his office door and turned to the two men, who were watching him. Aidan drew a long breath down into his belly, let it out. "Okay. Start off with, are there any reasons besides danger the trackers could have gotten turned off?" He knew the answer, but he wanted to get both men thinking instead of arguing.

Kevin shook his head. "They should be well within range, and the Force trackers in their tabs are one of the toughest parts in the machines. Waterproof and shock-resistant. They'd have to be intentionally smashed in order to fail."

Aidan nodded. "So, somebody smashed their tabs. Okay. What about vehicle trackers?"

Kevin nodded slowly, considering. "That's a thought. The main base reading states 'offline' on the truck as well, but they're quite easy to turn off remotely and quite difficult to find without taking the vehicle to bits. With any luck someone will have taken the lazy approach to signal blocking and we can turn the things on remotely as well."

"I'll get Dozer." Lazarus pushed his chair back fast enough to make it screech against the floor, but Aidan stood, catching the other man's eyes. "Laz. Sit for a minute. Talk this out. You know we want the girls back too. But we've got to get this right."

The anger in Lazarus's face and the fear behind it was a little bit terrifying to see. But he did force himself to sit back down.

"Once I know where they are, I can plan an attack," he ground out, "We've got everything we need for extraction maneuvers on a Fringe camp, a small EagleCorp convoy or a security contractors' crew. Those are the only groups that make sense for picking the girls up in this area. But the first forty-eight hours are the best window. After that they're probably dead or out of our reach. So can we please get to work and fucking *find* them?"

Aidan watched his face. Carefully, he nodded. "Go get Tweak and Dozer, and we'll see if the truck's tracking can get turned back on. Then we'll start planning. When we have a plan, you can go out."

Lazarus nodded. He nearly jumped out of his chair, running down the hall.

Two hours later, Aidan watched the munitions officer pace back and forth as the technical specialist and the transportation officer pored over their work. Kevin leaned against the wall, hiding behind his look of absolute cool. Dozer and Tweak compared quadrants to the route Sarah and Yvonne had logged, spiraling out and sending an auto-restart signal ping every ten minutes.

"Anything?" Lazarus demanded.

"You ask again and I k-kick you out," Tweak spat back, turning to glare up at him. "R-right n-now the t-truck thinks it's in the ocean. We gotta bounce the signal around to d-different areas and s-see if it r-reconnects. So, shut up. I'm working."

Lazarus picked up his pacing again. Finally, he slammed the door of the garage open. "I'm getting packed."

"Finally," Dozer grumbled. Aidan couldn't help but agree.

Kevin stepped out of his easy slouch. "I'll keep him occupied. Message us when you've got—"

The tab bleeped. A concentric set of rings spread on the screen, centered on a green dot.

Kevin stepped to Dozer's side, leaned in, then let out a sigh. "Thank God." Pulling out his own tab, he synced it with Dozer's map. "What do you make it Dozer? Half an hour to get there?"

"Forty-five minutes, you gotta wait for this." Dozer corrected, pointing to a low-fly drone.

"So, we'll need to get through that area either before or after the fly over. Roger. Can we make it tonight?" Kevin asked, every word sharp. Eyes narrowed, the big man studied his readouts of enemy movement, drone patterns, and weather.

"I'm gonna say... yeah. I want you guys on bikes though, 'case you gotta haul ass."

"Agreed." Kevin turned to face Aidan. "I'd like to take Laz and Alice and go out myself. Can I get your approval on that?"

Aidan considered the words, watching the fear coil in his boyfriend's eyes behind the steel wall of Kevin's officer persona. A logistics officer trained in route planning and communication, a munitions officer trained in short-term tactical planning and a medic specialist ready to fix up anything that happened in the field. It was a good setup for a small run. Not so good if there was a large group of enemies.

Aidan turned to Tweak.

"Can we get into the truck's camera and sensor reads? See if you can get an infrared read, maybe look for heat signatures and see if there are any people around?"

Tweak nodded, stepping in front of the two men to type. Dozer and Kevin both took quick steps back to stay out of the little coder's personal space.

Five minutes later the screen lit up with a grainy image, green on green. Two figures were in the foreground, lying on their stomachs in the pose of snipers ready to fire their weapons. In the bright area that seemed to be the mouth of some sort of canyon or cave, four figures clustered.

Kevin turned on his heel and took off running. Heart in his mouth, Aidan turned to Dozer.

"Get the bikes ready."

The mechanic nodded. "On it."

<u>Event File 10</u>
<u>File Tag: Recovery Detail</u>
<u>Timestamp: 20:00-11-16-2155</u>

Kevin and Lazarus rode side by side, cutting Dozer's safety margin of forty-five minutes down to twenty and nearly spinning Lazarus's bike out when he hit a prairie-dog mound. Neither of them cared, though Kevin did keep half a synapse on Alice's tracker behind them. They'd told her to ride safe and let them take point, and he was absently glad to see her doing so.

Kevin's emotions would have had him skidding up in a cloud of dust and leaping into the mess, but his training and his common sense reined him in. They cut engines behind red rock outcroppings tipped out of the ground a few hundred meters from the GPS signal.

Stepping off his bike, Lazarus tossed him a rifle. Kevin caught it in midair, activating his slick suit and noting Lazarus doing the same. Kevin pinged Alice.

Pull up behind the rocks. Wait here for communication. We are engaging.

That done, he caught Lazarus's eye and pointed two fingers in the direction of their target. Lazarus nodded.

Kevin took the safety off on his weapon. The indicator light on the scope flashed green in his infrared.

Moving in silence, the two men stole down into the small gully between the boulders.

Kevin moved with economy, every gesture efficient.

Something moved in the corner of his vision. His brain registered the shape of a jackrabbit as his body swung towards the light. No threat. He kept moving.

Lazarus moved like a hunting coyote at his side, stalking ahead. He checked their safety at a bend in the gully, motioned Kevin forward.

The smell wafted down the arroyo to greet them. Copper and sugar. Gunpowder. Gasoline.

Kevin froze.

Ahead of him, bodies lay fanned out around the mouth of a cave. They glowed faintly in the night-vision. None of them were as bright as a living body ought to be.

Slowly, he lowered his weapon, glancing at Lazarus.

"Thoughts?"

Lazarus made two visual sweeps of the area. "Clear," he stated finally, voice tight in Kevin's helmet mic.

"Verbal contact?"

"Yeah," Lazarus agreed. He shoved up his own visor. "Marco?" he called into the darkness, using the team's favorite recognition call.

"Polo!" The shout rang out from the cave.

The utter stillness inside Kevin broke like a sheet of ice. He grinned at Lazarus, who took off running. Kevin jogged to catch up.

By the time he made it to the cave, Laz had already swept Sarah up in a bear hug. In the light of the lamps the two men carried the little woman was grimy, but she was thumping Lazarus on the back with enthusiasm. Kevin left them to go over event details.

Yvonne's greeting was a little less effusive when Kevin knelt beside her where she sat between the wall and the truck's front tire, her rifle across her knees and her pistol in her hand. Kevin noticed the slick white plastic of an auto-pad shining in the lamplight beneath her ripped pants. The fabric around the tear was black with blood. She gave him a wan smile.

"Hey."

"Hey. How's the leg?"

"Really good graze. Bled like anything. I think I can walk. Thanks for coming."

"What sort of chevalier would I be if I didn't?"

Yvonne rolled her eyes, a smile flitting across her face. "You're such a—movement, down!"

Kevin dropped without a second's hesitation. Yvonne's pistol hissed out a shot.

Slowly, Kevin stood. Yvonne craned her head. "Did I get him?"

Lazarus's tone was all wrong in Kevin's ears when he called back, flat and quiet.

"Yeah. He's down."

Kevin stepped to the mouth of the cave, the tone in Lazarus's voice tightening his muscles.

In the lamplight, a body lay half-covered by another. He must have been hiding beneath the dead man. The youngster's eyes stared up at Kevin, registering nothing but surprise. He couldn't have been more than twelve. Younger, possibly.

Blood seeped slowly from the hole in his forehead.

Sarah turned blank eyes to Kevin. "Don't let Yve see," she ordered, voice soft and filled with steel.

"See what?" Yvonne asked, limping over. "Where was the bastard—"

She froze at the sight of the body. Sarah turned and shoved herself under the taller woman's arm.

"Baby, we gotta get you home."

Yvonne said nothing.

Yvonne waited in the truck while Alice tended her and the rest of them searched the bodies for the cutoff switch that had been used to stop the truck's electric engine. With that disabled, Alice helped them tie her bike to the truck and drove the girls home. Kevin and Lazarus rode point.

They were in Damian's office before Yvonne spoke again, adding her part to the explanation her wife gave while Damian worked on her leg. Sarah, as always, delivered her report like a reading program set to double speed, spitting out facts for Aidan as she watched the doctor see to her wife.

"They thought they could use our base for ransom. We made friendly contact with Sanctuary Station, but they were out of what we needed. They directed and vouched for a group called Amana, all according to regulation. We got to their main camp at sixteen-hundred and they talked and bartered a while. Kept asking for high-grade meds, we kept saying we couldn't give those away right now. That must've been when they stole our tabs. They said they'd take us to their supply cache for materials. We got halfway down the gully and I got the feeling it wasn't right, so I hit reverse. That's when they kill-switched us and kicked in a signal blocker. Had just enough time to reverse into the cave on inertia. We set up a defensive perimeter, fired a line of warning shots and told them not to cross. We tried to negotiate, but they weren't hearing it. After that they tried rushing us. We defended."

"They did it for medicines," Yvonne added, her voice quiet. "They wanted a bunch of medicines, stuff we can't afford to give away. They've got sick people at their main camp. I told them we could requisition stuff for them, but it'd take time to get them the supplies."

"So, the fuckers decided they'd get our base coordinates out of the truck and hold those until you guys gave in. Either you'd give them our stuff, or they'd give us all to the Corps. That was their plan," Sarah rattled off, finishing her wife's thought. She squeezed Yvonne's shoulder gently, giving Aidan a rueful smile. "Guess we're not bartering with them again. Maybe not Sanctuary either. I'll get it documented tomorrow."

"Sounds good," Aidan agreed with a smile, nodding at the munitions specialist. "Good to see you guys back in one piece."

"Good to be back." Yvonne murmured, her voice quiet.

Damian tossed the casing for the muscle-repair auto-pad he'd just put in place. "Alright, leave that in place for two days and let those mast cells integrate and start to grow new tissue. You want something to help you get to sleep tonight?"

Yvonne shook her head. "No worries. I'm beat. Can I go sack out?"

Damian tipped his head in the direction of the door. "Try not to do anything energetic for a week. Go on."

Yvonne nodded wearily, sliding off the examination table. Lazarus steadied her on one side, Sarah on the other.

"Dude, what do you eat, nothing?" Lazarus asked, and Kevin could hear the attempt at teasing in his voice. "I mean, look at this." He lifted his cousin in his arms. "You're so light I don't even break a sweat."

"Laz, seriously, don't start," Yvonne grumbled, but Kevin was heartened to hear a little humor in her voice as the banter followed the two out of the room.

"Watch, I'll carry you to your room and I still won't feel it. It's like carrying a barbie doll."

"I'll barbie you, you gamma dipshit. Will you——"

"Thanks guys," Sarah added, giving the room a quick, grim smile before trotting after her partners in crime.

Kevin raised his eyes to Aidan's, giving him a tired half-smile.

"Never a dull moment."

"You sure they're okay?" Aidan asked, glancing between him and Damian. The bald man nodded. "Physically, yes. We'll have to keep an eye on everything else. Killing thirteen people at once isn't good for anyone's emotional stability."

Aidan nodded. "Got it. Should I—" a yawn cut off his words.

"Go to bed?" Damian put in dryly. "Why yes, yes you should."

Aidan gave the taller man an acknowledging smile. "Okay. Thanks."

Kevin spared his boyfriend a smile as he stepped out of the room.

Alone with the doctor, he turned back. "Damian?"

Damian's black plastic eyes met his. "I thought you had something else to say."

Kevin cleared his throat. "One of the casualties was a pre-teen. Yvonne made the kill shot. She saw the body."

Damian ran a hand over his face, weariness showing for a moment. Opening a drawer, he extracted a bottle. "Propranolol. Should keep the trauma from settling in too deep and ending up PTSD. You got it?"

"I'll handle it. Thanks," Kevin murmured, taking the bottle. Damian nodded.

"That dose would work better if she talked to me about this and took it now. But I know she won't."

Kevin shrugged, resigned. "I'll wait until she cracks. It'll be some time tonight."

Damian eyed him. "I want you to sleep tonight too, you got that?"

"Doctor's orders," he agreed. He didn't have much trouble obeying either: after the night he'd already had, he plummeted into sleep like a stone thrown from a cliff.

It was a soft sound that woke him, deep in the belly of the night. If some part of him hadn't been listening for it, he probably would have slept through.

Turning over in bed, he listened. The sound of sobbing filtered through the thin plastic of the wall.

Finding his glasses and lifting the little white bottle, he slipped on a ragged sweater and a pair of boxers and cat-footed into the hall. He slid the door of the next room down open gently.

"Can I come in?"

In bed, Yvonne sat with a pillow pressed to her face, sobs racking her body. Sarah looked up from her embracing hold of the other woman with that hopeless, helpless look she had when Yvonne was hurting. She propped her chin on her wife's shoulder and gave him the ghost of a smile, a jerky nod.

Gently, Kevin took a seat on the edge of the bed, reaching over to rub Yvonne's back softly.

"Some days are hell," he whispered.

Yvonne's sobs shuddered out. Sarah gave him a worried look. He carefully held up the white bottle. Another twitch of a smile was his reward.

"Oh god. He was so little." The words came out as a wail.

Sarah leaned in, stroking Yvonne's hair. "Shh, honey. It's okay."

"No, it's not," Yvonne moaned, dropping the pillow into her lap. "I shot a... I shot a baby! A little kid!"

"You shot an attacker," Kevin murmured gently. "There was no way you could have seen his face in that situation. You saw a body moving a gun."

"That's what I saw, but what I shot was a...a..." Yvonne's words dissolved in a heaving groan.

"Sammy. We got introduced. His-his name was Sammy. He-he wanted medicine for his baby sister. Oh god!"

"Ssh now. It's all right," Kevin soothed. "You did what you had to do. You protected me. You protected everyone. You did the right thing."

"Take a couple of these, okay baby?" Sarah whispered, holding two propranolol tablets against Yvonne's lips. "Just slide them under your tongue. Please baby. Just take these."

Yvonne eventually opened her mouth, admitting the dose. She gulped. "I don't... I don't think I can do this anymore."

The words sent a small lightning bolt of fear sizzling through Kevin. Not again. Not Yvonne too. Peter had said those words exactly.

I don't think I can do this anymore.

He'd said that just a few days before he'd asked for decommission paperwork and stated his intention of going Fringe. He'd said those words a few days before he'd made Kevin choose between the fight he needed to be a part of and the love they'd shared.

I don't think I can do this anymore.

He'd already lost a lover to the sins this world forced them to commit. He couldn't lose the girl who he thought of as a foster-sister as well.

Think, he ordered himself. *Find the right words. Give her a reason to stay. Say something!*

"I think you can," Kevin began softly, trying to sound sure. The words came to him as he spoke. "You're fighting for a world where little boys don't have to die that way." The breath he drew was ragged, but the words came with conviction. "One day we're going to win, Yve. We're going to win, and then there won't be Fringe camps and drones. There won't be little boys holding guns. That's why you need to fight. That's why we're going to keep fighting. All right?"

Yvonne didn't look at him, but she nodded.

"You going to be alright?" Kevin asked quietly. Yvonne's head shook ponderously.

"I'm going to go to Hell," she whispered. "I deserve to. I shot a little kid."

Leaning in, Kevin put an arm around Sarah's shoulders, ensuring that Yvonne was completely enfolded in warmth. He kissed Yvonne's brow. His voice sounded odd coming through the lump in his throat.

"I think the Almighty has a lot more discretion in His grace than we mere mortals. And Heaven has more room in it than you'd imagine."

Tear-streaked blue eyes met his. "Y-you think so?" Kevin nodded solemnly, holding her eyes. "I believe so."

Yvonne's lips twitched in the barest remnant of a smile. "Yeah. Maybe you're right."

Slowly, she used the sheets to wipe her face. "Sorry about the snot and the waterworks."

"It's okay, baby," Sarah managed, her voice choked. "We're crying too."

"So, this is what we got." Tweak pointed out the six images on the screen.

"These guys. Your best bet. All social media engineers, w-working on the c-core programs. They've got all the access c-clearance you're gonna need. Here."

She brought the first one forward. Aidan watched Kevin lean in, adjusting his glasses absently as he studied the six faces.

"Hm. Adele Anderson. Ritra Varati. William Sinclair..." He read the names aloud with slow deliberation. Aidan guessed it was mostly to help him remember; he didn't seem to be talking to either of them.

For a couple breaths Kevin sat absolutely still, studying the dossiers of gleaned information beside each image. Then he relaxed and sat back.

"Well done Tweak, thanks for this. Really, at this point, it's only a matter of making a choice among the candidates."

"We're sure they all hang out in the same pavilion?" Aidan asked. Tweak nodded. "T-timestamps in their social feeds, pics, metadata all show the s-same spot. Two guys don't go as often, but the other four are there about every d-day."

She tapped her tab, and the screen lit up with a new image. The internal layout of the TechoCo workers' recreation area turned, showing an uncomfortably blank interior. Aidan hated that blank space.

"Are you sure we can't get some more information on the area layout before Kevin goes in there? I'm not feeling real good about this." Aidan remarked, giving the diagram the fish eye.

"I got as m-much as I could out of the pics and stuff, but the p-plans aren't an-anywhere I could get at w-without c-c-clearance," Tweak retorted crossly. "I know it's all consumer-g-grade, no crazy security stuff. Just the usual. B-but if you want perfect s-schem-matics I n-need a m-m-month."

"Which we certainly don't have," Kevin added. "And really, I'm not unduly concerned. I'll take along credentials for a CSS social media writer, a CPS janitor and a CSS engineer. Oh, and a CES futures trader, just in case. I'll use what works in the situation and do a little reconnaissance on the ground. Give me six days or so—make it eight to be on the safe side—and I'll get the amenities and security setup plotted out. In fact, I can probably squeeze in a check on the prices for used stockbots that Ag is done with if I swing east on my way home. I'll make that CES set for ZonCom, that should cover all eventualities. Sound good?"

Aidan turned his chair. "I'm really not liking this Kev. This is all the intel we can get about what the inside of the engineers' pavilion looks like, but it's not a lot."

"There isn't an-any more," Tweak muttered.

Aidan nodded. "Yeah, that's why I'm worried. You got us what there was, Tweak. Thanks. We got it from here if you want to head out."

Hands stuffed in her pockets, the little coder slouched out of the room. Aidan hoped she wasn't going to sulk too long. But now that she was gone, he could focus on checking in with Kevin. He turned back to face his logistics officer. Right now, they needed to be officer and commander.

"We don't even know which door they use to get in. Sending one of my people in there blind weirds me out." He shrugged, holding Kevin's eyes. "But it's your call. I need you to be sure first. If you feel like you can do this, I'll give approval."

Kevin nodded slowly, glancing from his face to the screen.

"It's a bit of a gamble, but it's a gamble I'm willing to take. Give me the approval and I'll run reconnaissance at least. I'll head out Thursday, and I'll abort if the mission doesn't seem feasible once I've had a look." He drew a cross over his chest. "Cross my heart, I'll only do this if I'm comfortable with the danger level."

Aidan held his eyes. Slowly, he let out a breath, managing a smile. "Okay, I can live with that. Just be sure."

Kevin returned his smile with interest. "Oh, by the way. Personnel file says it's your birthday. Happy birthday."

Aidan rolled his eyes. "Crap. You guys aren't going to act all crazy like you did on Topher, are you?"

Kevin chuckled, shaking his head. "It isn't your twenty-first birthday, though I have heard a rumor that there will be cake and a very short bout of singing at dinner."

Aidan smirked. "I guess I can survive that if I have to."

"Good, because I doubt the unit will give you much of a choice. And now I'd better be about my business." Kevin stood, shooting Aidan a quick grin. Tapping at his tab, he hurried out of the office.

Under his hand, Aidan's personal tab pinged. He flicked the screen to life.

Kevin's message handle scrolled across the hologram.

Aidan, come over to my room once you've survived the horde, and we'll celebrate in style. Wear a tie.

Grinning, Aidan shook his head.

Kevin had been right about dinner. No sooner did he step inside the canteen than the kids glommed onto him, dragging him to the table. "Sit, sit, sit!" Donny crowed. "We got you something!"

"We surprised you!" Dilly squeaked on his other side, grinning wide enough to show him every one of her white teeth.

"Guys!" Andrea sighed, "after dinner, didn't we say after dinner we'd surprise him?"

The adults gave one another knowing looks, and Aidan caught a couple of eye-rolling grins sent his way.

"Okay can we eat pleaaaase?" Tommy begged, "And then we can surprise him?"

His mother gave him a smile of amusement and chagrin. "Okay, okay, come on and let's get dinner served."

The kids bolted down their dinners, and Aidan got the sense that a few of the adults slowed down just to tease them.

"Now?" Tommy asked, and Alice shot Aidan a grin. "Brace yourself Commander. You're in for it."

"Yeah, I know," Aidan acknowledged with a rueful smile.

The kids ran for the kitchen, and came back with, to Aidan's absolute shock, a real angel food cake with strawberries on it and a tall, slim bottle. Aidan stared at the spread, then at the crew. Cautiously, he took a bite of cake.

"Holy... how the hell did we get real strawberries?"

"Um, did you forget that you're dating the logistics and *requisitions* officer?" Blake asked, dramatic emphasis dripping off every word as he jerked a thumb at Kevin.

The younger man gave his mentor a smirk, crossing his arms. "I do my humble best."

Aidan chuckled, shaking his head.

"Hey, jackass! I helped!" Tweak snapped.

Kevin shot Tweak a weary look. "In case you hadn't been informed, she helped," he agreed dryly. "There's champagne in the bottle. Shall we have a sip with our cake?"

Between the adults the single bottle was gone in record time. Kevin passed the last sip to Aidan with a small, secret smile, leaning in to kiss his throat.

"My room, remember," he whispered in Aidan's ear as he pulled away. Aidan's skin tingled.

As the crew broke up to find their own amusements for the night, he padded back to his room for a tie off one of his dress uniforms, killed a little time to let everybody settle down, then slipped to Kevin's door and knocked quietly. Glancing up and down the hall reflexively, he froze when Topher came out of his room. The young man gave him a grin and two thumbs' up as he walked away, and Aidan forced himself to grin in return, hoping it didn't look too sheepish. It was going to take him a hell of a long time to get used to being chill about this whole relationship in public thing. But he was starting to get the feeling that the guys would get him over it, one of these days.

Soft turn-of-the-century music played when the door opened, something gentle and rock at the same time. Kevin leaned against the door frame. The sight of him made Aidan's pulse jump. Kevin was in a pair of his tight black Grid-quality jeans. He hadn't put on a shirt. A black tie graced his milk white chest. Aidan raised his eyes to meet Kevin's rain cloud gaze.

"'Ello sailor," the redhead smirked, that heinously fake cockney accent he'd ripped off an old vid with a magic nanny going strong. "Fancy comin' in for a night?"

"If you stop the terrible accent," Aidan said with a crooked smile, trying for a tone as relaxed as his boyfriend's. His eyes ran up and down Kevin's bare torso as he slipped into the room and closed the door behind him. "What's all this for?"

"Your birthday, what else?" Closing the door and setting the lock, Kevin leaned against it, head cocked coquettishly. "I've got a bottle of proper wine and something with your name on it," he added, tipping his head in the direction of his jerry-rigged bedside table. An open bottle, two glasses and a box wrapped in shiny paper stood waiting.

That made Aidan's brow furrow. "Wait, wine? On top of the strawberries and the champagne? Where did you get real wine?"

"Now that'd be telling." Kevin smirked wryly. "I've got a few favors owed me here and there. And an idiot in ZonCom who was extremely eager to avoid his little habits turning up on video. We made a few trades. Who says capitalism doesn't work?" For a moment, his smirk was bitter. Then he shook the expression off, stepped to the bed and filled the glasses.

"Ah," he added as Aidan reached for the box. "In a bit." He held a glass out with a sly smile.

Aidan watched Kevin's face, but took the glass he was offered and sipped the wine all the same. It was bitter on his tongue, sweet in the back of his throat. Shit, this was real wine, not the terrible stuff they usually drank for alcohol.

"Where did you... tomorrow we really need to talk about these requisitions runs done on the side. But thanks. This is nice."

"Mmhm," Kevin agreed, sipping delicately as he took a seat on the edge of the bed. "So, read a good article today..."

Half an hour later they were halfway through the bottle, fingers twined together as they kissed. In the background, something old and soft played.

Kevin ran his hand down Aidan's spine. "Think it's time you opened that present," he murmured invitingly.

Aidan's skin tingled with Kevin's touch as he pulled the box to him. Kevin's teasing half smile didn't give anything away. He warily unwrapped the package, careful of the paper. They could re-use that. He blinked at the result.

The box was a long lozenge of plastic, black and slick to the touch.

"The release catch is on the side." Kevin murmured, leaning in to push the button.

The lid slid smoothly open. The lining was soft silicone and obviously bio-tech. The thing inside it looked organic.

Aidan's breath caught.

Kevin cleared his throat. "I thought this might..." Pulling off his glasses, he polished them. "It's DNA locked, I got a few hairs when you used my brush. It's a full-sensation model, so it'll feel just like it was...er..."

Reaching over, he downed the last of his wine before looking at Aidan. "Don't take this the wrong way, but we've had a few conversations on the subject of you...topping? I think we'd both like that, so... I picked this up for you. I thought we could try it out tonight?"

Aidan sat frozen, staring at what was in his lap. After a geologic age he got his brain and his tongue reconnected. "Kevin, I-I can't take this. This much money should go for base requisitions, not...this."

He pushed the box's lid down again with trembling hands. God, he wanted this. But it was a waste of funds and requisition resources. If Kevin got caught buying stuff like this, he could get demoted, or transferred, or...

"I got it when we took the signal broadcasters in. It was picked up on a break during an approved Grid run, and I used a false payment card," Kevin murmured, his quiet voice breaking in on Aidan's thoughts and short-circuiting the nibbling panic that had started to race through his chest cavity. "You know I wouldn't use base funds for luxuries, but if I can find another means then we can indulge in something...special, don't you think?" His hands were soft on Aidan's. "We don't get many frivolities, Aidan. We can afford this one." Lifting Aidan's hand, he kissed his knuckles softly. "Please."

In the background, the song changed. A woman earnestly sang something about the power of two and chasing away monsters.

Aidan looked up at Kevin, searching his face. Kevin actually wanted this, didn't he? The expression on his perfect face was so hopeful.

So why was it so hard to accept this gift? Because it wouldn't be a permanent fix? Because it might help him forget what he had been? And God forbid he let himself forget and be really happy? Wasn't that some bullshit thinking. Finally, he shook his head, a smile quirking his lips.

"I can't believe you. But I love it. Thank you. I..." He opened his mouth to say more, but the words wouldn't come. Instead he leaned over for a long, languid kiss.

"I take it you approve after all?" Kevin's words slipped out between kisses. "Oh, and I got a special feature. Self-lubricating. Could be fun."

"You're just too impatient to wait for lube," Aidan teased, kissing Kevin's jawline.

"Impatient... mmm... in some cases," Kevin agreed easily, tugging on the hem of Aidan's shirt. "Besides, I need to find out if I got my money's worth. Set your glass down."

"Okay, okay," Aidan laughed and gently pushed Kevin away. He set the wine bottle and both glasses carefully out of the way, took a breath and opened the box once more. Glancing up, he met Kevin's eyes.

"Um...I never tried one on...how does it work?" God he sounded helpless.

Kevin smiled softly. Taking the toy, he turned it so that Aidan could see a small cup filled with bumps in the blunt end, surrounded by two rings of—he squinted—yeah those really were tiny suction cups.

"You just put this over your existing endowments. It's full of proprioceptors—sorry, touch receptors—which will send signals up your own nerve endings. It's designed to feel like it's part of you. Body heat triggers the attachment, and the release signal is sent by the box when you push here," he added, pointing to a small button on the box's lid. "It also has a bio-feedback feature, so it'll start lubricating itself in time with your excitement. I'll get it calibrated for a sensation level you like once it's on."

Aidan gave his boyfriend a puzzled look. "How did you learn so much about this?"

Kevin countered with one of his 'I'm being patient but don't waste my time' expressions, looking at him over the rims of his glasses. "There is such a thing as a user's manual, my love. I do my research."

My love. Those words still sounded too good to be true coming from Kevin's lips.

With a long, slow breath to calm himself, Aidan carefully pulled the strap-on from its lining and held it balanced across his palms. Aidan glanced up at Kevin for a moment, feeling the fear in his gut fighting with the tingling excitement.

Kevin leaned in and stroked his cheek softly, running his fingers through Aidan's hair. He didn't look away as he got down on his knees and unzipped Aidan's pants. Kevin took a moment to get Aidan's boots undone and off. Then he slid back up to press against Aidan for a long, slow kiss.

"Let's get rid of that shirt."

"You gotta get the tie off first I think." Aidan whispered.

Kevin made a dismissive noise. "The ties stay."

"Weirdo."

"Yes, and your point is?" Kevin chuckled, working Aidan's shirt up and over his head. Long fingers stroked the skin below his binder, sending waves of sensation through him.

"You want your binder on or off?" Kevin asked softly.

"On." Aidan whispered, loving the man with almost painful intensity in this moment. How had he ended up with a guy who was this good to him?

"Roger," Kevin agreed, fingers moving lower. Gently, he leaned his weight against Aidan until he was flat on the bed, then stood and slid his pants down, taking off his boxers and packer while he was at it. Kevin's hands stroked his legs, running over the scars that crisscrossed his thighs.

Aidan sat up when Kevin lifted the strap-on, watching with nervous interest as he carefully put the thing in place. It grafted seamlessly over what little dick he already had, pinching him so hard it made his eyes water. For a moment, it felt as if pins and needles pricked over his skin. When that sensation passed, he shifted his legs. He felt heavy and hard. His heart leaped. He ran his fingers along his new shaft, wanting to feel how real this was.

"Aidan, wait for—" Kevin didn't get his warning out fast enough. Sensation so strong it burned ran through him. He yelped and jerked his fingers away. When he caught his breath again, he glanced up at his wide-eyed boyfriend.

"Are you alright?" Kevin asked, expression almost funny in its shock.

"Yeah," Aidan gasped, "yeah, just...wow."

Staring at Kevin's face as his breathing evened out, he couldn't help but chuckle. Kevin relaxed, grinning and reaching out to stroke his hair. "Let me get that for you, love," he quipped, lowering his eyes as he pushed his glasses up his nose. His black tie swung with the motion of his breathing as he reached out a hand. Kevin did something at the base, then stroked the shaft with one long finger.

"How's that?"

Aidan shivered as the sensation of Kevin's touch slowly lowered from intense to pleasant. Thank god he'd read the manual beforehand.

"That's great," he sighed in relief, his tight muscles relaxing. "Thank you."

"Good. Device lock," Kevin stated. Aidan didn't feel anything different, but he assumed that the receptor setting had worked.

"Contrary to what my subordinates think, I'm not a sadist." Kevin added lightly, tugging gently at the strap on. The warm pressure made Aidan gasp. "Looks like the attachment's good. All set," Kevin quipped. He splayed his fingers against Aidan's chest and leaned in for a kiss, pushing him back onto the bed again. Aidan lay back willingly, watching Kevin above him.

Kevin held himself over Aidan, the tip of his black tie tickling Aidan's collarbones as it swung. His eyes gleamed softly in the low light. In the background, a new song began slow and built in a wash of chords.

Aidan grabbed Kevin's tie and pulled him down for a thorough kiss. Kevin chuckled against his lips. The singer's rough voice caressed lines about staying together for the next one hundred years. Even for Kevin, this song was over the top. But maybe tonight that was okay. Maybe it was even true.

Every brush against the strap-on was a thrill through Aidan's pelvis. There was a fire starting in his gut. If this was what it felt like to have a normal guy's body, no wonder Kevin was so easy to tease with light touching.

"Time to get these off," Kevin muttered, pulling away so that he knelt over Aidan undoing the button of his own jeans, fingers racing through the motions.

"Don't rush it," Aidan murmured, sitting up and putting his hands over Kevin's wrists. "I want to make this last. Undress so I can watch?"

Kevin glanced down, copper brows raised as he smirked. "Thought I gave you a present," he teased, one finger drawing circles on the very tip of the strap-on. Aidan swallowed a gasp at the new touch on the prosthetic and the zing of energy that ran up his nerves.

"Okay, fine, fine," he managed, his voice a squeak.

Kevin's lips twitched. Then, very slowly, he slid off the bed, with a lick for the tip of Aidan's new toy on the way that made him bite his lip. Standing, he unzipped his jeans, and slowly slid the band away from his waist, rolling his hips to shed them of the fabric before neatly stepping out. He repeated the performance with his boxers, until he stood bare save for the tie around his throat. Tipping his head invitingly, he ran one finger up his own shaft, already standing to attention. "You approve, sir?"

"Very much," Aidan agreed, his voice coming out ragged around the edges. His eyes raked down Kevin's bare body. He sat up. "Come here."

Kevin obliged. Taking a moment to set his glasses in their case, he leaned down until he held himself over Aidan again, his dick and the strap on rubbing together.

"Oh. By the way. Happy birthday. And remember what I said about not being a sadist?"

"That you weren't one?" Aidan breathed as his eyes flickered shut from the wonderful sensation of Kevin's dick against his. His real dick. For now, at any rate.

"Exactly. While I'm not, I may have a touch of the corollary condition." Kevin agreed, burying his fingers in Aidan's hair, lips tracing his throat. "Because tonight, I'm offering you the chance to take me so hard that I scream." Rolling in one quick movement, he continued in a tone that would have been conversational if it hadn't been rough around the edges, grabbing the little bottle they kept under the head of the bed. "A little preparation does the trick..." Standing, he caught Aidan's eyes again and poured a dab of lube into his hand, stroking himself slowly as he spread the gel. The way he moved was so damn hot.

"Of course, you're already prepared in this department, otherwise I'd do the honors," Kevin continued. Surprised, Aidan glanced down. Beads of clear gel had spread over the strap-on, lining it in a glistening sheath. There was something weirdly exciting about that.

"By the way, did you know that the human body still shares a number of features with quadrupeds?" Kevin asked in his attempt at a casual tone as he returned to stand beside the bed. "We do. Everything's a bit more aligned when you're on your hands and knees. All the muscles and *tubes* are just that bit elongated. For our purposes, that should serve nicely." Eyes still locked with Aidan's, he tipped his head. "Care to test the assertion?"

Aidan's eyes kept drifting downward, lingering on Kevin's dick, until he forced them up again. He grinned. This daydream they'd both been having was real. They were really doing this.

"Oh hell yes."

Kevin's smile was languorous, and so was the way he moved as he climbed onto the bed. He pulled Aidan with him as he did until they were sitting in the center of the bed, touching and teasing. With slow grace, Kevin turned in Aidan's arms and leaned forward, positioning himself on his hands and knees in front of Aidan. Aidan felt his breath catch. He stroked Kevin's long white back.

"Don't let me hurt you," he whispered, rolling onto his knees and shifting until he knelt behind Kevin. His heart pounded against his ribs. Whether it was eagerness or fear, he wasn't sure. One hand rested on Kevin's hip, his thumb tracing idle circles on his lover's ass. He ducked his head and tasted Kevin's balls for a moment, tracing them with his tongue.

Kevin chucked low in his throat. "Oh, don't worry. I think I'll live."

Aidan hummed gently against the soft skin, slowly pulling away. Running his fingers over his strap-on, he covered his fingers in lube. He watched Kevin's body as he softly slipped a finger inside the man, stroking. Kevin gave a sigh of pleasure. Aidan added a second finger, and Kevin pressed back against him.

Aidan teased with his fingers, watching Kevin's body tense and twitch with anticipation. He glanced down at himself, and excitement blossomed in his chest.

Keeping one hand braced on Kevin's hip, he very carefully guided his new prosthetic to his boyfriend's entrance with the other.

"Say something if I get this wrong."

Kevin's reply was ragged. "The only thing you've gotten wrong so far is pacing. You don't need to hesitate so much, love."

Aidan bit his lip. Slowly, he tilted his hips forward. His breath hitched in his throat as tight heat swallowed the tip of the prosthetic, a sensation unlike anything he'd felt before.

"Oh wow… "

"Good, hm?" Kevin murmured, amusement and excitement twining in his voice. "Don't stop there," he added as Aidan stroked his dick with one hand, "Certainly not now…"

To Aidan's surprise Kevin leaned back, murmuring low. Aidan couldn't help the soft groan that escaped his throat as Kevin's body invited him in. Waves of pleasure lapped up from his core to run over the rest of his body. His hand tightened on Kevin's shaft, and he struggled to find a rhythm as every ounce of his awareness centered on the sensations between his legs. Kevin pulsed in his hand, hot and hard.

Balancing himself on one hand, Kevin reached back with the other and squeezed Aidan's hip, pulling him forward and pushing himself back at the same time. The thrust pulled an inarticulate noise from them both.

"Like this," the redhead whispered, leaning forward just slightly, pulling away, then pushing himself back again and enveloping Aidan in heat. "Like this, Aidan. Just like this…"

"That's not too hard?" Aidan asked breathily, but his hips fell easily into the rhythm Kevin set. The sensation was unbelievable.

What had started as a chuckle came out of Kevin as a pant, and his body rocked in sync. His words came out disjointed.

"Thinking too much. Said I want to scream… remember?"

Aidan took a shuddering breath and braced both hands on Kevin's hips, muttering, "If you really want that, then sit still."

Kevin's body relaxed completely, waiting. Only the shivering of his muscles and his panting breath gave away his excitement.

It was hard to overcome the sheer sensation and focus, but Aidan got his hips to change angle. Slowly, he thrust himself in, burying himself deep. He pressed his fingers to the skin between Kevin's balls and his ass, reminding himself of the spot. Once he got going on this, he wanted to hit Kev's prostate every time.

Kevin groaned. "Aidan..." The word was a whimper.

"This good?" Aidan asked, his body alive. He wished he could hold them here all night. Hearing Kevin on the edge was never going to get old.

"Please love, please God please pick up the pace!" Kevin panted, pleasure and desperation tangled in his voice. "I'm losing my mind here…"

Aidan grinned. "You asked for it."

This time he let himself plunge forward. Tight heat enveloped him again and again. The muscles of his belly clenched. Holy shit, what a feeling! He leaned over Kevin and panted, sliding one hand around to stroke Kevin in time with his thrusting. He screwed his eyes shut tight as the sheer feeling pounded through him.

Kevin gave a long, shuddering cry as he tipped over the edge. Aidan swore his heart stopped as Kevin spasmed around the prosthetic. He tilted his head back and tried to remember to breathe as his own climax overtook him, turning his knees to water and his blood to fire.

Kevin's scream petered down into a moan, then a whimper of senseless joy. The man trembled, head hanging limply, shaft throbbing as it relaxed.

There was the hollow *thunk!* of a boot hitting the left-hand wall.

"*Kevin*! You sound like a fucking siren man! Turn it down you guys!" Sarah's voice yowled.

"Seriously! You drowned out our vid! Jesus," Yvonne added through the wall. There was some other comment, but Aidan didn't catch it. Weakly, Kevin began to laugh.

Aidan snorted breathlessly as he rested himself across Kevin's back, the prosthetic still connecting them. He kissed Kevin's shoulders and the back of his neck over and over, muttering half-sensible thanks and trying to find the strength to move.

"Love you too... pull out, because I want to fall over," Kevin replied giddily. He murmured the last of his pleasure as the strap-on slid out, then turned and curled against Aidan.

"Sarah can complain all she wants; I'm not turning you down," Aidan whispered, and that got them both laughing. Kevin fell over as he snickered, burying his face in a pillow to smother the laughter. Aidan flopped an arm over his waist and they leaned against one another, wheezing with laughter and euphoria.

"Thank you," Aidan whispered when the laughter gave way to quiet cuddling. "Best birthday ever."

"Glad to hear it," Kevin breathed, curled against him. A moment later, he wrapped both arms around Aidan's waist. "Going to be gone for a while. Stay with me tonight."

Aidan knew he shouldn't. Tomorrow was a duty day. He really shouldn't. But Kevin had given him the most wonderful night of his life. Couldn't he give the guy a couple hours of companionship?

He settled back down into the pillows, shifting closer. "Okay... I'll stay. Let's get cleaned up."

They wiped each other down and put the strap-on back in its box, which turned out to be self-cleaning. Kevin really did think of everything. The man dropped his head onto Aidan's chest, nuzzling like a cat. Aidan loved the feeling of his lean body relaxing so completely.

"Love you, Aidan." Kevin whispered one last time, words slow with sleep.

Aidan chuckled softly and nuzzled closer. "Love you too, Kev" He unzipped his binder and let his eyes fall closed.

Chivalry, Kevin mused, really did have its uses. He'd used the oldest trick in the book, holding the outer door for a lady entering the CSS employee recreation area like the gentleman he was and following after her. She was so busy giving him a blushing smile that she keyed him into the pavilion without a peep of comment. He didn't even have to give the new Citizen Card in his pocket a try.

The open-air pavilion was lined with restaurants, a scattering of coffee shops and a handful of bars. Kevin blinked four times in succession, signaling the recording chips in his contacts to start their work. He ran through the images of the people he was looking for in his mind as he took a seat in a coffee shop. Ideally, he'd get a look at a few of them while they worked outside their offices or took lunch. Failing that, he was sure of a good chance to observe while they gathered for after-hours drinks.

It wasn't a terrible place to kill time. The holo ads were muted and discrete, the people friendly and relaxed. They knew their place in society was secure. He made a few casual conversational gambits while he sat his watch, keeping his cover story of a bored social media writer shipped in from out of state and killing time until the corner office decided where he was most useful in the process. The conversations also let him get a closer look at a proper coding tab. The retro designs were back in again, and Techo's coders were using tabs as long as his forearm. The things were solid slabs of plastic, at least three times as thick as the wafer-thin tabs most people used. Since the machines weren't wasting processing speed on creating holographic screens, they were also incredibly powerful. All the same, Kevin was glad he didn't have to use one. They looked like bulky monsters and he imagined they weighed rather a lot. Of course, he'd be able to check that theory soon enough when he 'borrowed' one.

One hacking candidate he crossed off immediately; in two days of Kevin's watch the man was never alone. He always had a gaggle of friends with him. Too complicated.

Two other candidates never appeared. Perhaps they had other places to spend their time, probably less easy to observe and secure than this was. Tracking each candidate was tempting, but not nearly as efficient as sitting quietly and waiting.

In his hotel room after each day's surveillance, Kevin re-ran the clips his contacts had been sending to his tab, circling important points and adding his own notations. He encrypted each clip in amusing memes and put them up on his favorite Grid persona's Social Feed account. The base could get them from there. It would have been faster to send them directly to the gang over the Greynet, but it would also be a risk he didn't want to take. TechoCo didn't take kindly to Greynet signatures turning up on its servers, and they had a nasty habit of spreading their displeasure around.

The fourth candidate showed more promise the longer Kevin watched him. He was a reedy little man with the tells of somebody who'd been gene-modded for a high IQ and a sedentary life. The gene-mod that allowed for a lifetime of close reading without eye strain had given the man's eyes that signature lime-green color that Kevin had learned to spot a mile off. Other hints were subtle, but they were there if you were watching. That gene mod package also came with a tendency toward hyper-focused attention, which was perfect for their needs providing they could find a way to keep his attention on something other than what they were doing with his work computer. Misdirection and timing were going to be the keys to pulling this mission off.

Attention to detail was another common trait in what people called the Cubicle King gene-mod bundle and, wonder of wonders, the man actually brought a detachable keyboard with him to the coffee shop. He sat with perfect posture while he worked, protecting the asset of his wrists and shoulders from carpal tunnel and all the other modern man's physical ills by typing on the foam-and-plastic pad in his lap with his tab in a folding cradle. He sat for exactly two hours and absently sipped the same order four days in a row; double-shot latte with hazelnut flavoring. Kevin made a note of the coding computer's make and model as well as the drink and the type of bag the man carried.

Every evening like clockwork the little man would go down to the same bar, order Grey Goose, and chat with a few work colleagues. When girls laughed at other tables, he'd give them wistful glances. Kevin noted that, too. Yvonne would be an asset on this run. She was pretty enough to keep his attention.

Sipping a neat whiskey on his fifth night in the bar, Kevin made his decision. A better social engineering target than Mr. William Sinclair couldn't be asked for.

He recorded the choice of target that night, along with his intention to set the preliminary groundwork for their plan into motion. He got back a pic of a smiley face, which worked as an approval signal.

It took a day to get ahold of the right cleaning crew uniform. After that it was simple enough to use a back door in the system that Tweak had coded, get into the pavilion's work schedule and insert a new set of credentials from the selection he carried. He checked the attachments for the surveillance cameras while taking out the trash and found their control box while getting 'lost' looking for the supply closet. A signal broadcaster easily affected the low-grade security fixtures in the hall, giving them the electronic equivalent of 24-hour flu. Kevin killed the requisite fifteen minutes to ensure the bug had gotten a foothold by polishing door knobs. Then he slipped into the control closet. He carefully pierced the thick casing on the fiber-optic wires running along the wall, connecting the building's camera hardware to its recording computers. Carefully, he reached in his pocket and retrieved the primary and backup devices. The direct-uplink splices sank their connection spikes through plastic. Their little attachment legs snapped down, and each tiny device showed a blue 'on' light for a moment. Hidden in the wire bundles, they would be practically invisible to the casual eye.

Kevin nodded to himself, satisfied. That would allow them to control what the cameras showed. What work he could do here and now was done.

Scrubbed and CSS in credentials again that morning, Kevin did something he really hated to do. Casually passing the table while his target was in the restroom, he dropped a pinch of powder into the open mug. Resuming his seat and reading with ease, he waited.

Sinclair sat back down and took a few sips. Typed. Took a few more. Then he made an odd little 'urp' noise in the back of his throat. A moment later, he vomited on the table. His coffee tipped over his machine.

Kevin really didn't like doing that to the poor fellow. But needs must, given the situation. He jumped up and pulled on the persona of Surprised Good Samaritan.

"Steady, steady, I've got you," he murmured as the little man groped feebly for his bag, one hand clutching his gut. "No, I'll get your stuff, let's get you to the bathroom."

Around him people relaxed, glad to see an unpleasant situation fixed. Kevin shot the barista an apologetic smile. "I'll get his gear cleaned up."

She gave him the pained smile of a subordinate who needed to be polite despite the situation in return.

Poor little Sinclair threw up for nearly ten minutes. Kevin had to admire the man's dedication to his work. Between convulsions, the little fellow managed to eke out a plea to get his machine checked and cleaned before the coffee could harm it.

"No worries, I've got the back open, it's dry." Kevin called, making a great show of dabbing at the machine's insides with a paper towel. It was the perfect cover for sliding a new chip inside. Kevin felt it click into place. Now the input-output connection that transmitted the keystrokes from Sinclair's detachable keyboard to his machine would also send a copy of the keylog back to Tweak. He screwed the coding computer's casing back into place and hit the power button for the cameras.

"Turning on just fine! Now let's worry about you."

Kevin did his best with aspirin and a chewable to counteract what he'd slipped the poor sap. He cleaned the desk jockey up as best he could with paper towels. The man looked up at him with grateful green eyes, his sandy hair wet with sweat.

"Thanks man, you're a lifesaver."

"I do my best," Kevin replied easily, feeling like the slime of the earth.

In his room that night, he documented what he'd done and despised himself. He hated doing things like that to innocent people trying to get through their days.

He'd be glad to get out of Dodge the next morning. Checking his time tables, he found that he'd calculated right: he still had the time to run and check on used stockbot availability with a reliable contact. Of course, that involved a really miserable trip. But if he could make some headway on the Ten Year Plan, it'd be worth it.

He moved to a new hotel in the morning. This time, he checked in using the CES level credentials he carried. They'd be his only protection in an American AgCo community.

Two hours later, he was on enemy ground.

The old American flag fluttered high overhead, emblazoned or defaced—depending on how you saw it—with American AgCo's logo. Kevin opted for the latter description.

He pulled the wide brim of his suit's matching hat low, glad he'd brought it. You'd think American Ag could pay for awnings over the streets of their only Community in the city.

One more reason he hated it here.

A few men watched him idly from the shade of a doorway as he passed. He nodded and tipped his hat politely. They nodded in reply, but their faces were blank.

Kevin passed a mural of two children staring with saccharine devotion into a wide blue sky graced with waving sheaves of wheat and the shadow of a cross. He was always reminded of an old movie about evil children in corn fields when he was on Ag land. But this was not the place to kick up any sort of fuss. As much as he despised American AgCo, the feeling was mutual.

In spite of the down-to-earth-farmer facade they loved, Kevin had always thought that American AgCo had been one of the most strategic Corporations when it came to consolidating their authority. He kept his mind on the history and the strategy of the Corporation as he walked.

American AgCo had taken a fanatical type of Protestantism as its standard, and they called an awful lot of things 'against God's Law.' Here the Morality Laws would kill you if you were caught breaking them. You wouldn't die quietly either. The vids of morality executions that went around made Kevin itch to hide in the crowds with a bullet for every one of the executioners in his gun. It would be suicidal, and it wouldn't be effective. Those were the only realities that stopped him figuring out how to make it happen. The idea still tempted him some days.

He passed another sickly-sweet mural on a building, this one depicting two kids holding a pig wearing a ribbon. One of the children was in a wheelchair. The words 'God Loves All His Children, Just the Way He Made You' circled the picture in a curling banner. Kevin repressed a sneer for the thing. They caught him coming and going with their vitriolic hatred for gene-editing on 'all beings with souls.' If he wasn't carrying CES credentials from ZonCom right now he'd be fair game for an unofficial beating in this area. Human gene editing of all kinds was banned in Ag's Morality Laws for its employees. They let it be known that they didn't welcome outsiders with gene modifications visiting their residential communities from other Corporations either.

Kevin had always seen the policy against human gene-editing as a very cynical and clever dodge. It meant that American AgCo could do what they liked with the genomes of the plants and animals that fed the nation, and still allow their employees a platform of moral superiority to look down on others from. Not only did the agricultural super-corporation hold money, power and authority over the people born into contracts with them, it held religion. Ag-raised people saw everyone else in the country as sub-human and physically no longer acceptable to the Lord. It did create a sick sort of loyalty, and there was power in that.

It galled him, what they'd done to his religion. Granted, he was a Jesuit Catholic and not a Protestant—and considering how long it had been since he'd seen a priest, not a good Catholic either—but it still made him ill. His mother had taught him her own Jesuit beliefs, and they were beautiful. They'd helped him handle the garbage Cavanaugh had taught him about his own worth and the worth of others. The stuff Ag plastered across its branding and its walls was a warped travesty of the religion. It didn't encourage anything but blind obedience, fear of whoever was speaking on behalf of God and hatred of anything unusual.

Finally getting past the first few blocks of the Wheat-Sheaf Community and the endless murals, he gave himself a mental shake. He had a job to do. The faster he did it, the faster he could leave.

It didn't take long to finish his haggles for the stockbots he wanted with the third-hand machine dealer who also helped out the Grapevine. Standing in his shop with the dusty sunlight filtering through the blinds, Kevin tipped his hat.

"Thanks Tip. Keep your head down."

The skinny man smiled his gap-toothed smile. "Hang in there."

Stepping out of the little side-street, Kevin pocketed his tab with its new pricing information and braced himself. He pulled the jacket of his suit a little tighter around himself. The sunlight slammed into him as he walked to the vehicle rental kiosk.

At least American AgCo liked their Communities clean and quiet: the worst of the popup ads were absent and the people in the inadequately air-conditioned glass shelter for a Go rental were secure enough about where their next paycheck came from to be polite.

"We look forward to working with you," the hologram set in the wall beside him stated in sugared tones, appearing as a happy old manual car that had been called after some insect. What had it been, Kevin asked himself. Ladybug? Beetle? Bug, that had been it.

He must be getting Gridbuzzed, forgetting details like that. He was looking forward to thinking without distractions again when he got home.

"What rate will you be paying at today? Economy, Express or Elite?"

"Express, please. I'm in a rush."

"Too much of a rush to talk to an old friend?"

Kevin whipped around.

Kevin couldn't help but grin at the squat, adobe-skinned man who stood in the doorway. Stepping out of the kiosk, he enveloped the old man in a hug.

If the man had been a nanoid mimic of his godfather, he would have just killed himself. The thought flashed across his mind, but it was gone when Umberto laughed.

"Jesus boy, you hug too tight!"

"Umberto! I heard they upgraded your Standing! Are you living here now?" he asked, unable to hide his grin as the old plant geneticist looked him up and down.

"Three streets that way," the man replied with a spark in his eyes, "and Maria wants you over for dinner. Don't you eat?"

"I swear by the Virgin, I eat, I eat!" Kevin protested as Umberto poked him in the ribs, "Lay off!"

"Well, you're coming home with me for a decent meal," the older man retorted, "so come on, Maria will have something cooking by now."

He was right. The scent of cooking rice and spices filled Kevin's nose the moment he stepped inside, and he breathed it in. Glancing down at Umberto, he smiled slightly once the old man had closed the door.

"Is today a good day to come in out of the storm?" Kevin asked quietly. Umberto flapped a dismissive hand.

"You think I don't know how to get a house taken care of? I was the one who taught your mamma. Besides, who's looking so hard for you? You're dead, I mean I went to your funeral. You're buried. And since when has Ag liked Cavanaugh sniffing around their security turf?"

"Just checking. Thanks, Tio Berto," Kevin murmured, slipping back into his childhood name for the man as he relaxed.

His godfather looked him up and down with grave eyes now that they were indoors, studying him.

"You really aren't eating enough, son," he stated eventually. Kevin shrugged.

"I've got my needs covered. We do our best."

Umberto grunted into his grey-streaked moustache.

"Come into the kitchen and let Maria fuss over you."

Kevin rolled his eyes, smirking.

"Oh, mijo!"

Kevin braced himself as the round little woman's hug caught him around the waist. These days his mother's best friend had to reach up a lot higher to cup his cheeks in her wide, soft hands, but she still managed it. The botanist frowned at him.

"Kevin, when did you get so skinny? And so tired! Look at the bags under your eyes! And have you fixed those eyes yet?"

"I'm fine Tia Maria, really. Really! Being svelte's in my genes and my eyes are my problem!" he laughed, but his godmother clucked her tongue.

"Every time I see you, I tell you the same thing and I know you hate it, but you—"

"Should have gone to England," Kevin finished for her with a weary roll of the eyes, "Yes you do say it every time I see you, and it's been nine years. I could start asking the same question; you two were supposed to head back home years ago. What happened to that, hm?" he asked, leaning against the counter.

"Our work's helping—" Umberto began, and Kevin finished that sentence too.

"Helping people, I know, I know. Your legitimate genetic work and your Grapevine work both. But you could be doing even better work in Argentina, open source work, and you'd be safe there. You'd be in a decent country with a real democratic government. You guys aren't young anymore, and—"

"Oh, like you?" Maria asked, pointing a spoon covered in finely chopped vegetable matter at him. Kevin acknowledged the jab with a nod. "Yes, like me. I'm allowed to be crazy; I'm young. It's going to be a long time before America's a good country to live in; I wish you guys would—"

Maria slapped his shoulder gently as she passed with the serving bowl.

"Oh stop. Now, sit, sit, and we'll all eat."

Kevin took the seat he was offered between the old man who'd saved his life and the old woman who'd been his mom's best friend. He was so lucky that he'd been able to keep this one precious tie to his old life. He'd been able to justify the connection to Sector as a secure contact. But Umberto and Maria were a lot more than that.

"Tio Berto, how did you know I'd be coming around?" Kevin asked as his plate filled with matambre.

"I keep an eye out, you're not getting sloppy," Umberto replied, watching Kevin dig in. "I asked Tip to give me a buzz if you came by, now that I'm here. He let me know when you researched an order with him," he added, gesturing at the discreet wall screen in the corner of his kitchen. Kevin nodded carefully.

"Just be careful who you give the word to, Tio. I don't want you two or Tip or anyone in the Grapevine in trouble because you wanted to see me, all right?"

"Don't worry about us," the old man deflected, muttering at his dinner.

"All right, then you be careful because you're worrying about me if you like that better," Kevin retorted, exasperated, "I've got every intention of living to forty if I can."

That got him a dour look. "I plan for you to live a lot longer than that. And I was doing this before you were born, hijo. Before I met your parents too. You remember that."

Kevin nodded his acknowledgment. "Sorry, Tio."

"Yes, well. Eat."

Kevin did as he was told.

"Been hearing a lot about you on the Grapevine," Umberto added as Maria took a seat beside him, "you remember a man named Saul? You saved his life a few months back. He would have died in the crossing if it wasn't for you."

"It was my new commander who saved him actually," Kevin deflected with an easy shrug.

Aidan. One more reason he wanted to get home.

"Well, Saul sent us a message," Umberto continued, "he had trouble with it so it's later than is good, but it's here. There's going to be an exchange of seed stock from the Co-Wy grid to the Tex Grid to keep up gene diversity. Vegetable crops: tomatoes, carrots, all that. Saul used to be a courier. He sent along the validation codes and the time and place."

Kevin paused. Seeds. That was tempting. But he wasn't here for seeds. Risking himself for a set of seeds when they had no way to plant them and none of the chemicals that triggered germination was a fool's errand. He shook his head, smiling ruefully. "Thanks for telling me Tio, if I was on my own time, I'd jump on it but—" Umberto raised his eyes, and Kevin fell silent at the calculating look on his face.

"Saul says they're sending something else too."

"What?"

"Hard copies of the gene-mod software for their plants, and 3-D printing specs for gene-modification tools as well as chemical mixing instructions. They're paranoid, AgCo. Every time they update their software, they send hard copies to install. They don't trust sending it over any kind of net. That's in the briefcase too."

Kevin blinked, his brain kicking into overdrive.

"Are you saying..."

"Printing the tools and supplies you need to work with seeds is easy once you have the designs. And it's even easier to keep the seeds alive once you can change their code. Maybe you can even take out that germination prevention and the programmed second-generation sterility that makes everything on the commercial market worthless." Umberto took a bite of dinner.

Kevin stared at him. Gene tailoring programs. Designs for tools. Actual seeds and a way to tailor them. With their own tailored seeds and the water Janice had found, they could do so much. They could make Taylor's Ten Year Plan start to happen.

But if it didn't go exactly right, if he was caught, then...

"Is it to be a delivery or are they using a courier on this?"

"Courier," Umberto replied, and Kevin's rising hopes deflated. The old man studied him out of the corner of his eye. "But if that courier was kept busy, and his gear was blocked from sending a message, somebody else could show up and..." he sucked a meaningful breath between his teeth.

Kevin nodded carefully. "That's quite the idea. When's the drop?"

"Tomorrow morning, at the greenhouses out on 78th."

Kevin flinched. "That leaves me precious little prep time, Tio. I should really get this approved and make some solid plans with my Commander before I walk into American Ag and ask them to hand over their seeds."

"Can you get it tonight?"

Kevin shook his head. "Mm, no, not safely. All I can do is drop a quick message..." Then he glanced up into two watching faces. Slowly, he drew a breath.

"But I've never been one to turn down a gift," he finished with a brittle smile, "so I suppose you can sign me up."

Umberto nodded once, solemn.

"I'll do that. I've got a complete information packet with your name on it, I'll send it to your tab. You'll need to be at the Cavanaugh Central Library at nine. Look for a car with Welb logos, that's your ride."

"Right," Kevin agreed. He raised his glass in a toast. "Thanks, Tio Berto. This is going to do a lot of good."

Umberto grunted rather than responding, lowering his head to dig into his meal. He always had been embarrassed by genuine emotions and thanks.

"Now we want to hear more about you," Maria put in. "We never see you properly! Six and eight months at a stretch, we worry! Tell us everything. Has your crew calmed down? Are you out of trouble?"

"Yes and yes," Kevin agreed with a smile and, knowing the drill, launched into a few of the more amusing stories about base life: the prank with the lizard the kids had played on Aidan on his second day, Lazarus sneaking a bug onto Kevin's tab that turned into an irritating dancing vid which executed its program in the middle of dinner, Janice telling the twins to go find her a box of elbow grease so they'd leave her alone and the fact that they'd spent the rest of the day ransacking the base for it.

He considered and discarded the story of Sarah and Yvonne trying to have sex up against their door and falling out into the hall when the brittle pre-fab gave way. No sense in shocking these sweet people who were embedded in the most conservative Corporation. Kevin knew they believed in a world that allowed real freedom as much as he did, but they still didn't really get alternative lifestyles.

Umberto brought out a bottle of cheap rum, and they shared a drink as the stories wandered back into the old days.

Maria gave a small, happy smile as she packed the dishes into the washer. "There never was a woman for roses like Julia. So many roses! And the two of you always looking to breed one more," she added with a fond smile for her husband, "what a hobby! She had you in and out of the house all the time!"

"Who else could get creosote genes into roses without ruining them?" Umberto retorted teasingly, "Why do you think American Ag contracts us and pays us so well? But that blue and red rose, that was the best thing Julia ever pulled off. I've still got the patent on it. Julia's Jubilee. You remember, Kevin?"

"Yeah," Kevin agreed quietly. He wished his gut didn't still tighten when they talked about his parents.

Out of the corner of his eye, Umberto caught Kevin's expression. Slowly, he pushed his seat back.

"Maria, this boy needs his sleep. He's got a day ahead of him."

"Oh…" Maria turned from her work to give Kevin another tight hug. "Be safe, mijo," she murmured. Kevin hugged her back just as tight, wishing he could do more. He wished he could promise her that he'd be safe. He wished he could protect her.

"You too, Tia Maria."

"Come on son. I'll walk you out." Umberto said quietly.

In the foyer, Umberto put a hand on each of Kevin's shoulders.

"If you do ever want that way out... your mother was good people, Kevin. She'd cry to see you living this kind of life."

Kevin's heart turned over at that, but he spoke as calmly as he could.

"I've stated my reasons before, Tio Umberto."

"You can't live for revenge Kevin," the older man replied quietly.

Kevin shook his head.

"I did for a while, I'll admit it. But these days… it's not like that. I've got… well, you know. I've got something like a family to take care of. I love the guys, even when they're a load of jackasses. And… Tio, if every man who doesn't believe in the way this country's run leaves it, how is it ever going to improve?"

Umberto sighed irritably. "Some days I think I should've slipped you a pill and put you on that plane when I had the chance. I wish to God you weren't so much like your father." Then he gave in and nodded. "You know, they'd be proud. I mean, I think you're crazy…but they'd be proud. They were crazy too."

Kevin's throat tightened. He gave the old man a smile.

"Thanks."

Umberto pulled him into a hug, clapping him on the back once before releasing him.

"Adios, little Mr. Craydon."

Kevin cleared his throat. "McIllian, Tio. My name's Kevin McIllian."

The old man gave him a lopsided smirk. "How many times boy? This house is safe."

Kevin shook his head. "It isn't that. It's… I'll always be my mom and dad's son. But I'm not the little boy I used to be. And maybe I'm a little bit proud of that."

For a handful of heartbeats, the old man studied him. Then he nodded once, slowly.

"Then adios, Mr. McIllian."

"Adios." Kevin agreed, opening the door.

That night, he managed a quick message for the base: 'Hit a snag, may be late getting home.' He couldn't wait to see the looks on their faces when they found out what the snag was.

Aidan probably would take him to task for running something on the side. He'd been getting nervy about the extra work Kevin and Yvonne tended to do while they were out and about. But Kevin could deal with that later; this opportunity was one in a thousand. He couldn't pass it up.

He was there to take the Corporation car that arrived red and plastered with 'WelbCo: A Subsidiary of American AgCo' in cheerful colors. The validation card was lying on the seat inside. He checked, but Umberto had done his work well. The car was secure.

As he rode, he double checked his own preparations. He'd paid an extortionate price to use a DIY clothing printer for his suit and briefcase the night before, but it had been worth the money. The machine hadn't recognized the tiny QR code in the subtle blue-on-blue pinstripe pattern he'd given it to use for the suit, but the groan of the next customer in line as he left had proved its utility. The code had done its work, wiping out the machine's programming once it processed the image. As long as it did the same to the security cameras he was set.

As a precaution, he uncapped a bottle of what looked like lotion and smeared the clear gel in a careful pattern across the bridge of his nose, one cheekbone and just under his eye. The infrared reflecting compound was invisible to human eyes, but it would turn up in cameras as bright red blots and make a nice mess of their facial recognition software. Between the two methods and the tinkering he'd done to the briefcase, he should be fine on the tech angle. Now he just had to hope he and his new validation codes passed muster with the human security measures.

His car crunched over the gravel in the greenhouse's main drive, stopping just short of the concrete wall surrounding it. It was a good thing that this handover was routine enough to happen in a low-security distribution center that mostly produced ornamental flowers. No guards on the walls, several gates, only a few ground crew on security. Nothing fancy either; they were equipped with simple guns and uniforms. Nobody really thought the news of an exchange like this was going to get out, apparently. Or that anyone who could do anything about it would want to.

All the better for him.

The security guard at the gate stepped to his window.

"Morning, sir."

"Morning," Kevin replied with polite cheer, handing over the validation card. *Don't hold your breath*, he ordered himself.

The man ran his scanner over it, heard the ding of approval and smiled, stepping aside.

"Have a nice day."

"You too."

The greenhouse complex was an expanse of white sizzling under the sun. The sound of cooling fans was deafening.

The silence inside was shocking by contrast.

Kevin listened to his footsteps as he walked down the immaculate public halls. The only color existed in the holos of the plants the company was famous for: all-nutrient potatoes, golden rice, perennial corn, low-water tomatoes. They glowed in their optical-illusion niches in the walls, each one perfect.

AgCo could and did create biological perfection. If you could afford it.

Or steal it.

The handle of the briefcase was slick in his hand.

"Good morning," the dark-haired woman in the public office greeted. It was a relief to look at something that wasn't white.

"Morning!" Kevin replied cheerfully, "Atkinson from the Tex establishment, I assume I'm on the schedule?"

The woman glanced at his card and put it face down on her pristine white desk. "Of course, Mr. Atkinson. May I see your validation?"

Kevin passed over his validation card and laid his briefcase on the desk, tapping the lid to bring up the industry specs for a reading that purported to report the contents and their fertility rates. *Thank you again, Tio Berto,* he thought to himself. If the old man hadn't recorded every detail about how these exchanges worked in house, he'd already be dead in the water.

The woman smiled and did the same. The list boggled Kevin's brain. *So many seeds!*

He forced his face to retain its bland smile.

On the woman's desk, something made a nasty little bleating noise.

She glanced at it with a frown, lifted Kevin's validation card and set it down again. The bleat repeated.

"Please validate with biometric data." a digitized voice warbled.

The woman glanced up with a professional 'I hate days like this, but they pay me' smile.

"This reader, I tell you what. If you'll just wait a minute, I'll call someone up."

She activated the 'bud in one ear, smiling. Smiling.

When the smile began to fade, Kevin knew he was in too deep.

The silence was brittle.

The woman deactivated her 'bud with a new, sickly smile.

"If you'll just wait a moment, we've got some formalities to run through when a validation doesn't quite—"

Kevin grabbed the woman's briefcase off the desk and bolted for the door.

"Message says 'hit a snag, may be late g-getting home.'"

Aidan gave Tweak a smile. "Thanks. Do you have enough to start thinking out a plan with the rest of Logistics before Kevin gets home?"

Tweak shrugged. "Sure, we got enough. Where're they?"

"I'll ping them and tell them to meet you in the logistics office, Kevin won't care. Three hours work for you?"

Tweak turned in her coding chair. "Cool."

Aidan tapped distractedly at his tab as he left Tweak's lair and strolled down the hallway, his mind turning the message over. Hit a snag? What kind of snag?

That intel he'd given Kevin hadn't been much good. Was that where the snag was?

Was Kevin okay? He would have said something if he was in trouble, wouldn't he?

Okay, no sense going down this road. Deep breath. In for a count of seven. Out for a count of seven. Missions ran long. No big deal.

Still, he really wished Kevin could've sent home something clearer than 'hit a snag.'

Contracting a Grapevine operative to pick out their stockbots for them and helping with the details for a sting on a ZonCom exec that another base was running ate up most of his afternoon. It kept him mostly distracted, but the words of Kevin's message were still rattling around in his head when he headed down to dinner. He studied his tab as he walked in hopes of getting his mind off things.

The self-induced distraction only made the yelling that came blaring out of the logistics office more of a shock. He jumped about a foot. Catching his breath, he flipped his tab off and backtracked.

"The hell's going on in…here…"

Jim was pressed flat against one wall, Tweak's fist inches under his chin. Fat sparks crackled from it. Jim twitched as they fell on his unprotected throat, the light from the electric knuckle dusters reflecting hot blue in his dark eyes.

"Tweak," Jim managed, his voice very quiet, "that's enough."

"Not!" Tweak snarled, her chest moving as fast as a bird's. "Fuck you! Send me back. Bastard! You said! You all said we c-c-c-could stay! Liar! Not! Going!"

"Um. Tweak? Let him go and let's talk," Aidan said. He carefully slid his tab onto the nearest table and stepped forward like a man approaching a wild animal, catching Yvonne's frightened eyes for the skin of a second as she carefully typed on her own tab. "Just calm down."

Tweak's breath was loud in the little room, overlaying the crackle of her knuckle dusters. "F-f-Fuck you. All. Not going. N-not. Going. NOT!"

"All right." Jim swallowed hard. "All right. You're not going. I copy. Sorry I asked."

Tweak shook her head hard, her hands trembling. "C-can't." she repeated. "N-Not going. C-can't. C-c-c-can't."

The electric knuckle dusters dipped with the movement, and the smell of burning cloth unfolded. Jim gave a strangled yelp.

Tweak gasped, her eyes widening into black pools. She took one step back, her entire body shaking as if she was the one electricity had gone coursing through. Then she gave a whimper, turned and bolted, shoving past Aidan and out the door. Her boots clattered down the hall.

"What the hell just happened?" Aidan asked, his words barely above a whisper. He glanced after Tweak, then hurried to his subordinate's side. "Shit, Jim, you okay?"

Jim slumped back against the wall, his eyes closed. "Holy shit," he breathed, the words sounding like a prayer of thanks. He sucked in a lungful of air and met Aidan's eyes. "I'm fine. We've gotta get that thing away from her before she runs into one of the kids. Aidan, she's batshi-fuck, ow!" He winced as he moved, a hand instinctively pressing itself to his chest. The smell of burnt cloth and burnt hair filled Aidan's nose.

"I think I might need to see Damian," Jim muttered, "and you might want to get some tranqs from him for the nutcase. One minute we're talking mission details, then this." A hiss of pain whistled between his teeth. "Damn her!"

Aidan frowned deeply and slung an arm around Jim's waist. "Let me worry about Tweak. Let's get you to the med bay."

He'd taken his first step towards the door with the wounded man when Liza skidded into the entry, two throwing knives in one hand and a gun in the other. Aidan gave her a grim smile. "Stand down Liza. We're good."

"What the..." Liza straightened. "I got a message that Tweak had flipped her shit and you guys needed backup." Her eyes met Yvonne's and narrowed. "If that was a prank—"

"It wasn't," Aidan cut in. Now that he had time to think, he realized his mistake and slid carefully out of the stance he'd taken to support Jim. "Can you take Jim to the infirmary, Yve?"

"I can get there on my own," Jim ground out. "It's just a burn. Go deal with her before someone else isn't so lucky."

Yvonne stepped over to support him regardless.

Aidan could hear his pulse pounding in his ears. He nodded. "I'll check on you soon as I can."

Once he'd seen his people head off, he turned to Liza.

"We need to find Tweak," the personnel officer stated flatly. Aidan nodded. He really didn't like the look in her eyes.

"I have no idea where she's gone, she took off so fast. So let's start with the obvious."

Five minutes later, he knocked on the door of Billie and Tweak's room. "Tweak? You in there?"

There was a tiny, animal sound from inside the room, but no voice answered him. The barracks wing was breathless in the heat of the afternoon.

Inside Tweak's room, there was another tiny sound that might have been a sob.

"Tweak?" Aidan asked again, just a bit louder. "Can I come in? We need to talk."

Silence. A creak inside the room, barely audible through the room's door. Distant sounds of life floated down the hall, but the barracks wing was a pool of quiet.

Liza grabbed the door. Then she glanced at Aidan. "Commander… the reg books say base discipline is my job. You want me to do this, or do you want it?" Slowly, she stepped back.

Aidan took a deep breath. "Give me a sec. Let me think."

He studied the scuff marks on the wall and let his churning thoughts settle. He wanted his mind to do the thinking. Not his adrenaline. Beside him, Liza waited quietly.

When he could breathe easily again, Aidan met her eyes.

"Sometimes I get through to her. Let me give it a shot. Back me up if you hear me yell."

Liza nodded. "I copy. I'll stay by the door."

"Thanks, I—" Aidan began, when Billie came racing up. Liza caught her around the shoulders.

"Tweak," Billie panted, "Is Tweak... oh god she fucked up! Is she okay? Is everybody okay? Can I—"

"Calm down. Take a breath," Liza instructed quietly. She nodded at Aidan. "He's going to talk to Tweak. You're going to stay out here and talk with me, okay?"

Well. That was his cue. Aidan tested the door panel, chest muscles tight with tension. He had to know what the hell was going on and if it was going to affect this operation. He just had to hope she'd put down the knuckle duster. Heart pounding in his throat, he pushed the door open and peeked inside.

"Tweak?"

The room was a dim cave. The only window had been covered with a cloth, toning harsh sunlight down to filtered dimness.

Another tiny sound came from the wardrobe cupboard that stood against one wall, almost hidden in the shadows.

"F-f-fuck-k-k off." Tweak's shaking voice had a broken dissonance to it, the sound of something cracking under pressure. "G-g-g-get out."

Aidan swallowed hard and carefully closed the door behind him. He hesitated near it a moment before gingerly approaching the cupboard. He didn't try to open it. He leaned against the wall instead, his stomach doing backflips. He kept his voice quiet when he spoke.

"You want to tell me what happened in there?"

"N-n-n-n-no." Tweak's breath came in pants, easy to hear through the thin plastic. "F-f-f-fuck you," she wheezed, her word ending in a tiny, ragged sob.

"Look," Aidan muttered as gently as he could manage, "I'm not the bad guy here, Tweak. I want to help you, but I can't do that if I don't know what's wrong. Is this about the mission?"

"C-c-c-c..." inside her hiding place, Tweak gasped for air. "C-c-c-c-can't-t-t."

"You didn't realize you'd need to go on Grid with the crew sending the Folder?" Aidan asked. "I guess we all kind of assumed you would. You're fast, Tweak. We need good work at high speed for this thing to happen. That kind of means you."

Tweak made an inarticulate noise halfway between a groan and a sob. What was probably a fist thumped the inside of the wardrobe. Silence filled the room for a moment.

"C-c-c-c-can't g-g-g-g-go."

"It's not a real hard hack, is it?" Aidan asked softly. "It's going to be dead easy for you. The hardest part is getting you to the physical machine. That's what the logistics team is for."

Tweak gave a tiny bark of a laugh. In his pocket, Aidan's tab blipped.

"P-p-pick up." Tweak managed. "Me."

I can't go back.

The words scrolled across the screen of Aidan's tab.

I can't go back on grid. Not on TechoCo's ground. I can't get caught.

He slid down the wall with a sigh and positioned his tab so that it was easy to see against his knees. "Course you can't get caught. We don't want you to. But you already know these systems, you're fast as hell, and we need to pull everything off fast for this to work. That's why we're getting you set up with a fake ID and a set of synth. On-Grid you don't exist anymore. None of us do. We haven't had any problems with ID chips in years, and Kevin's team will make sure you get in and out safe. We have a work around for facial recognition too. We're good at this, Tweak."

His cursor blipped.

You don't get it. The ID I'm carrying doesn't matter. None of that matters. I know they're still looking. If I go back, I'll get caught. And this time they'll give me to Cavanaugh and they'll dissect me.

There was a tiny, broken groan inside the closet, and the sound of Tweak trying to blow her nose quietly.

"There's millions of people in the city, Tweak." Aidan made his voice as gentle as he could. "You never even showed up as an escapee on the news vids. I think you're letting being scared do the thinking for you right now. Believe me, I've been there enough times to know how it looks. Try taking a couple of really deep breaths, and—"

This time the words flashed onto his screen.

> They don't publicize it when they go hunting for somebody like me. They wanna hunt things like me quiet. That's why it's not on the Feeds. When Ag or Eagle hates you, they parade you around like a trophy and splash your blood all over. When TechoCo hates you? They make you stop existing.
>
> I want to exist.

Aidan's brow furrowed as the words moved around in his mind, trying to form something coherent. So, Tweak was hiding a secret about herself as dangerous as his own. Definitely not the same something, not if she was scared of TechoCo. The tech giant couldn't care less about sexuality and gender. What was just as dangerous on TechoCo grounds? Something that would make her interesting enough to hand over to Cavanaugh? Maybe there was something going on with her brain that caused some of the stuff she showed, and that made her worth dissecting?

That didn't make sense. TechoCo didn't care if you had three heads as long as you paid their prices, didn't steal from them and didn't start trouble.

He tilted his head back against the wall and released a breath in a slow, steady stream. What else could get you on Techo's shit list?

What could he possibly say to calm her down?

"Dusters know how to do this, Tweak," he tried, but the words sounded lame even to him. "You're one of us now. I know there are a lot of vids around of Dusters getting caught, but—"

There was a snort inside the wardrobe. New words flashed on the screen.

You ASSHAT. You think I'm scared because I think I'll get shot for being a Duster. You think I'm chickenshit & stupid?! I'm not. It's not about that. It's—

The cursor blinked for a handful of heartbeats.

I got other reasons to be scared.

"Yeah. Me, too," Aidan replied quietly. He adjusted the tab on his knees, his hands shaking. He took another deep breath and let it out slowly. The sick joke was that he probably knew better than anyone how she felt about keeping her secret, but he couldn't tell her without giving a couple hints about his own. That could be a really, really bad idea. But it could be the one thing that got the kid to listen, and she had to listen to him. Without her technical skill on the mission this entire plan was dead in the water.

He swallowed. "Tweak...you're not the only one out here because you're on the Corps shit list for...for something you can't control. First time we met I was freaking out to be on Grid. I still went. I know some tricks for helping to handle the fear, and Damian's got some meds if you—"

Inside her hideout Tweak let out a weak little groan. The cursor on Aidan's tab raced.

I don't need a shrink and I don't need a social worker. Just leave me alone. You have NO IDEA how something being out of your control feels. NO FUCKING IDEA!!! I'm not going to hurt anybody else and I'm sorry OKAY?! I didn't mean it. It was an accident. I got freaked. I CAN'T

> GO ON GRID. If you want us gone, we're gone. Just shut
> up and go away right now. You don't know what the
> fuck you're talking about.

"I don't want you to go anywhere. You're a part of my team," Aidan insisted quietly, trying to keep breathing deeply. How was he going to get this through to her?

He could tell her just how much he really did know about things he couldn't control. How much danger he was in when he went on Grid. But if he did…

He gripped the sides of his tab to try and stop the trembling of his hands. The thin plastic wafer bit into his fingers.

His words came out jagged. "Tweak, I… listen. I don't…I don't think you… I know more about what I'm talking about than you think. We need you there. You're the only one around who can do this in the time frame we can keep the owner distracted for. It's either you go, or we try drugging the guy, knocking him out and pretending to be buddies from work taking a drunk home. Then we either take him to his own house and try to knock out the surveillance systems, or we take him to one of our safe houses. That way's a hell of a lot more dangerous. It could get the whole team killed. You know the other options, you were the one to tell me not to use them. I…I understand about the Grid. Really. But you've got to talk to me about what you're worried about and how we handle this."

The cursor stared back at him, blinking blankly. Silence filled the room. Aidan felt as if the air was thickening, growing harder and harder to breathe.

The screen blipped.

> You don't get it. I. CAN'T. Tell. You.

Aidan laughed despite himself, a bitter sound. "I understand a lot more than you think I do. I've got my own secrets, Tweak. I ever get hit with a DNA scanner in the wrong territory and…poof. No more Aidan."

There was a sharp gasp inside the wardrobe. This time, the silence lasted only a breath.

You too?

Out of the corner of his eye, Aidan could see the wardrobe door creak open, just the sliver of a dark eye watched him through the crack.

Aidan very carefully kept his gaze on the tab instead of letting himself look at the wardrobe. Looking at her might undo whatever progress he'd just made. He took another breath and leaned his head back against the wall, closing his eyes for a moment. "Tell me your reason and I'll tell you mine. Deal?"

There were a few long, drawn out breaths. Then the cursor began to move on the screen.

> **Some of us have brains that work faster than normal. If they catch you, they stick you in special holding and test you out. If your brain wiring's good, you work for them. If you don't work fast and good, they got a deal with Cavanaugh. They sell you to the docs to take apart. The docs always want to see what's wrong with your genes, so they don't make mistakes again, I guess. You have to see the docs every month anyway, answer questions, give blood. If you live to 18, they sterilize you. They don't want more freaks around. If you get loose and get caught again, you die. No second chances. Not for a—**

The cursor stuttered to a halt. Several letters were typed, erased, typed, erased again. Tweak gulped loud enough for Aidan to hear.

"G-g-g-" she drew a shuddering breath. "G-g-gamma."

The tab blipped.

I'm a Gamma.

"Oh," Aidan breathed, feeling all the pieces click into place in his head. He hadn't known what he was expecting, but that was a surprise. A Gamma. A child of the poor bastards TechoCo and Cavanaugh had contracted with China and Kenya and places like that to create during the Beta Project. Beta babies had looked so perfect. They'd thrived on half the nutrient resources normal humans needed. Beta kids had been a success story until they were old enough to have their own kids, and the Gammas started getting born with unbelievable genetic weirdness. Three stomachs. Cow ears. Brains outside their skulls. Brains that didn't work like normal human ones.

Tweak was a Gamma. A walking, talking Corporate mistake. And the Corps hated people remembering their mistakes.

Aidan stared at the wardrobe door as one more puzzle piece fell into place. If he didn't give her something in return for that secret, she'd hate him for what she'd been forced to give away. He needed her to feel like she was trading secrets here, not like she'd gotten suckered. He needed her to feel like she was part of this unit.

He'd have to do it.

He swallowed hard and licked his lips. "Guess that makes us both enemies of the Corps born and bred, huh? I… my parents named me…um. Amanda. When I was born. Always hated it."

The wardrobe rocked on its little feet. Slowly, Tweak's tear stained face peered out, her eyes wide.

"Ser-r-r-rious?"

"Yeah," Aidan muttered, closing his eyes. "Got the body to prove it. Don't exactly want to show it all off though, you know?"

Tweak swallowed hard. "Y-y-yeah…"

Wary as a wild animal, she crawled out of her wardrobe to sit against the wall, her knees drawn up to her chest. The light of her tab reflected blue in her eyes.

Aidan nodded at her hands where they clutched her tab. "So, gamma. That's what's up with the arms?"

A tiny nod of the head.

"Does what's under there need anything medical?"

A shake of the head.

"You sure?"

Tweak sighed. "You d-d-don't w-wanna show off? M-me either."

Carefully, Aidan nodded. "Got it."

Tweak studied him for a few seconds too long. "On Grid. H-h-how y-you s-s-s-stay s-s-s-s-s..." she swallowed hard, then typed on the tab. Aidan's screen blipped.

How do you stay safe?

Aidan stared at the typed question for a long moment, trying to put his jumbled thoughts into words. He was never safe. Not really. So how the hell could he tell Tweak how he managed it?

"Um. I...I trust my team, I guess. Kev and Yve know all the tricks on Grid. Topher invented the Synth when I told him I'd get killed if somebody scanned my genome in the wrong place at the wrong time. That's helped. For me, I watch who owns what neighborhoods and try to stay out of places that'll kill me for my body." He smiled weakly. "I mean they'll all kill me for being Duster, but that's easier to hide. And I guess I keep my head down as much as I can. If you don't give them a reason to suspect you, they're less likely to pull out the scanners."

Tweak gave a tiny parody of a laugh and typed.

> Like they're not going to suspect me. I look weird, I talk
> weird and I've got wrapped up arms. A dead guard
> would sit up and look at me. Only reason I lived at all
> was Jazz letting me stay inside 24-7.

Aidan shrugged. "We get you some long-sleeved shirts, pretend you're deaf or something so you never learned to speak, and...it's not perfect, but...with Jim and Kevin and Yvonne and me, we'll keep you safe. I promise."

Tweak's face pinched. Her fingers flashed.

I came out here to get away. Going back——

Tweak typed, erased, typed, sighed, then met Aidan's eyes and shrugged her thin shoulders helplessly.

"S-s-s-s-s-scared." she finished in a stuttering whisper.

"I know," Aidan replied in a voice just as soft. He set his tab carefully aside and placed his hand on the floor, stretching it out toward her slowly. He kept it far enough back that she knew he wasn't going to touch her, but hopefully the gesture reminded her that he was there to listen. "I know, Tweak. But our only other option is…well, someone's got to get into that tab and navigate every step of the Feed engineer's back-end work. You already know it. If you're not there, you're going to have to walk someone through the code. Less scary for you, but it's dangerous. We'd have to take all those extra measures."

"M-measures." Tweak shook her head. She drew a long, shuddering breath. She glanced at his hand and drew away. "D-don't t-t-touch. Okay?"

"Wasn't going to," Aidan assured gently, but he pulled his hand back all the same. "Look, Tweak, I won't force you to go. But just… if you go, we'll be out there with you, okay? We'll have each others' backs. Promise."

Warily, Tweak studied his face. "I get c-c-c-caught, you g-g-get me out?"

"Only if you'd do the same for me." Aidan smiled weakly, amazed that this was actually working. He'd walked into this room expecting to get punched in the face. Now he was apparently bonding with his prickliest base mate. Life was full of surprises.

Tweak gave a tiny, bleak smile. "D-deal." She took a breath. "J-j-just d-don't…. n-nobody gonna know? Ab-b-b-bout m-m-m-me?"

"Promise," Aidan said. He forced himself to meet Tweak's eyes again. "Same here, right?"

After a moment, Tweak nodded. "R-r-r…" she wiped the back of her hand across her face, smiled and nodded.

Aidan nodded. "So we're square. Now... do me a favor and put those knuckle dusters in munitions instead of keeping them on you? No one's going to hurt you on this base, I swear."

Tweak glanced away. "Y-yeah... He okay? J-jim?"

Aidan's smile faded. "I have to go see. He went to see Damian. Want to go check on him with me?"

Tweak flinched. "Gonna be p-p-pissed."

Aidan raked his fingers through his hair and carefully hauled himself to his feet, tucking his tab back into his pocket. "He's kind of got a reason. But I don't think he's going to take it out on you. Maybe you can talk to Damian later, ask how Jim is and talk to him about your stuff. He knows about me. He keeps secrets really well."

Tweak's shoulders hunched. "Docs are b-bastards."

Aidan's lips quirked. "Yeah, but this one's on our side. Think about it?"

Tweak nodded slowly. "Think," she stated shortly. "Maybe."

Aidan nodded, looking down at the little bundle of a girl. "Okay. Hey, Tweak? Thanks. For telling me."

Tweak managed a shaky smile. "You tell anyb-body, I c-can always f-fuck you up later."

Aidan spread his arms and gave her his best innocent smile. "Yeah. You can. You've got plenty of dirt on me now."

Event File 15
File Tag: Information Applied
Timestamp: 15:40-12-1-2155

Damian looked up when Aidan poked his head into the medical bay. His thin face set like concrete. "I want a talk with you." He nodded curtly down at Jim, who sat on an examining table without his shirt. A wide auto-pad gleamed against the skin of his chest. "Tweak did this?"

"Yeah." Aidan agreed. He glanced up at Damian. "How bad is it really?"

"It's a second-degree burn. He'll be fine for duty, but I want him back in here tonight and tomorrow morning for a check. I'm getting really sick of this base wide 'stick an auto-pad on it and forget it' attitude," he added, giving Jim a look. "And don't hold Hen against your chest for two days. I mean that."

Jim gave the doctor a cockeyed look. "Damian, she's not even two. If I'm not supposed to hold—"

"Second degree burn, do those words mean anything to you? Hold her against your side because if she presses that wound, we'll hear the yell from here. I'm not giving you pain pills for stupidity, got that?"

Aidan bit the inside of his cheek to keep from smiling. When he got himself under control, he nodded. "Do what the doc orders, Jim. Can't have you getting infected."

Jim sighed. "Two against one isn't a fair fight. I got it."

Damian, unimpressed, waved a hand. "Go on, I'm done with you. Don't come crying to me if you ignore what I told you."

Jim shrugged back into his shirt, giving Aidan a half-salute and a small smile as he left the room.

"And am I going to have any more patients today?" Damian added over his shoulder as he cleaned up the burn tray he'd been using. "Psych work to do on Tweak, maybe? A tranquilizer for her? Or a medical signature on decommission paperwork?"

"You think I ought to decommission her?" Aidan asked quietly.

"I think this is the second time in a year she's landed somebody in my space. I think I want to know why and set up a treatment plan, or I want her out of my people's safety zone." Damian caught his eyes with those black implants, brows raised. "Personally, I'd prefer the first. But I can't help people who won't take help."

Aidan sighed as he considered the best way to respond. He couldn't tell the doctor that Tweak was a Gamma. He had promised. But he had to tell him something.

"I convinced her to put the knuckle dusters in munitions. I'm sure she needs psych work, Damian. But I think…she's got reasons to be scared of doctors."

Damian crossed his arms, saying nothing. One finger tapped slowly at the fabric of his coat.

Aidan looked away from his eyes. Damn he was looking forward to talking about all this with Omi and trying to figure out some better answers. Nothing he was saying sounded right, and Damian was still staring at him, and—

Aidan blinked.

Omi. A private way to get talk and feedback therapy. A quiet, safe way to start easing towards talking to people about problems. Exactly what he had, exactly what Tweak needed.

He raised his eyes to Damian's.

"Look, we've got work to do before we can get her on your table, but I've got access to a damn good psych wellness coaching program. Let's get her started using a copy of that until she feels safe enough to come to you."

Damian studied him for a long, long moment.

"How good?"

"Good enough to get me through some of the shit I deal with." Aidan replied as honestly as he knew how.

The rangy doctor sighed. "I'm not feeling exactly generous at the moment. But if you're sure..."

Aidan's smile felt weak, but he nodded. After a moment, he sucked in a breath and found one honest thing to say.

"Think of it this way, Damian. If... when Kevin told me I had to go on-Grid without knowing that there needed to be special precautions taken? I freaked, in private. This isn't the same problem, but it's about as bad. "

Damian's finger stopped tapping. "Really. That bad?"

Aidan nodded.

Damian raised his head from his work, eyeing him with slow deliberation.

"And am I getting more information than that?"

Aidan shrugged. "Soon as she clears me to give it to you."

Damian's ocular implants whirred as he raised a brow.

"If what I'm missing in this conversation is the reason I'm still missing a medical file on her? Do me a favor, tell her about patient confidentiality and that it does still exist, at least around here."

Aidan nodded. "I already kind of told her you'd keep a secret, and you had for me. But I imagine it's going to take time."

Damian grunted, turning back to the cleaning of his work area. "Just don't let her injure anyone else," he agreed dryly, setting the tools into his autoclave. "I hate listening to grown men whine when they get beat up by girls."

Aidan chuckled despite himself. "Shouldn't be a problem."

Closing his door that night felt like putting down the weight of the planet. Aidan curled up in the corner where his bed met the wall, leaned his head back and closed his eyes.

His tab's fan whirred.

"Hello, Aidan."

"Hey Omi," Aidan replied. He didn't bother to open his eyes. "Is it possible for you to make a copy of your base program? I need my personal information stripped out of the copy. I've got a kid who needs a program like yours."

"Of course. One moment..."

The image of his sister froze. The tab whirred loud enough to make Aidan open his eyes, a little nervous.

Omi flickered. Then she smiled.

"There is an executable labeled 'Wellness Coach 2' on your home screen. Shall I send it to a specific handle?"

"Not yet. I'm going to talk to her about it first."

"It must have been an interesting day."

Aidan gave a weak bark of laughter. "An interesting day. Yeah. You could call it that."

"Do you want to talk about it?"

Aidan let out a sigh. "I don't really know what to say yet...found out what's up with Tweak."

"Yes?"

"She's a Gamma. I mean, really a Gamma. Messed up genes and brains. Explains a lot."

"It does indeed. Can you tell me about how you found out?"

Aidan did. It took a while, but getting it out felt good.

"And I'm hoping working with a version of you will get her in good enough shape to go see Damian." he finished eventually.

"That sounds like a good plan." Omi agreed quietly. "I think you did very well, Aidan."

Aidan gave a quiet bark of laughter. "I hope so. Hope she gets around to seeing Damian sooner than later too..."

Leaning back, he closed his eyes. "Damn I wish Kev was home. I wish I could go to his room and sack out, watch some vids or something..."

"When is his return scheduled?"

"He's off schedule," Aidan sighed. "He sent a message. All the thing said was 'hit a snag.' I have no fricking clue what that means. And that's all we got from him."

"He is very skilled in his work. Assume that he's doing well unless you hear otherwise. It is much healthier for your mental state."

Aidan closed his eyes. "Easier said than done, Omi."

"Whatsit?" Tweak eyed the file that Aidan had projected. Aidan eyed her.

"It's something I want you to start using once a day, okay? It's a psychological wellness coaching program."

Tweak rolled her eyes. "I'm not—"

"Tweak." Aidan cut in, "if you're going to say you're not brain-fucked, guess what? That's bull. You're a little bit brain-fucked. So am I." He pointed at the holographic file. "This is a copy of what I use, okay? It's private. Nobody has access to it. You put in your own personal history—all of it, seriously—and put any firewalls you want around the thing. And then you use it. I can tell you it helps." He held her eyes. "I'm also going to tell you this is an order. If you don't want to see Damian or anybody else, your last choice is this. I can't let you work with people if you're going to get violent whenever they scare you. You start taking the anti-anxiety pills and you start using this and you start dealing with your shit. I want you here, but I want everybody else here to be safe. So, I want you to start fixing this. Okay?"

Tweak's eyes flicked from the file to his face. She swallowed hard. He could see her little body trembling.

Reaching over, she tapped the file, brought up the menu, and hit 'send'. She selected her own handle.

Raising her eyes, she gave him a twitch of a smile. "This thing's d-default setting. It isn't an old white d-dude with g-g-glasses, is it?"

Aidan smirked, shaking his head. "Jackson—the coder—wasn't that much of a geek."

For a moment, Tweak's knife-sharp grin flicked out. "G-good. Too many g-geeks around."

Behind him, there was a knock on the doorframe of his office.

"Aidan?"

Aidan shut down his screen and turned in his desk chair to give Yvonne a smile. "Hey. What's up?"

Giving Tweak a wary look, Yvonne stepped inside his office.

"Can you come and authorize some Sector paperwork? I don't have the clearance, but I don't want Kev to have an insane backlog when he gets in."

Strings pulled in Aidan's chest. He did his best to ignore the feeling.

"Sure, no problem."

Together, they ran through requisitions and inventory reports, vehicle supply requests and mission schedule requests to and from sector. It was lunch time when Aidan glanced at the clock, and Sarah stuck her head in the door with an impatient look for Yvonne just as he was standing.

"Baby, you aren't skipping out on—"

Yvonne's tab pinged in her hand. She rolled her eyes with a smile for her wife.

"Stuff just never ends."

She glanced at her tab. When she raised her eyes to Aidan's, they were huge.

"Aidan?"

Aidan's skin prickled. "What?"

"Check your tab."

Aidan glanced down and read the message on his own device.

Message Handle: KingofHearts

Authorization:1407-R-234

Message: 911. Available personnel. Need emergency transport 22:00.

Coordinates attached. 911.

The coordinates flashed beneath the message. Aidan stared at them numbly.

"Those coordinates...are those..."

"Those are in fucking Wyoming." Yvonne's voice was a brittle croak.

Kevin's feet skidded on the slick white tile. Pressing a signaling disc hidden against his wrist, he started the countdown in his head.

One one thousand.

"Stop!"

Two one thousand. Pounding boots behind him.

The indoor guards wouldn't have guns. The outdoor ones would.

Three one thousand. Thank God he'd taken the extra precaution with the briefcase.

Four one thousand.

"Stop! You're ordered to stop by—"

Five one thousand.

The soundless explosion hit. He didn't dare glance over his shoulder, but he could hear the sound of violent retching as the hyper-flashing light diode and the supersonic sound emitter worked together to throw anyone near that office into such a state of disorientation that they vomited. That'd stop them from calling anyone for backup for a bit. Hopefully.

Forcing himself to a walk when he stepped outside the door, he schooled himself into a casual posture. No sense giving the exterior guards something to react to. A running man was worth chasing, after all.

He slid calmly into his car.

"Destination?" it asked pleasantly.

"Denver Metro Station." Kevin stated calmly, his heart racing.

There was a pause. He closed his eyes.

"A security issue has been detected. Please wait calmly."

"Bloody hell." Kevin hissed. Reflexively he tried the door. Locked. Of course.

"Please wait calmly." the car warbled. Kevin snorted.

"Like hell."

Digging in his pocket, he yanked out his backup plan, pressed the EMP to the car's dash and activated it.

The car died. The back of Kevin's neck shot pain into his brain for a split second. Then he was out of the unlocked door, throwing his travel bag over his shoulder, grabbing the briefcase and pelting for the nearest loading bay.

They'd expect him to head for the gate. A rookie would head for the gate.

He was no rookie.

He leaped the lip into a small-vehicle loading bay and took off, dodging stockbots loading flats of bacopa and men with carts full of lantana. He dodged and raced across the plug rooms where new plants were beginning life and found what he was looking for, the dahlia room. Dropping to his knees, he slid under the benches beneath the enormously tall blooms. Mud and grit slid between his fingers.

The pound of boots raced by. Eventually they'd get around to searching, but right now they were looking for a running man. *That's right boys, keep going.*

On his hands and knees, Kevin crawled beneath the benches, gravel in the mud cutting into his palms. When he reached the wall, he followed it to the end of the benches, breathing in the scent of dirt.

Dahlia rooms were always closest to the back of the building in WelbCo greenhouses, he'd learned that. And behind that was the parking lot where the long-distance delivery semis were loaded.

Slowly as he could stand, he slid out from his hiding place beneath the last bench, freezing when his travel bag caught on a strut and made a tearing sound. This was not the time for noise. Besides, losing the travel bag really would be the end of him. All the supplies he had were in the thing.

Very carefully, he untangled its strap and pulled it out. Slowly, he moved into a position that allowed him to study his exit.

Nobody around. Of course not, they'd all gone to the front to see what the fuss was about.

Perfect.

Sliding along the wall, he slipped out a back-end loading bay and sprinted for the nearest semi he could see. Already half packed with tall ornamental citrus, hibiscus trees and patio pots, it was the ideal hiding place.

Worming his way into the shadows at the very back of the truck, he slid a scrambler out of his travel bag as quietly as he could and slapped it to the side of the briefcase, trusting that the little device would take the signal any GPS device inside might have and rewrite it with satellite information to make it appear to be heading away from him very, very fast. They'd think he'd gotten out by vehicle after all through one of the other gates. Leave them scratching their heads over that.

There was a certain amount of yelling outside. Eventually, it faded down into the sounds of a working day. Kevin listened as the front of the truck was filled and the door was locked, and finally allowed himself to relax. Luckily for him, transport rigs were climate controlled for the sake of the plants.

Three hours later, the rig started to roll. He smiled. Now all he had to do was wait until the truck was moving well and use the program on his tab to reroute it near enough to home for a quick pick up.

Just to be on the safe side, he unlatched the briefcase and removed the seeds in their vials and the precious data stick, storing them in one of the secure inner pockets of his jacket.

He gave it an hour, plenty of time for the rig to be well away from the city. Then he flicked on his tab and brought up his Go program. Homing in on the signal of the vehicle he was in, he sent his program digging, disguised as a command from the facility he'd just left.

A warning window popped up.

Codesign required.

Kevin set the program to work finding the password and waited.
And waited.
Fifteen minutes later, his tab beeped.

Unable to decrypt codesign. Codesign required.

"What?" Kevin whispered in irritation, pushing swaying leaves out of his face and restarting the program.

Unable to decrypt codesign. Codesign required.

For the next two hours Kevin fought with the truck's programming on his tab, looking for any outlet he could and checking his GPS position more and more frantically. They were heading further and further north, further and further from his home or anyone who could help him. And about the only system he could get into was the damage-detection routines.

"God damn it all to Hell and back!" He growled at his impassive tab screen. Finally, he let his head drop.

So. ArgusCo had finally fixed the loophole in their Go programming that the Dusters had been using for three years. Either that or American AgCo had their own secondary encryption. All he could do was stop the truck somewhere.

Work with that.

He checked the time and his location. He'd have to wait for darkness if he wanted to stand any chance of survival at all. In another four hours it'd be dark, and he'd be somewhere close to Laramie.

It'd have to do.

Quickly, he typed out a message at the Regional level.

Message Handle: KingofHearts

Authorization:1407-R-234

Message: 911. Available personnel. Need emergency transport 22:00

Coordinates attached. 911.

Once it was sent, Kevin caught what sleep he could in the cramped space, knees drawn up to his chest, and woke to pain in his back and legs three hours later.

At precisely ten that night, he brought up the program again and hit 'engage damage detection.'

The truck shifted as its systems were fooled into thinking it had blown a tire. Kevin felt the deceleration as it slowed, parking itself by the side of the road. An EMP burst unlocked the door, and his shoulder slammed against it pushed it open.

The night was cool, wind kicking up off the asphalt. Wary of incoming cars that could catch him in their headlights, he jumped to the gritty soil and took off, getting as far as he could from the road. Kochia and rabbit brush scraped at his legs.

Ducking under the slim protection of a mesquite shrub, he checked his tab, updating his coordinates.

Then he waited.

The night crawled by like something injured. When no one had picked up his signal in two hours, he checked the drone patterns in the area.

"Damn."

Sighing, he stared at his travel bag for a moment. He had to move. He couldn't sit out here so close to the road. That was where low-fly drones swept most often for human heat signatures.

He had twenty minutes. Then he had to move.

Digging in his bag, he extracted a pill bottle and popped the top. The StayWake fizzed under his tongue. At least the chemicals in the drug would keep him from ruining his brain chemistry permanently in the run he was going to have to make to get home.

Unfortunately, they wouldn't stop him from dying out here.

Standing, he shouldered his bag and started to walk.

Event File 17

File Tag: Personnel Recovery

Timestamp: 12-2-2155/12-7-2155

System x87, Designation Base 1407

Calculating Viable Route

Calculating

Route Not Found

"Sorry Aidan," Topher repeated quietly, "I've already tried six times. Dozer'n me both. There's no safe route there from here for another three days."

Aidan's eyes flicked to Dozer's. The older man was more experienced. He'd have a route.

Dozer shrugged. "I can't make things happen, Commander. Drone patrols overlap too much. Anybody who tries to run a hundred an' forty miles across that corridor's dead."

Aidan's hands tightened on the back of the chair. "Try to get ahold of bases up that way. There's got to be somebody close who can pick him up."

Dozer's small eyes studied him patiently. "I did that yesterday, sir," he repeated as if he were talking to a child. "You had me do it yesterday, remember?"

"Do it again," Aidan demanded tightly. "Reach out further, to non-Force contacts up there maybe. Maybe there's a vetted Fringe group that'll help."

He hated the pity in Dozer's eyes. He stood and stared at the screens as the transport team worked. It was too easy to nod off if he sat down.

It was amazing that he was still on his feet, if he stopped to think about it. He hadn't slept since Kevin's communication. He'd barely eaten. Food felt like an intrusion in his guts today.

Half an hour later, the big man looked up. "Nothing. Sorry sir. I'm getting nothing on response."

"Fuck," Aidan whispered. He shoved back the chair he had been holding onto. It slammed into the wall with a metallic clatter. As the sound died, he took a deep breath and shook his head. "Sorry, Dozer. Topher. Keep trying. Please."

"We will. No worries," Topher murmured, watching him with wide eyes.

Message Handle: KingofHearts

Authorization:1407-R-234

0500-12-3-2155

Message: 911. Available personnel. Need emergency transport

N 40° 54' 24.146", W 105° 29' 5.968"

On the second day, Kevin ran out of food. He hadn't exactly packed to be out in the Dust, and the two calorie bars in his emergency stash only went so far.

He rested in the heat of the day, letting his tab recharge on solar as he sat. If this had happened in the summer, he'd be dead already. Thank Heaven for small blessings.

He hid during low drone flybys. The rest of the time, he walked.

For once, he appreciated his gene edits. At least the coating on his skin cells was preventing sunburn.

He didn't dare to sleep: there were far too many things to watch out for. The drones whose patterns he watched obsessively. Fringers from any direction with any sort of agenda. A pickup crew sicced on him by American AgCo. No. He couldn't risk it. An update of his coordinates, a refresh of his SOS and a StayWake at dawn and dusk would get him out of this. All he had to do was stay sharp and keep walking in the direction of home.

System x87, Designation Base 1407

Calculating Viable Route

Calculating

Route Not Found

Aidan woke from another nightmare with a gasp, his heart thundering in his throat. Kevin was dead. For a moment, he knew that for a fact.

No, no he wasn't. That had been a nightmare. He was out there. He was only four hours away by truck, if they could just fucking get there.

There had to be a way. There had to be somebody who could help.

Fingers trembling, he grabbed his tab and typed, studying the maps and coordinates. The transport guys could have missed something.

In his hands his tab whirred. Omi's loading screen flicked up, the colors of the load hologram casting the room in rainbowed shades.

Aidan just about jumped out of bed. "What the—"

"The biometric sensor in your tab sensed elevated heart, breathing and skin resistivity readings," Omi explained quietly when she appeared, 'seated' beside him. "I think you might need to talk?"

Aidan swallowed hard. "Kev's still out there."

"He is trained for this kind of emergency," Omi stated gently. Aidan's laugh sounded hollow in his own ears. "Nobody's trained for no food and no water in the middle of nowhere. You've never switched on when I picked up the tab stressed before."

"You haven't picked up your tab in this level of unexplained heightened state before. My programming takes into account alerts and warnings. You have activated your tab in a heightened state without a cause. That is a sign of distress."

Aidan gave a little groan. "Goddammit Jackson. Did you have to code every damn thing you knew about me in this thing?"

"In order for me to be effective, he did," Omi replied. Aidan ran a hand over his face.

"Omi... fucking Wyoming. And there's hundreds of drones between us and him, and... every time I try to sleep I dream he's..."

"Your brain's doing its best to translate the state of fear into scenarios you can act on. That's not a bad thing. That's normal. But you do need sleep. I recommend a sleeping pill."

Aidan shook his head. "I don't want to end up using those every time I have a problem. You end up addicted."

"You are afraid of dependence? It isn't in your personality profile."

Aidan rolled his eyes. "My mom was addicted to the things, Omi. I'm not doing that."

"Then let's run through a meditation." Omi put a holographic hand on his knee. "Start with—"

"Damn it!" Aidan pushed his sheets off, his feet thudding into the floor as he stood. "Kevin could die out there and you want me to sit here doing fucking breathing exercises?!"

"Yes," the hologram agreed calmly, "because you're right. He could die. And you cannot control the situation at this time." The words brought such a rush of pain up Aidan's chest and through his thoughts that he barely heard the next words.

"But you can control how you react to the situation."

Aidan snorted. "That is such bullshit," he whispered.

"Aidan. Please consider this. Do you feel you are more useful to Kevin well rested, focused, and ready to work on the problem tomorrow, or focusing on the problem and losing sleep tonight?"

Aidan hid his face in his hands. There was a storm cloud in his chest. His head felt as if it was full of hot insulation.

Kevin was going to die out there. He'd sent Kevin into a situation without the right intel, and that was going to get him killed.

He'd probably gotten the man who'd given him everything killed.

"Why don't you sit down?"

The words filtered into his brain slowly. He obeyed on automatic pilot.

The hologram's words lulled him into sleep.

Message Handle: KingofHearts

Authorization:1407-R-234

0500-12-4-2155

Message: 911. Available personnel. Need emergency transport

N 40° 54' 44.146", W 105° 29' 5.982"

Stay sharp. Keep walking.

Kevin sang to himself. He recited all the poetry he could remember.

It was cold at night. He found he was shivering. His fingers were numb in his pockets.

Red buttes reared around him. Spiky grass slapped at his legs.

He reminded himself of the waste it would be if he died out here after all the effort he and others had put into his survival. How embarrassing to do all this work only to let these seeds lie in the Dust beside a skeleton.

Besides, if he died the bastards won. He wasn't about to give them the satisfaction.

System x87, Designation Base 1407

Calculating Viable Route

Calculating

Route Not Found

"We're calling around. We think we might have a lead with an old buddy," Sarah rapped out, her dark head framed between two bright ones as the Three Stooges leaned over the same tab. Kevin always called them the Three Stooges.

Another little stitch of pain ran through Aidan's gut.

"Thanks guys. Keep me posted."

Turning, he headed for his office. It might be four in the morning, but nobody seemed to be in bed tonight. Sarah, Lazarus and Yvonne were all up calling everyone they knew. Topher and Dozer were up trying to fight with routes and find one that worked. Damian was circling them all like a pissed off vulture.

And Kevin was out there with nothing. He'd let Kevin go out there. He'd known the intel they had wasn't enough for a run. He'd known it was dangerous. But what had he told Kevin?

"Okay, I can live with that. Just be sure."

Why the fuck had he said that? How stupid was he?

Message Handle: KingofHearts

Authorization:1407-R-234

0500-12-6-2155

Message: 911. Available personnel. Need emergency transport

N 40° 35' 42.146", W 105° 29' 5.988"

Stay sharp. Keep walking. Everything had distilled down to those two necessities.

The terrain was growing rocky now, and he found himself climbing from time to time. Pines had begun to appear the night before. He must be somewhere around Red Feather.

He found a small stream and risked a drink. He'd heard it wasn't a great idea and he knew for a fact that there could be diseases, but there wasn't much choice in the matter. He hadn't had water for two days.

The water felt good in his empty stomach. It eased the ache a little.

He followed the stream uphill for three hours, until the cramp in his gut doubled him over. Grasping at a tree trunk to keep himself upright, he clutched at his gut.

Not *could be* diseases in the water then. *Were* diseases.

He spent the next three hours throwing up bile.

Finally, he forced himself to his feet, his knees rubbery.

Stay sharp. Keep walking.

System x87, Designation Base 1407

Calculating Viable Route

Calculating

Route Not Found

It took Aidan a moment to process the fact that Liza was in his extra chair when he stepped into his office. She met his eyes, trying for a smile. "We're up to date on all our Sector paperwork. I took care of it."

"Um...thanks." Aidan tried for his own smile. It came off as badly as hers. Liza nodded. She cleared her throat, staring at the screen.

"It's Friday. We're going to need to make contingency plans for getting supplies if Kevin doesn't come back today."

Aidan nodded curtly. He was the commander here. He had to act like it and get his ass back to work, regardless of how shitty he felt. Kevin was just one person. He had to remember that.

One person he loved.

One person he'd probably gotten killed.

"Right. Yeah. Thanks. Um. Give me a minute. I...I need a stay-awake and a shave. I'll be right back."

"Maybe you need some sleep," Liza suggested carefully.

Aidan snorted and shook his head, standing carefully. "I can't. We have work to do."

Liza opened her mouth to say something, shut it when her eyes met his.

"Yeah. Okay."

The water was warm and weak coming out of his sanitation station. He didn't need much. Just enough to wet his razor and shave with trembling hands.

The blades bit a little too deep. Blood welled from a cut on the angle of his chin.

The tiny sting was like a burst of light in a dark room. The sting of washing the cut out felt even better. For a moment, he was completely in one place. Completely in his body.

The razor glinted in the harsh light, the edge gleaming silver as it moved.

The drops of blood in the basin stood out stark until the water washed them away.

Message Handle: KingofHearts

Authorization:1407-R-234

0500-12-6-2155

Message: 911. Available personnel. Need emergency transport

N 40° 35' 42.146", W 105° 29' 5.987"

At least he didn't run out of StayWake, Kevin thought as he watched a shooting star. It had started to taste rather nice, too. That was a good change.

Or was it?

He couldn't remember.

He wished Aidan was here to see these stars. They were so beautiful. He'd have to tell Aidan about this when he got home.

He needed to get home. Aidan would be worrying.

It was amazing how clear his thoughts had grown out in the desert, he thought as dawn began to tinge the starry sky. Waiting out a drone, he lay on a warm rock slab and watched the stars. No distractions out here. Not even his body. He wasn't even thirsty any longer.

All he had to do was walk. Stay sharp. Walk. He'd have to get up in a few minutes.

Or maybe he'd take his time.

The stars were so bright. His mind was so clear. He was paying such attention to the things around him that he thought he could feel the turn of the world. Heartbeat of the land, he mused. Whatever they did, whatever they fucked up, the land itself was forever.

He'd forgotten about that.

System x87, Designation Base 1407

Calculating Viable Route

Calculating

Route Not Found

"Aidan, instead of using self-harm, let's try something that releases the tension in a healthier way. Push-ups and crunches will help build your muscle mass and—"

"Switch off Omi."

The sting of the razor against his leg set off a firework inside his mind.

"This is not a good coping mechanism."

"I said switch off."

"Aidan, I'm here to help you. Please don't stop using the tools you have. You've done a great deal in the last year and come such a long way. I know you're hurting right now but falling back into old and unhealthy coping mechanisms isn't the solution. This may feel good now, but it isn't helping you and it isn't helping Kevin, and—"

Aidan surged to his feet, rage and pain boiling through him.

"System shut down!" he snapped.

The tab went into a hard shutdown. The hologram blipped out of existence.

Aidan dropped onto the bed, staring at his bleeding legs. Putting his head in his hands, he groaned like a wounded animal.

His sheets were stained with blood in the morning. The slices along his legs burned when he pulled on his clothes.

He looked like shit in the mirror.

He'd just started to brush his hair when a hammering came at his door. Topher gave him a breathless grin when he opened it.

"We got ahold of somebody!"

Message Handle: Coyoteboi

Authorization:1101-TT-051

1700-12-7-2155

Message: KingofHearts, Copy. We need your coordinates.
Please reply.

The sound of a truck's wheels broke the silence like a desecration.

"McIllian?! Kevin McIllian! You out here?!"

Slowly, Kevin sat up. He felt as if, were he to let go, he might float up into the endless field of stars. But two people were running up, grabbing him. Holding him here.

"Evening," he croaked, smiling in his best attempt to be polite. A warm blanket dropped around his shoulders.

"Christ man, what happened to you?"

"Adventures." Kevin murmured, fingers clutching his bag.

The next several hours blurred in his mind. He remembered the sting of several injections, and the taste of water. He remembered explaining that his bag couldn't be left behind. He remembered giving Liza and Damian a smile when they helped him into the base.

"Somebody needs to tell the Commander...I did it..." Kevin remembered hearing the giddiness in his own voice. "I did it. I got them. They're in my jacket...Liza, go tell Taylor...I got them…"

He remembered wondering why Liza's expression was so heartrendingly sad as she helped settle him on the med bay's bed.

"You can tell anybody anything when you wake up." Damian's quiet voice replied as the slight sting of a needle sank under his skin, "But right now you're going to sleep."

Kevin slid into blackness.

"How long was I out?"

Aidan raised his head from the pillow at the sound of the voice, letting out a breath he felt as if he'd been holding since Kevin had sent his first SOS. Kevin rolled over in his arms and watched him with clear grey eyes. Aidan's chest expanded.

Kevin was awake.

Kevin was going to be okay.

"About two days," Aidan replied quietly, the cuff of his floppy sweater folding over his hand as he reached up to brush Kevin's hair out of his face. Damian and Alice had sponged him down before they put him in his own bed, but his hair still looked dusty.

Kevin closed his eyes and sighed.

"Damn. That bad?"

"Yeah," Aidan agreed, "that bad. You were in the med bay with a couple IVs in you until last night. How do you feel?"

Kevin considered the question.

"Mm... well my eyes ache and my whole body feels like cured jerky. Other than that... tired."

"Damian said you'd need to sleep through part of today too," Aidan agreed, "you're pretty messed up. About the only thing you didn't get was a third-degree sunburn, but you've got all the other fun things that go with being out there. Your eyes hurt because you had your contacts in too long, and you were dehydrated as hell. Damian said the only reason you lived was all your fancy gene-mods and nanites."

Kevin nodded, closing his eyes.

"Did you lot open my jacket pockets? I think I asked you to. Did you see what else I got?" he asked, his lips quirked up. Aidan smiled his own helpless smile at that. He still couldn't believe what had been on that data stick.

"Yeah. You're nuts, and we need to talk about it later, but...yeah. It's pretty amazing." He rested his head carefully against Kevin's shoulder. He'd considered just waiting until the man was recovered before checking in on him. That's what a normal commander would have done.

A normal commander also would have torn a few strips off Kevin for being such an idiot the minute they were in the same room. He needed to get the story and find out just why the hell Kevin had thought it was a good idea to go hunting around for seeds and agricultural gene-mod tech while he was out on a critical mission. But that could wait until Kevin was all the way online again. Aidan had been too worried about him getting back on his feet to waste time deciding how angry he was.

He knew he should have trusted Damian's opinion and checked on Kevin tonight, not last night. But the longer he'd waited the more anxious he'd gotten. He'd needed to see Kevin's face, to feel him breathing, to know for a fact that he was all right. Damian had said nothing would wake him for nine hours after he'd taken out the IV the night before. Sneaking in and lying down beside Kevin after lights out had been the only way he could calm his fear.

Now he was wondering if he'd just done the creepiest thing imaginable.

"Is it okay that I'm in here?" he asked, half-terrified to hear the answer.

In his arms, Kevin smiled more widely and snuggled closer against Aidan. They'd gotten his stained shirt off him, and his bare skin was warm. That was good too. He'd been so cold last night.

"Is it okay if you stay?" Kevin asked softly.

The spring wound up inside Aidan's gut released. He breathed a chuckle.

"You're on bed rest, but I've got duty. I'll come back after hours, okay?"

"I'll hold you to that," Kevin replied in a murmur, the ghost of his usual laugh in his voice.

Aidan put his lay-around clothes on top of Kevin's clothes hamper and pulled on the fresh things he'd brought with him. The hall was mercifully empty when he slipped out.

He distracted himself with his work. He checked in with Yvonne and made sure she got the help she needed finishing up paperwork while Kevin was out of commission. He made a report to Magnum on what had happened with Kevin, as much as he knew. He stared at the message he got back for longer than he should have.

Message Handle: Sector40COM

Message: Grapevine contact who gave McIllian the intel he decided to act on has filed a report. I'm forwarding it to your tab. Turns out this isn't completely your officer's error, but I'm not happy about it. I'm instituting a two-month review of all McIllian's work and mandatory full

> mission statements from him for all off-base procedures,
> filed with you and with me.
>
> I reminded you. The Folder is top priority. Remind him.
>
> Discipline beyond this is at your discretion.

Aidan felt like his throat was lined with sandpaper. He swallowed hard.

Discipline is at your discretion.

Carefully, he read through the report from somebody with the handle EcharPanza. Things made a little more sense once he'd gone through it. Kevin had been presented with a huge opportunity and time-sensitive information on short notice. He'd gotten the materials from a trusted informant. At least it hadn't been as insane a stunt as it had looked before they'd gotten this.

But still.

Discipline is at your discretion.

Aidan set his tab aside and stared at his hands. He never should have let himself get this emotionally tied up with somebody in his chain of command. And Kevin never should have tried for the seed shipment. He should have turned the informant down. He could have died pulling this stunt. The materials and the information he'd gotten them were amazing, it was true. But it hadn't been mission-pertinent and it had nearly cost his life. It had cost their base a ton of working hours, medical supplies and a gigantic favor called in.

Kevin should have known this. He should have known better. And this wasn't the first time he'd decided that getting something good was more important than his safety.

Aidan raked a hand through his hair, lifted his tab and read the message again Not that it was going to change.

How the hell did he handle this? How did he get through to Kevin?

He covered his eyes with his hands, thinking.

Eventually, he stood.

Aidan was in luck. Blake was in his office, holographic windows open on every side. The setup made him look like a chubby spider sitting in a web of blue light. The holographic windows reflected blue off his scalp, beneath his thinning hair.

Aidan tapped on the door frame. "Hey Blake? Got a minute?"

Blake glanced up, a frown pulling the lines of his face into brackets around his mouth.

"A minute I can spare. Then I need to get back to explaining to Base 1470 that they are fiscal *morons* who can't *type.*"

Aidan chuckled. "They mess up their funding request and reroute their cash to us again?"

"And I'm tempted to *keep* it to teach them a *lesson*," the older man shot back tartly. "Their so-called financial officer needs to go back to training."

Aidan realized his fingers were tugging at the hem of his jacket. "Yeah. About training...mind if I shut the door?"

"Feel free." The pudgy man switched off the screens as Aidan sat. When he turned back, his expression was blank.

"Let me guess. This is about Kevin?"

Aidan nodded. "Good guess."

Blake waved a hand. "Oh *hardly*. He's gotten good, but I *really* should have told him off more often for playing Robin Hood. He's gotten *cocky*, that's the problem. Somebody around here needs to take that cocky young thing *in hand.*"

Blake gave him an expectant look. In spite of the mess, Aidan snorted. "That was awful."

The older man reached over and patted him on the shoulder. "There. You needed a good laugh. So, tell Auntie Blake what's going on."

Aidan shook his head. "Okay, so..."

Carefully, he laid out what he knew. He sighed when he'd finished. "I guess what I'm asking here is, you trained Kevin. I need some advice. This is the second time in nine months that he's done something without approval that could have got him killed. I need to get an idea for what discipline he'll respond to. Something that will get him to quit this."

The financial officer nodded, elbow of his right arm cupped in his left hand as he stroked his chin.

"Discipline, hm? Well *basically*, what gets through to Little Red is grounding him. Every time he did something *gamma* on me, I'd leave him at home the next time I went out."

Aidan raised a brow. "Little Red?"

Blake gave him a smirk. "You'd get it if you'd seen him at sixteen. Skinny as a pipe cleaner with the *cutest* mop of red on top. Aaanyway... this is a big step. But you really want him to sit up and pay *attention*?"

"Yeah?" Aidan asked.

Blake studied his fingernails, mouth pursed. "Remind him that Commanders can take away rank if they need to."

Aidan blinked. "Y-you think that's what will get through?"

Meeting his eyes, the older man nodded slowly. "That little boy is *stubborn*. I mean he trained with me, *me* of all people and managed to hold onto that purity complex of his. He still blushes, I mean *really.*" Then his expression sobered. "But you know he *lives* for his work. When he realizes he's put *that* in danger, I don't see him stepping over the line again for a good *long* time."

Aidan nodded slowly, feeling his body weigh itself down with lead. Blake studied his face, then reached over and patted his shoulder.

"You're a *sweet* little boy, Aidan. And *frankly,* you're sweet on him. If you want somebody else to go queen bitch on Little Red, Janice or I make a better bitch than you."

Aidan shook his head. "It's my job and I know it... but thanks."

The financial officer eyed him measuringly. "All right then. Keep this in mind: bitches are meanest when they're protecting puppies. And that particular puppy is going to end up road pizza if he doesn't get his leash *yanked* sometimes…. Mm. Leashes. Speaking of *discipline,* you know there's a whole kink for leashes, that kind of thing. Ever tried it out?"

Aidan shook his head, smirking in spite of himself. He might be sour as a lemon when he was pissed, but Blake really did know how to lighten people up.

"I don't think we're into that. But I get the picture. Thanks for the idea."

"Any time," the older man agreed airily, bringing his screens back up.

Kevin was still dozing when Aidan slipped into his room that evening. Shucking his work clothes with his back turned, he lay them over a chair and set his binder and packer on top, then pulled on his old sweat pants and floppy sweater. The cuts on his legs burned beneath the auto-pads as he brushed cloth over them.

He crossed to sit on the bed.

"Hey." Kevin murmured without opening his eyes.

"Hey." Aidan replied just as quietly.

Kevin laced his fingers behind his head, making him appear relaxed. Aidan had started to realize this past month how misleading that look could be; it meant Kevin was telling himself that he wasn't worried.

He must know how stupid he'd been.

"You're going to need to write me up, I imagine," Kevin remarked eventually. Aidan watched him.

"Kev… I basically already did. You in the kind of shape to talk about this?"

"As much as I'll ever be," Kevin replied quietly, "what's the damage?"

"You're going to be on a two-month review. You're going to need to write up schedules and purpose statements for every run you go on with contingencies and get a copy to me and Magnum before you go. If you don't keep the schedules, you're going to lose your rank."

Kevin was silent for so long that Aidan wondered if he was going to start yelling. Then he wondered if Kevin had fallen asleep.

The wiry man sighed. "I've really pissed off Magnum this time, haven't I? He's never threatened to take away my rank before."

Aidan swallowed. "Um... yeah. That was me."

This time, Kevin did open his eyes. Slowly, he sat up, staring Aidan down.

"Why would you suggest that? I excel in my work. You know that."

"Yeah. I do," Aidan replied, holding Kevin's eyes. "That's why I suggested it," he stated carefully, walking through the rehearsed speech. "I know that this was the only thing that would get you to take this seriously."

He drew a slow breath before he continued, "Problem is, you know you're good at your work too. And it looks like you think being good means you can pull off just about anything without backup. Kevin, you almost died out there—" He held up a hand when Kevin opened his mouth, "—and it was because you left me and everybody else in the dark. You told me you were going on a routine six or eight day run to get our intel and set up the next steps for the Folder. When this seed thing came up you didn't check with anybody, you—"

"There wasn't time!" Kevin exclaimed. Aidan gave him a beat of silence, holding his eyes. "You took a risk you could have passed up and it almost killed you. The seeds and the gene mod stuff are really amazing. They are. But we would've been okay without them. The base doesn't need seeds nearly as much as it needs your work. If I have to knock you down to specialist to keep you doing that work, I'll do it."

Kevin's face had gone still, distant and cold as the moon. Aidan's insides felt like a clenched fist.

"Pass me my glasses." Kevin's voice was frightening in its quiet.

He took his time adjusting them once they were in his hands. Finally, he raised his head to look Aidan in the eye, his face blank.

"If I lose my position, I'm worthless to the base," Kevin stated flatly. "I can't do anything worth a damn as a specialist."

Aidan's heart flopped over. He couldn't resist any longer. Leaning in, he took Kevin's hand in his.

"The only one who thinks that is you. I see the way you work, Kev. You think it doesn't matter how much danger you're in as long as the rest of the base is safe. I've only been here six months, I know, but here's a heads up: keeping yourself safe is what keeps them safe. They're going to suffer if you end up dead. I'm... I'm going to suffer, okay? We need you around and healthy enough to do your job, because you're right, you're fucking amazing at it. We all know that. You don't have to keep proving it with crazy-ass stunts like this one, okay? And I'm not saying this because you're my... because we... I'm saying this because I'm a commander with a great logistics officer he wants to keep alive first. I'm also saying it as a guy with a boyfriend he..." he had to swallow to get the words out, "he loves. We don't need stunts and seeds and cool stuff. We need you to come home from every run."

Kevin sat still for a long time, holding Aidan's eyes, emotions Aidan was too afraid to put names to flitting across his face. Then he sighed, dropped his eyes and reached for Aidan's other hand. The brush of his hand against Aidan's leg set the cuts there on fire.

"You make a rather excellent case. Wish I could refute it." His voice was unexpectedly soft as he continued. Aidan had expected yelling, had expected to see that temper of Kevin's again. But Kevin only shook his head like a defeated man.

"I really had intended to do a simple run, but when I was offered something like this... I let it get out of hand. Speaking as an officer, I'm sorry about that. Speaking off duty...I'm sorry I scared you. Very bad form on my part, frightening my boyfriend." His thumbs softly traced Aidan's knuckles. When Aidan got up the guts to raise his eyes, Kevin was smiling.

Aidan couldn't help it. Leaning in, he put his arms around Kevin and hugged him close. "Don't scare me for stupid shit again, okay?"

Kevin rested his hand on Aidan's thigh, leaning in for a kiss.

"I'll do my best."

Aidan inhaled sharply, pulling away as the new cuts on his leg burned. Kevin's eyes flicked open. "Aidan? What's the matter?"

"Nothing," Aidan replied tightly, doing his best to resist the urge to protect his legs. It was his own damn fault that he was hurt. He had done it to himself. He smiled weakly. "I'm fine. Just decompressing. Go to sleep, Kev. Seriously."

Kevin's copper brows rose. "I'm not particularly tired; just a touch stiff and off color. And..." Tentatively, he put out a hand to touch Aidan's thigh. "I know this is sophomoric, but I haven't seen you in a while. I thought we could spend some time together. Not... well, I don't have a lot of energy. Watch a vid with me?" He squeezed Aidan's leg gently, smiling. Pain flared over Aidan's skin, and Kevin's smile fell away. Shit. He'd seen.

"Did you strain a muscle again?" With deft fingers, Kevin massaged Aidan's leg through the fabric. Then he sucked in a breath. "Aidan...what...are you wearing auto pads under here?" His hand splayed out over Aidan's leg, fingers feeling the outlines of each plastic pad under the fabric.

"Holy... how many do you have on?"

"Fuck," Aidan breathed, jerking his body away. "Just... I just kept running into shit while you were gone. Stay-awakes fucked with my spatial awareness or some shit."

When Kevin spoke again, his voice was flat. "Then you'd be bruised. You wouldn't have series of injuries in a straight line down your legs that require auto-pads. I'm not an idiot, Aidan." Reaching out, he gripped the band of Aidan's sweatpants. "Let me see what's wrong."

"No," Aidan retorted, attempting to squirm out of his lover's grasp. "Kev, drop it. Please…"

"Why?" Kevin asked. In the low room lights, his eyes were the color of twilight. "Why won't you let me see? Because I know what it looks like. Tell me I'm wrong."

Aidan couldn't answer the questions. He pulled out of Kevin's hold and sat further down the bed, staring at his hands.

After a moment, hands wrapped gently around his midsection, and Kevin lay his head on Aidan's shoulder. "You did this when I got into trouble, didn't you?"

Aidan shrugged again. He was too tired to try to squirm away again, but he sure as hell didn't feel like he deserved Kevin's comfort.

Kevin sighed. "God, Aidan… this is my fault, isn't it? You thought… what were you thinking?" The words should have been an accusation, but in Kevin's tone there was only honest asking.

It took Aidan a long time to organize his thoughts into something semi-coherent. When he managed, his voice was uncertain. "I thought I'd…I was the one who let you… if you had died, I… Kev, I… the intel I gave you. It was bad. I thought I let you go in on bad intel and that got you killed."

Gentle hands pulled at his sweatpants, Kevin's voice murmuring all the while.

"You gave me intel, and you told me you thought it might be less than impeccable. I decided to act on it. You didn't give me an order, remember? You gave me the option. I took it. That's my decision. I took a gamble to get us something I thought I wanted us to have. A gamble I didn't give you the chance to approve. That's my responsibility. None of this is your fault, love. I decided what to do. If I'd died, that would be my oversight. Not yours. I knew I might pay a high price, but if I'd known you'd pay it too… Please love, just let me see this."

Aidan jerked his body away again and shook his head. "I… I'm commander here. I could have… I should have…."

"Expected your officers to use their discretion in their areas of expertise." Kevin countered gently. "Which you did. Expected me to do my work well. Which I failed to do. And gotten something more than first aid pads on your injuries, which I don't think you did. We don't need a commander with gangrene."

He held Aidan's eyes, skin oddly luminous in the low orange night-cycle light. "I hurt you. Let me help you."

Aidan jerked his head in disagreement. "I took care of it. It's fine. Drop it. Please." His voice cracked.

"Aidan, I can't just 'drop it.'" Kevin whispered. "You cut yourself up like a slab of meat. I can't 'drop it.'"

Aidan swallowed hard, the gulp audible. "I'm sorry, Kev, I just... I've always... I've always been this fucked up and I don't... before I transitioned, I was...diagnosed w-with...I..." The words dried up and he shook his head again.

"With what? Aidan, are you sick?" Kevin asked, voice gone tight and breathless as a man who'd been hit in the gut. His arms tightened around Aidan's waist. "Diagnosed with what?"

Aidan took another shaky breath and licked his lips. Finally, he breathed, "Major depression."

"Oh." Kevin cleared his throat. "Did you ever try any medicine for this?"

Aidan shook his head weakly, wrapping his arms around himself. "Can't. They'd... I can't be a commander if...if they knew. Was wiped from my records when I transitioned."

"You idiot," Kevin sighed, leaning his head on Aidan's collar bone. Then he raised his head and kissed Aidan softly. "All right, fine. Then you'll talk to Damian and I'll start getting you something unofficially. And you'll take it, all right? And you won't do this again on my account. Promise me."

"I...I can't...I can't promise that," Aidan whispered. He took another shuddering breath.

Kevin's soft voice was relentless. "Those old scars on your legs aren't from barbed wire, are they? You told me they were from barbed wire."

Aidan shook his head. He could hear accusation in Kevin's voice now. It was like a knife twisted into his belly.

"It's how I used to handle things when my brain started getting fucked up. I thought I was getting better. But you don't get better from this kind of shit."

"If you call yourself fucked up one more time," Kevin stated flatly, "I swear I'll...I'll...I'll make you regret it in some undecided but heinous and dreadful way. And you don't need to get better. But you have to find some better coping mechanisms, because what you're doing isn't working."

Aidan stared at the fabric hiding his wounds. Coping mechanisms. Everybody tried to give him coping mechanisms. He had Omi and that helped, until he got too far gone and shut her off. He used to have the real Naomi, but he'd burned that bridge making sure she was safe. She needed to believe he was dead and get on with her own life.

Physical exertion had never worked for him. What else had people suggested when he was still pretending to be the little girl that they all loved? He couldn't even remember, but he knew it hadn't worked. Nothing had ever worked like the pain had.

"Tell me what to do to help," Kevin asked, voice choked. "Tell me something."

"There's nothing to tell," Aidan muttered, his voice barely audible, broken. "I... I'm a fuckup. That's all there is to it."

"Don't." This time the word was raw and edged in anger. "Don't even try to hide behind that label and give up, do you hear me?" Kevin's voice tightened, taking on a sharper note. Kevin's fingers forced Aidan's chin up until he was looking into grey eyes that had a glint of steel to them. The pale man's voice grated. "And don't you ever dare to assume that you know what I can and can't do something about and hide from me what you've decided I can't handle. Don't you dare. I just dodged armed guards, a drone grid and everything the Dust could throw at me to get back to you. I walked nearly a hundred miles, and I got through the days by thinking about you. And you've got the nerve to lock me out when I'm finally sitting beside you by telling me there's a problem you've decided we can't solve together? You're actually going to tell me not to try to fight this? Don't. You. Even. *Dare*."

Aidan stared into Kevin's face. Hot tears trickled down his cheeks. He didn't deserve this man who wanted to fight for him. He wasn't good enough for this.

"I... I can't... I don't... Kev..."

"I said. *Don't.*" This kiss was fierce, a demand instead of a request. Kevin yanked Aidan against him, kissing him until they were both breathless. "And learn to trust me, God damn it. I'm a reckless jackass who thinks he's bulletproof and tries to move Heaven and Earth without asking for help. High-handed. Arrogant. Those are valid complaints. But I don't lie to you if I can help it. If I say I'm coming home, I'm coming home. If I say we can fight, we can. And if you'd *tell me* things like this, I could *help*. But I can't do anything about what I don't know about. So stop hiding things from me, damn it!" Another bruising kiss rounded out the words. His fingers found and counted auto-pads.

Aidan couldn't meet Kevin's eyes. Waiting for Kevin to say something, do something, was like waiting for a bomb to drop.

"Please say something," Kevin whispered, holding Aidan close in the dark. "Please tell me what you need. I'll do anything."

Aidan let his head hang. His eyes hurt. His legs hurt. Everything hurt.

Finally, he forced himself to raise his eyes. "I need you here." His voice strengthened as he looked into Kevin's eyes. "What you were saying? About me lying to you?"

"Yes?" Kevin asked softly.

"I'll take the pills and tell you the truth. But this is a trade. You stop making me wonder when I'm going to have to write your death certificate. You stop taking risks you don't need to take. Stop pushing so fucking hard and doing stuff on your own. We both stop hiding shit from each other. Deal?"

Kevin smiled crookedly. Lifting one of Aidan's hands gently, he kissed Aidan's knuckles. "You have a deal, Aidan my love. First exchange: how often does the issue get this intense?"

Aidan picked distractedly at his blanket. He allowed himself to be silent for a long time before whispering, "Not often. I… the last time was around the time when I…when my home base got taken out, I think. Four years."

He looked up into searching grey eyes. Kevin seemed to relax, though his body didn't move. "Are there signs for me to watch for?"

"Get quiet, I guess," Aidan muttered at his hands, still playing with the loose edge of the plastic. "Don't sleep. Don't eat a lot either."

Kevin nodded. "All right then." One of his hands reached out and rested on Aidan's. "Good to know."

Aidan leaned back against Kevin, closing his eyes. He was still so tired, but he wasn't hungry yet. His appetite would return eventually. It always did after a while.

"I love you, you know," Kevin murmured into the quiet. "If I had known what this would do to you, I would have shot myself in the foot before I tried it." He kissed Aidan's throat softly.

Aidan gave a weak parody of a laugh. "Try remembering that the next time a batshit stunt seems like a great idea."

Kevin chuckled dryly. "That I will. And like I've said before. You don't need to worry about me in the field."

"I think I kind of do," Aidan replied softly, "four days in bed doesn't count as being alright."

"Touché," Kevin agreed quietly.

In this safe, dim pocket of time, Aidan listened to Kevin breathe.

"So where do we go from here?" Kevin asked eventually. Aidan studied their intertwined hands.

"I guess... you spend one more day on recuperative leave. And then you and me work harder at this whole thing."

"You still want to do that in the knowledge that the man you're working on it with is a single-minded, high-handed and rather obsessively fixated jackass?" Kevin's voice was soft.

Aidan smirked, keeping his eyes on their joined hands. "Yeah. I figure your baggage looks pretty good beside mine."

"Touché redux," Kevin murmured, a trace of laughter in his voice. "Let's just agree not to scare the shit out of each other in future?"

"I can't... I can't promise anything," Aidan replied in a whisper. "We're in a war."

"I suppose I can't either, given the situation." Kevin's lips trailed along Aidan's throat. "I am a requisitions man, after all. But I'll try. Will you?"

Aidan nodded weakly. "I'll try."

"All right." Soft fingers cupped his cheek, caressing. Kevin's fingers stroked up along his jaw, gently tousling his hair. "Missed you," he whispered, kissing the ridge of Aidan's ear.

"Same here," Aidan muttered, smiling weakly and tilting his head to give Kevin better access to his throat.

Kevin's lips trailed down to the hollow of Aidan's throat, and his hands languidly trailed through Aidan's hair. "You know, now that I'm awake, I'm finding a little more energy. You up for...?" he trailed off.

Aidan hesitated. He wanted the comfort of sex so badly, but he was tired, he ached, and Kevin still wasn't in great shape and...

He nodded weakly. "If you've got the energy. And if—if you want me."

Kevin smiled. "Aidan my love, there's no if about it."

They made love more slowly than they'd ever done before, mindful of one another's wounded bodies. Afterwards, they lay quiet in one another's arms, breathing together.

Event File 19
File Tag: Prep Work
Timestamp: 09:00-12-14-2155

"It's the best Synth we can print, you'll be fine. I knew you were on Techo's search list, so I double checked it against all the scan models. It's good." Topher's tone was bright. Tweak's response wasn't.

"It better be."

"You know, the words 'thank you' have a valuable place in the English language."

Tweak shot Kevin a sour look where he leaned against the wall. "Don't start."

Aidan carefully watched the team put itself together for the run. The plan had gotten final approval. Sarah and Yvonne would take Tweak in, Lazarus would watch their backs and Kevin would be running everything from the logistical side of things in a nearby hotel room. On paper it looked good.

Of course, on paper a lot of things looked good.

"Guys?" Aidan interjected. "Let's walk through this one more time, okay?"

Kevin glanced at him, managed a small smile and left his slouch for a chair, studying the windows floating at eye level.

"Right. We'll equip with sub-vocal molar mic sets—yes Sarah I know you hate the bone resonance mics but the voice box models in the necklaces are too obvious—and we'll use those to keep in touch. We'll head in and arrive at noon the day before. I've planned for us to go in from three separate directions: Sarah, Yvonne and Tweak by bus, Lazarus in by car, and myself on the train. The sensory load's going to be intense. Everyone has been running through their mental exercises morning and evening, right?"

"Yes Dad." Yvonne, Sarah and Lazarus chorused in perfect lockstep.

Kevin rolled his eyes. "See if I try to save what passes for your sanity again, ingrates. We'll take separate hotel rooms in the same building, the Hotel Barbados. Both day and night shift clerks and the security guard are working with us, we won't have to worry about anything beyond basic safety measures. That evening I'll get Lazarus and myself in on the cleaning crew at the pavilion. We'll make a last check of the premises and... Laz? What are you planning?"

Lazarus flashed a bulletproof smile. "Remote-detonation flash bangs hid around the place with smokescreen attachments, in case shit hits the fan and we need a fast out. Phage nanoids to make the Corps think we're trying to cover our own DNA footprints, so they don't figure out the synth. Nothing real fancy but it'll work."

"Sounds good," Kevin agreed, eyes distant as he thought through the situation aloud. "We can get you in as the cleaner for the locker room, if you bring in a bag and store it there... yes that should work. Tweak, we're going to need you to verify the remote hack on the cameras while we're in and put the cameras on a loop to keep them from showing Lazarus getting his supplies out of his bag or my work checking our splices and such."

"Easy," Tweak agreed.

"What're you packing besides the stuff you're setting up that night?" Aidan asked his munitions officer.

Lazarus gave him a shrug. "Four plastic pistols armed with tranquilizer darts, four with bullets. One set of electric knuckle dusters." He glanced at Tweak and winked. Tweak gave him a quick, feral grin.

"We need to be to the bar and set up by four," Kevin pointed out thoughtfully, tapping their maps. "That gives us two hours to get situated and blend in. Mr. Sinclair comes in for his drink at six in the evening and stays 'til nine, regular as a clock. I put a splice on the cable panel for the surveillance cameras when I was in last, and I'll ensure that's still in place on our evening visit. All I need to do is initiate the connection and start sending the signal to my tab. So, once I'm set up in the hotel, I'll bring up the remote camera feeds. That will get me a complete oversight of the premises and I'll be able to watch everyone's backs through the cameras. I'll send the initiation signal once I'm ready."

"Which is when we start chatting up Kevin's new friend," Sarah remarked easily. "We take about half an hour to get him out of his chair one way or another."

"And that's when Tweak walks by with a bag identical to the guy's and switches it out," Yvonne continued.

Tweak nodded. "I g-got a v-virus that'll m-make an ad m-malfunction and show up inside. It covers m-me when I switch the bag. I go down to the m-maintenance r-room, get on his tab. Get to work. Give me half an hour to w-work, f-fifteen m-minutes to m-make it b-back. Forty-five m-minutes, tops."

"Forty-five minutes of the charming Sister Act later, Tweak puts the bag back and you girls can leave our target in peace," Kevin finished.

"Then we all ride off into the sunset."

"It's gonna be night-time Kev," Yvonne remarked with a smirk.

Kevin rolled his eyes. "Figure of speech, do look up the concept some time."

"Jackass."

"Hee-haw."

"Guys," Aidan remarked, repressing a smile. "A little focus here? We've got a route and a safe room for Tweak set up?"

Tweak hit the tab's screen, and the image flared with a bright red line. "This's my route, this my room. All set. Only one thing we still gotta do. Test the Folder. S-send it to a secure G-grid c-c-contact with the same c-code I'm gonna use to attach it t-to an update, m-make s-sure it l-loads okay f-first time and opens r-right."

"Go ahead and send that file to me." Aidan added, "I'll send it to a secure contact. Something this big looks better with a Commander's credentials on it."

"Gotcha," Tweak agreed, bobbing her head like a sparrow.

Aidan looked the plans over. Slowly, he let out a breath of relief. "Okay. This actually looks like it's going to work."

They covered a few last details before the meeting broke up.

"Tweak. A few details before you go," Kevin remarked as folks filed out of his office. His boyfriend's tone was brisk and friendly enough, but the words still made Aidan glance back.

Tweak and Kevin stood on either side of Kevin's desk, both stiff. Over Tweak's head Kevin caught Aidan's eyes and gave a subtle 'go on' tip of the head.

Aidan hesitated, body tensing. He really didn't want to deal with Tweak putting another person in the medical bay—for a lot of reasons—and she and Kevin rubbed each other all the wrong ways. If both of them were tense that could only get worse.

Finally, he made himself step out the door. It was a logistical planning issue, and Kevin really did kick ass at that. Tweak knew that she was walking a line. And he'd be right down the hall. He'd hear a disaster if it happened.

All the same, he was debating standing half way down the hall as backup when his tab pinged. Pulling it out, he blinked as a window popped up.

"Watch my back?"

The message blinked for a moment. A vid screen showing Kevin's office from one of the upper shelves replaced it a beat later.

Aidan picked up his pace, got to his office and closed the door, sitting down to watch the screen as Tweak spoke.

"Yeah?"

Kevin sat like a statue at his desk, hands folded neatly. "I understand that you put Jim in the medical bay while I was gone."

Tweak glanced at her hands. "Yeah. Did. Got s-s-scared. Was really s-stupid."

Kevin watched the head of glossy black hair, his face unreadable. Aidan felt his shoulders knot. That expression wasn't Kevin's coldest, but it wasn't good. He braced himself when Kevin spoke.

"We have enough enemies out there without attacking each other, wouldn't you say?"

Aidan held his breath.

Tweak said nothing. Kevin sighed, pulled his kerchief out of his pocket and took off his glasses, polishing them meticulously. "Is this going to be an ongoing issue?"

"Hunh?"

"Is it going to happen again?"

Tweak shook her head. Kevin replaced his glasses. "Can you accept that this base is a family and act accordingly? We trust one another. It's what keeps us alive. Especially when we're running together in enemy territory. If you're part of this family, you will protect us, and we will protect you." His voice had that slow, solemn tone it got sometimes, the one that made everything he said sound like it was some kind of binding contract.

Tweak raised her eyes, looking around the little room. She swallowed hard. Then she stood a little straighter, turned her eyes directly on Kevin and jerked her head in a nod.

"You guys, you prove that. You get my back. I get yours. It's the deal."

"It is indeed," Kevin agreed quietly. "If you keep your end, I'll keep mine."

Tweak took two long breaths, loud even over the speakers. She nodded.

"Okay."

Tweak started to turn, then froze. When she looked back, her eyes were narrow again. "One thing. Don't fuck Aidan over again."

Aidan read surprise in every line of Kevin's body. He practically jerked back in his chair.

"What?"

"You heard me. Don't f-fuck him over again. When you got in trouble. He walked around l-like a zombie. He looked like shit. For a week. We're a f-family? From where I stand, he's the big b-brother who brings home pizza. You're the one that makes him c-cry. You keep doing stuff that f-fucks him up. I d-don't wanna see that. So, quit."

For a moment, Kevin looked the way he sometimes did when he and Aidan were alone, vulnerable and lost for words. But only for a moment. Then he seemed to yank his usual manner around himself like a slick-tarp.

"Thank you for letting me know. You may have noticed that I like him rather a lot myself. And it's an issue I'll be rectifying in— excuse me. Yes. I'm going to try to quit doing things that freak him."

Tweak gave one of her jerky nods. "Good."

Then she turned on her heel and trotted out of the room. On the screen, Kevin drew a deep breath and let his body relax. Then he glanced up at what had to be his tab on the shelf, giving a crooked smile.

"Well, that went better than expected. See you at dinner. System shut down."

Aidan's screen went blank. He let out the breath he'd been holding.

Event File 20
File Tag: Duty Hours
Timestamp: 15:00-12-14-2155

Aidan's day filled up with paperwork: a detailed message Commander Magnum had asked to receive affirming that the mission was officially initiated and catching up on all the routine work he'd put off while he made sure the big mission was ready. He had to do a death report as well, and those always made him feel like shit. This one especially.

The Grapevine operative who'd contracted to buy stockbots for them had made a mistake in his credentials when he was trying to sign the delivery out of his neighborhood. The poor schmuck had panicked and run when security had started questioning him, and that got him shot.

That meant the stockbots they needed to create garden beds were still sitting on enemy land, which sucked. And they'd lost an ally, which sucked even more.

Aidan brought up the man's profile in the Greynet. Shit. He had a wife and three kids. Shit.

Carefully, Aidan took down the wife's handle. Bringing up a doc program, he started to search for the words to put in a condolence letter. Finishing, he read it over. They were all good words, and they were basically the right ones: he died helping us create a sustained food supply. He was a good man. Thank you for your service. We're rerouting a stipend fund to you.

It still didn't feel like enough. It never really did. But maybe that was a good thing. The day when death didn't feel like it was important was probably the day when he wouldn't want to look at himself in the mirror.

For a moment, he wondered how many of these Magnum had sent out when Rolling Thunder had been taken out. How many had he written when the base that tried this mission before Rolling Thunder had gone down in flames? How many condolence letters did a Sector Commander send out in a year?

Too many. That was an answer he could bet on.

It was nearly dinner time when he finally sent the condolence letter, turned in the stipend order and ran through his list of vetted Grid contacts. They needed somebody secure to send the test of the Folder to, Tweak had said. Somebody who could open the thing up and make sure her code worked first time out.

Looking down the list, Aidan considered names and dossiers. He didn't know a lot of Grid contacts, hadn't been in touch with very many folks on that side of things. He could send it to Kevin's contact Dilya, that wouldn't be bad. Or he could send it to...

His fingers and mind grew still.

Naomi. Naomi was a Grid asset these days.

He could message Naomi.

His kickass little sister didn't know he was alive, and she didn't need to know. But he could send her the Folder under his base code name and his Commander's credentials. God, Naomi would love this.

His fingers flew across the keypad as he searched. Five minutes later, Naomi's face turned up in the searches. He studied the image, feeling a smile tug at his lips.

The picture was in profile. In it, Naomi had that intent 'I'm working, why are you bothering me?' look that was her go-to expression, but there was just the hint of a smile in the cant of her lips.

She looked good. She looked healthy, confident, less angry and more on top of things.

Aidan tapped at the screen, bringing up her contact handle, and laughed out loud. "KaboomKid? Really Omi?"

Shaking his head, he typed. His baby sister had always been amazing at covert munitions, but the fact that she was still going by KaboomKid made him wish he could tease her in person.

But then she'd know he was alive. And he wasn't going to let that happen.

Naomi had been born four years after him, and yet she'd always been the one out front, the one who'd grab him by the hand and pull him along.

 She'd been the one who'd wrapped him in a blanket when stress gave him the shakes. It had been Naomi who stood up to their father. The bastard had broken her arm and she'd still stood up to him.

She'd been the one who'd found him in the morning after he'd tried to tell Sam who he really was seven years ago, lying in his own blood with a concussion and a broken jaw. And she'd been the one who beat the hell out of Sam.

It had been Naomi who stopped Aidan from killing himself. And it had been Naomi who got him through when the base their father had commanded had been eviscerated by drone blasts. It had been Naomi who'd figured out what was going on, grabbed Jackson and come running when that fucking medical assistant who used to be a Cavanaugh guy and his buddies had jumped Aidan on their new base.

Naomi had been protecting him since she was born, and he'd seen what it took out of her. She'd wasted too much of her life trying to protect her big brother already. It was why he'd asked Jackson to get in and write him off as dead after their new base got bombed and they got separated. She deserved a life of her own. One that didn't involve standing up to every asshole who decided she was sister to a freak. She'd deserved her freedom.

He'd never been able to give her much besides grief, but he could give her this.

Message Handle: AceOfSpades

Message Authentication:2343ddexcatfish

Biometrics: Validated

Secure Message, Command Authenticated

Message:

Contact from Base 1407. This is a high-security contact. Please open the attached file, validate full functionality on Grid-attached machines and reply with negative or positive result. Ensure security. This file is top security.

I hear good things about you, KaboomKid. Thanks for your hard work out there.

Keep your head down.

Two hours later, his tab pinged a reply

Message Handle: KaboomKid

Message Authentication: Dingorr3432

Biometrics: Validated

Message: File function affirmed.

Holy shit 1407, this is fucking amazing. Hope to see this on my news feed soon. Luck. Kick some corporate ass.

Feeling tears prickle behind his eyes, he smiled at the screen. Then he shut it off and headed down to join his crew for dinner.

Everyone seemed to be in the mood to decompress, and there was talk about new vids that had come in and a communal watch party that evening. Aidan didn't say anything about duty the next morning. The guys needed a morale boost tonight.

"So," Kevin remarked easily, "whose turn is it to choose?"

"Not yours!" The entire table chorused.

Kevin rolled his eyes. "I hate you all."

Hearing a squeak, Aidan glanced at Tweak. Holy shit, she was actually laughing.

"Mine!" Liza crossed her arms, smiling smugly at Kevin. "No stupid musicals this time."

"Yes, because idiot rom-coms are so much better," Kevin replied wearily.

"Hey, democracy!" Alice put in, white teeth flashing in her dark face. "We'll go and vote on it."

"What do you care, you're only gonna look at your knitting," Topher teased, pointing at the grey tube that got longer every time Aidan looked at it. For grey it was really pretty; there was a sort of warm cast to it.

"What's that gonna be anyway?" Topher asked.

Alice waggled a knitting needle. "You'll find out at Christmas, nosy."

The crew filed out, joking and calling out suggestions for Liza. Kevin took Aidan's hand as they left the canteen.

"God help us, if they vote before everyone gets in there it'll be another bloody gamma rom-com film." Kevin muttered, shaking his head. Aidan glanced over his shoulder.

"Y'know um... I've been thinking about that. We probably shouldn't use it."

"Bloody rom-coms? No disagreements from me," Kevin replied with a thin smile.

Aidan shook his head. "No, I mean 'gamma.' I mean... there are real people who are Gamma," he added as he walked. This might not be a great idea to bring up, but he'd been thinking about it since he'd sat in the dark with Tweak. "People with shitty gene mods that weren't their fault. I mean we hate it when people use 'fag.' Jim and Alice hate it when people give them shit on being black. Gammas probably feel the same about us using 'gamma.'"

Kevin blinked, a little chuff of surprise escaping his lips. "Where did this come from?"

Aidan shrugged. "Guess you got me thinking about words a lot lately."

Kevin considered the argument. "That's...actually quite a point, you know. I suppose I'd never really thought about it. Which is a bit ridiculous considering how much I hate that kind of garbage when it's thrown at my crew... I guess I've never met an actual Gamma who'd be bothered. But the ethical principle is sound."

Kevin glanced over his shoulder, steps slowing. "Wait. We're missing somebody."

He turned, took a few long steps back down the hall, and poked his head into the canteen. "Keep up girls, or you won't be in time to help us veto Liza's terrible rom-coms. Come on, we need the whole crew on this."

Aidan blinked. Billie's hesitant voice reached him.

"The whole… crew?"

"Well you are part of the crew, aren't you? You've got a vote. And we have to out-vote Liza and Blake or we'll be watching bloody chick flicks again."

After a moment, Billie's voice came down the hall to Aidan. "Um… yeah. No chick flicks."

A heartbeat later, Tweak's voice was added. "Yeah. No way."

"Well, come on then." Kevin ducked back out into the hall. Slowly, the two young women followed him.

It was a really awful movie, and a really good night. For a precious few hours, Aidan forgot about the morning.

♠

Morning sunlight set Kevin's hair on fire as he checked his bag one more time, going over his plans. Aidan watched him work, readying himself for the Grid again.

He'd almost died on the last Grid run. He could die on this one.

If Aidan was going to let himself love this guy, he was going to have to accept that as one of the terms. Kevin was a logistics officer. One day he might not come back from the Grid.

If he was going to be in love, he was going to have pain.

Could he make that trade?

Kevin raised his head, giving him a smile, and Aidan knew the answer.

"Well then, off into the wild blue yonder I go," Kevin quipped.

Aidan didn't move from his place on the edge of the bed for a moment. Steeling himself, he stepped across the space between them. He pulled the taller man into a kiss, hand cupping Kevin's cheek. Pulling away slowly, he stared into Kevin's eyes.

"You go and you do this." The words came from his lips slowly, heavy on his tongue. "And then you come home. In one piece. You get me?"

"I get you," Kevin agreed quietly. "And I will do this. We'll do this. And then we'll come home." He leaned in for another kiss.

"Promise," Aidan whispered.

"I swear," Kevin breathed, sealing his promise into Aidan's skin with another kiss.

Aidan drew a slow breath. Then he took a step back. His smile was lopsided.

"Okay. You better get going. You got a deadline."

Kevin nodded. Giving Aidan a casual salute, he slipped out the door.

<u>Event File 21</u>
<u>File Tag: Groundwork</u>
<u>Timestamp: 09:00-12-17-2155/ 02:00-12-18-2155</u>

The truck was already running when Kevin reached it, Topher in the driver's seat and Tweak tucked into the back corner where the risk of being touched was lowest. Kevin slid easily into the seat that had been left for him. "Shall we?"

The garage door rumbled open. Sunlight slanted across the truck.

Unobtrusively, Kevin took in the expressions of his team. Lazarus, grim as death. Sarah, stone-faced. Yvonne, picking at her cuticles. Tweak, pretending that everything she set eyes on was vaguely displeasing.

Yes, indeed. Everyone in this truck was terrified, in their own way.

"Well then," he remarked as he dug out his tab, "Let's get our blood pumping, shall we? I've got just the song."

Keeping his smirk to himself for a moment, he queued up Duran Duran's 'Hungry Like the Wolf.' The groans from his friends almost drowned out the bubbly tune.

Tweak very patiently leaned forward. "Kevin. Change tracks. Or I tase you."

Kevin affected a look of mute horror and tapped his tab. A synthesizer-spiced back-beat married itself to the lower, sharper tones of 'Another One Bites the Dust.'

Lazarus rolled his eyes. "Dude, you're gonna die before we even get to the Grid."

Kevin smirked as Freddy Mercury wailed.

Topher dropped the sub-teams at their own Grid entrances one by one. Kevin was the last to leave his seat, trekking for half a mile to a hidden culvert with cold wind carving through his slick poncho. He slipped down an access entry and took another half-mile walk through a neglected tunnel, the remnant of an old trash-removal system. He came up in a disused maintenance closet in one of ArgusCo's suburbs. Checking himself over, he slipped out and blended into the crowd, 'buds in his ears. Ads assaulted his eyes.

The train ride from the suburbs down into the Tech Center was a simple affair. Aside from one ad company that had figured out how to hijack the signal for 'buds to deliver their ads directly into his ears, he had no problems.

Checking into his hotel room, he stowed his gear. He set sound boxes to work putting out subsonic white noise that masked anything he did with innocuous sounds of habitation for the benefit of whatever surveillance the hotel had. That done, he pulled out his tab and typed.

Message Handle: KingofHearts

Message: Checked in. 12C. Everybody copy?

Moments later, his tab pinged.

Message Handle: BlackDiamond

Message: We're good! 14B

Message Handle: JOKER

Message: Copy. All set. 19F

Kevin smiled as he typed.

Message Handle: KingofHearts

Message: Right. Let's rock this.

That done, he glanced around the sterile room. He had a few hours to kill before they took their first step. He'd need to keep himself loose.

Sitting, he got down to coding a tab version of Hungry Hungry Hippos for Tommy's Christmas present.

He was deep enough into his work to jump when his tab pinged around seven in the evening.

Message Handle: TheTweak

Message: Can I come to your room? Want to talk.

Kevin blinked. He wasn't exactly thrilled, but he hit the thumbs' up.

"It cool to talk?" Tweak asked when he opened the door.

"In here, yes," he replied, holding the door wide. "We really should have finished mission-pertinent conversations back home," he remarked quietly once she was inside and the door was locked. Standing with her arms behind her back, Tweak shrugged.

"W-wanted to check. You think you can g-get that remote hack on the cameras g-going at what, twelve? One?"

"In the neighborhood of twelve-thirty. Why?" Kevin asked carefully.

Tweak stared at him, wary as a feral cat. Finally, she spoke. "We can spend some extra hours, maybe an extra day, I c-can use that hack. Track the uploads for TechoCo camera footage. G-get in where it's stored. You get me pics of the p-people they caught from that other base. Thunder. I can r-run a bot to search the d-database. We can find them. Find out where they got taken. I can hack Techo jails. M-maybe we take a c-couple extra d-days, g-get them out?"

Kevin quirked a brow, forcing down the flash of hope that had rocketed up his spine. "How sure are you?"

Tweak repeated her shrug. "Getting in the s-system? Totally sure. Getting them out?" She bit her lip. "I got me out. Got Billie out. If they're in, I think I c-can get them out. Probably."

Kevin nodded slowly, watching the girl as his mind raced.

A team of four from Rolling Thunder was still unaccounted for. If they were in prison rather than dead, they could be rescued.

Four good Dusters. Two friends.

"So, you wanna?" Tweak asked. Kevin sighed.

"Tweak, we… you should have told Aidan this. We should have planned ahead for this."

Tweak shrugged. "He'd say n-no. Too d-dangerous. You do this kind of stuff. So. You wanna?"

Kevin stared at her until he realized that she was squirming. He searched for words. "You… why did you circumvent Aidan and talk to me about this?"

Tweak sighed out her irritation. "What, you don't do that anyway? He'd say no, you m-might say y-yes. Just putting it out there. Thought you'd like it. D-don't get pissy."

Kevin swallowed down the first words that came to his tongue. "I didn't intend to 'get pissy.' And it was a well-meant gesture. I appreciate it. I suppose I hadn't realized that I'd given such a strong impression of operating outside my mandate."

Tweak cocked her head. "Hunh?"

Kevin raked a hand through his hair. "Give me until tonight to think it through. If I send you a video of the song 'Over the River and Through the Woods', the answer's yes. If you get 'Silent Night,' we're going with the mission exactly as planned."

Tweak pulled a face. "Holiday songs? Barf."

"Holiday songs. Cover." Kevin corrected.

Tweak rolled her eyes. "Whatever. Your buddies. Your call."

Closing the door behind her, Kevin leaned against it. It was his call. That was the problem.

He spent four hours working through the problem, pacing the room. It was very much like the Trolley Car Problem he'd learned as an ethics exercise. On the one hand, a mission that could change the trajectory of the country for the better, his good standing as an officer and the promise he'd made Aidan. On the other hand, the lives of four colleagues. Two of them people he counted as friends.

The logic was uncomplicated. The emotional ramifications were a dismal mess.

Around eleven, he grabbed his tab.

Message Handle: KingofHearts

Message: Come up here a moment?

Five minutes later, Lazarus smiled when he opened the door.

"Hey dude. We still got half an hour."

"I know. Come inside?"

"You're antsy." Lazarus observed quietly when Kevin had locked the door again. Sighing, Kevin sat on the bed. He raked his hands through his hair.

"I need to talk something through. You mind listening?"

Lazarus leaned against the wall. "Dude. What am I, your granny? Skip the intro. Give."

Kevin gave a weak chuckle. "Well then. Tweak thinks… she came up here and said she might be able to get Candace, Johnny Red, Martin and Bob out of jail. It would cost us a few extra days, and it's not a sure thing. It will make us a hell of a lot more noticeable."

"So what're you thinking?" Lazarus asked, his face blank. Kevin sighed, shaking his head. "That's the problem. I *think* it's an awful idea. But I *feel* like we owe it to them to at least try, if we can. I mean…." He raised his head. "I hate feeling that we'd choose to sacrifice them. Laz, if it were you in prison, what would you want me to do? What would you do?"

Lazarus studied his best friend for a moment. Then he tipped his head, smiling like a wolf.

"Okay seriously, you're asking me? You know that one, dumbass."

"Humor me," Kevin asked quietly. Lazarus shrugged.

"I'd tell you to fuck them over as good and hard as you can. Then I'd start a fight and get myself killed fast and clean. What'd you do if it was you caught, and me deciding?"

Kevin let out a long breath. "Tell you to get your ass in gear and give them hell from me. Then I'd take my exit." He tapped the back of his neck, where they both knew his personal kill switch was implanted. "But that's us."

"Yeah. It is." Lazarus agreed. "It's what we sign up for, when we start doing on-Grid runs. All of us. They signed up, just like us."

"I guess they did," Kevin said to his hands. He shook his head. "I wish Tweak hadn't given me the option."

"Why did she?"

"Because she thought I was crazy enough to take it, given the recent stunts I've pulled."

Lazarus gave a short laugh. "Yeah, you set yourself up for that one."

"I suppose I did," Kevin agreed quietly.

When the quiet grew too deep, he raised his eyes. Lazarus was watching him. He managed a crooked smile for his best friend. Lazarus returned it.

"I seriously thought you were dead last time. Aidan about lost it. Don't tell him we noticed, but yeah."

"I heard." Kevin drew a breath. "I promised Aidan I wouldn't do anything like that again."

"Then what're you talking about fricking options for?" Lazarus exclaimed, "Dude, this's you and you promised. You know you're not gonna break that. So let's play a couple rounds of something and then go do our thing."

Kevin swallowed hard. Then he nodded. "Right. I'll send Tweak the word. Then let's play Go for a bit."

Lazarus pulled a face. "Fuck man, that's worse'n chess."

Kevin chuckled.

At midnight, Kevin stood in the line of cleaning crew service men and showed the cleaning crew foreman his Citizen Card. The man grunted, eyes narrowed in his brick wall of a face.

"Thought you were off my roster. You gonna get lost looking for shit again?"

"No sir." Kevin kept his eyes averted, his shoulders slumped. Who needed disguises when body language changed the perception so easily?

"All right then." The heavy man eyed him for a moment, then moved down the line. Now it was someone else's turn to be reminded who was boss. This man was such a petty tyrant.

Without turning his head, Kevin checked on Lazarus out of the corner of his eye. He was looking relaxed, and he hadn't had any trouble stashing the bag he'd brought in the employee locker room. Since they'd slated Lazarus as the designated cleaner for that room, they were set. All Kevin needed to do was double check the camera splice he'd put in, and then they could get to work.

Once the foreman had put on his evening show, the line shuffled forward. Each man took the cleaning cart and fleet of clean bots he was assigned and fanned out.

Kevin's bots whirred away about his feet, following the master control embedded in the cart he pushed. He headed for the hall outside the control room.

Keying in the commands on the cart and spreading the sweeping compound across the floor, he watched the clean bots begin their work as he grabbed rags for the bathrooms he was assigned to clean.

As he moved, he tapped the tab in his pocket in the proper sequence to send the 'go' signal to Tweak. One buzz would mean the splice on the cameras was working, she had hacked in and replaced the camera feed with clips from the last time he was here, and he was free to work. Two buzzes would mean it had failed, and they'd have to go with Plan B.

He scrubbed mirrors for fifteen minutes.

His tab gave a single long vibration. Kevin smiled. Putting down his rags, he stepped out of the bathrooms and into the control room. The little devices were still clipped securely to the fiber-optic wires that connected the building's camera hardware to its recording computers. They were set.

Pulling out his tab, he tapped out a message to Lazarus.

Message Handle: KingofHearts

Message: Go for it.

Then he got back to scrubbing.

For three hours, Lazarus and Kevin passed one another without a word, both cleaning and keeping their heads down. The greatest difficulty was the sheer repetitive boredom of the work. It allowed entirely too much time for thoughts to come creeping in.

Had they covered every contingency?

Yes.

Were they missing anything?

No.

He'd checked the room Tweak was to use. It was secure. Was—

Behind him, Kevin heard Lazarus curse. He glanced down and felt his heart stop in his chest.

One of the flash-bangs had fallen from its hiding place in Lazarus's cleaning supplies and clattered across the floor. Matte black and square, it wasn't easy to identify on camera as anything but a box. But if any of the other men stepped within line of sight, they'd recognize it for what it was.

Kevin lifted a box of sweeping compound from his cart. *Slow is smooth, smooth is fast,* he told himself. He casually stepped out as if to put the compound down on a particularly egregious stain and made a show of tripping over a clean bot and going sprawling. The box of cleaning compound sprayed across the room.

Everyone caught within the cloud started to hack, sneezing as the dusty cleaning compound irritated throats and noses.

"The fuck?!" the foreman yelled, stomping over. "That cleaning compound comes out of your paycheck! Look at this mess! Get it cleaned up, right now!"

"Yes sir." Kevin agreed, putting his head down as the foreman continued to holler. When he looked again, Lazarus's cart was gone and so was the flash-bang.

He waited until he was back in his room and safe before he risked another short message to Lazarus's tab.

> **Message Handle: KingofHearts**
>
> **Message: What shape are we in?**
>
> **Message Handle: JOKER**
>
> **Message: Golden. Hit the sack. Big day tomorrow.**

Smiling, Kevin lay down to sleep. It was, indeed, going to be a very big day tomorrow.

Kevin checked his watch. Four in the evening.

"Show time," he whispered to the empty hotel room.

He drew three slow, deep breaths and lifted his tab. Working smoothly, he brought up two holographic windows, situating them to either side.

On his left, he brought up the video feed through the cameras in the pavilion. Eight moving images flicked into view.

On his right, he brought up his favorite alias's Social Feed and posted a picture of crossed vintage guitars, captioning it with 'for those about to rock, we salute you.'

He got two likes immediately. In the camera feed, he watched Sarah roll her eyes and smirk as he slipped on his 'buds and extended a long, flexible rod from the right one. He tapped the mic on the tip.

"Ladies? How's the reception?"

"I can hear you good," Sarah replied.

"Clear," Yvonne agreed.

"Tweak?" Kevin asked quietly.

A third window popped up with a message. In the camera feed, he watched Tweak type in the corner of the cafe.

Message Handle: TheTweak

Message: I hear you.

"Lazarus?" Kevin asked.

"Roger," Lazarus's voice murmured over the connection. Kevin studied his relaxed position near the main entrance and nodded.

"All right, we're all set then. Mr. Sinclair should come in between four to six minutes after six. Relax for a bit."

In Tweak's window, a new message popped up.

Message Handle: TheTweak

Message: Relax. Yeah, right.

Kevin sighed. "Play Go, Tweak. Maybe you'll actually win if you keep practicing."

Message Handle: TheTweak

Message: You're an asshat.

Kevin didn't bother to respond. For the next two hours, he watched his team chat, sip their drinks and play games on their tabs. Tweak fidgeted like a cat in a dog kennel, but she kept to her seat. It was the best he could have hoped for.

Sinclair wandered in at two minutes past six, his black bag over his shoulder, and walked over to his regular table. He ordered his Grey Goose and settled in.

"You see your man, ladies?" Kevin asked into his mic.

"Roger," Sarah sub-vocalized, the murmured words amplified into clarity as they vibrated through her bones and into the molar her mic was snapped around.

"Give him about twenty minutes to get settled, and then you can give it a try," Kevin judged, watching their target's body language. He seemed acceptably cool and collected. No issues that he could spot. Even better, he'd slipped his bag rather clumsily under his chair.

"He's a bit diffident, so don't overwhelm him. Yvonne should be the one to start the conversation. Go for peppy new girl in town, Yve."

"Si, mis jefe." Yvonne's voice popped through the mic.

Kevin's lips twitched at the corners. "Don't channel Janice when you're talking to the poor little fellow, you'll give him a heart attack."

"You got it."

In his screen, Kevin watched as Yvonne casually stood and sauntered over to the bar. He turned down the feed to her mic to avoid being deafened when she spoke at a normal level and watched as she bought a drink, turned, took a few steps and 'accidentally' splashed it across her shoes. True to form, Sinclair jumped to his feet and helped out with a handful of paper towels. Yvonne's friendly animation was pitch perfect for the situation. Kevin nodded to himself, leaning in. He noted Tweak watching in the corner of his screen, coiled in her chair with the replacement bag gripped in her hand.

"Hold up Tweak, not yet... remember, casual. Like we practiced. Give it a minute… any second now he'll... wait, what?"

The slim man gave a bobbing nod and, almost nervously, stepped back. He resumed his seat, eyes on his tab.

In the screen Kevin watched Yvonne stand for a second too long before returning to her own seat.

"Well crap," Yvonne's voice fizzed in his ear, "what now?"

"What went wrong?" Kevin asked, head cocked as he studied the scene. He could practically hear the shrug in Yvonne's voice.

"I don't know, I said I'd buy him a drink for being such a sweetheart and he sort of blushed and mumbled and sat right back down. Said it was no big deal, that kind of thing."

Kevin ran a hand through his hair. "All right, maybe that was too forward. Sarah. In ten minutes try the tourist routine. Pull up a map and ordering app and act like you're trying to decide. Ask him if he's a regular. Make sure it looks spontaneous."

"Got it."

Kevin watched as Sarah gave it her try and cringed as her friendly overtures failed even more miserably than Yvonne's had.

"Shit." Sarah's voice crackled down the mic. "Kev, this guy's shy! How the hell do we get this kind of shitty luck?! All the gropers and weirdos on Grid, and the one guy we need to chat up is fucking *shy* around *girls*."

"Oh good God." Kevin groaned, pressing the heel of his hand to the bridge of his nose. "Damn our luck."

"Maybe he's not into girls. I can jump in?" Lazarus interjected, his mic spitting and popping in Kevin's ear. Kevin shook his head.

"No, there's no plausible way to start a natural conversation for you, Laz. We already used Tourist and chatting up isn't something you'd be any good at falsifying. Sorry, but it's true. Besides, we need you on guard and I know for a fact the man's straight. Shy as a Sunday school student apparently, but straight."

"I'm not doing it," Tweak whispered flatly.

"Of course you're not," Kevin replied in exasperation. "All right, everyone, let me think for a moment..." He slowed his breathing, eyes studying the situation.

"All right, yes... Yvonne. Come take over my position. Sinclair's met me before and he thinks I helped him out. Those are grounds for a friendly and viable conversation. I'll take a crack at it."

"Roger," Yvonne agreed, voice distorted over the mic.

Fingers tapping, Kevin glanced at the clock. They were already behind.

Ten minutes later, Yvonne slipped into his room and handed him her mic.

"Better luck than I had," she remarked ruefully.

Kevin took the time to give her a quick grin. "From your lips to God's ear."

Stepping into the bar, Kevin strolled over to buy himself a drink. He nodded at one or two people he'd made the acquaintance of on his last run and got a smile from the bartender along with his whiskey. Meticulous in his manner, he held himself at ease. Appearing casual was one of the most difficult acts to pull off, but he'd had practice. He let his unfocused gaze sweep the room for just long enough, timing it in his mind until a natural period of observation had been reached. Then he gave an affected jolt of surprise.

"William!"

Striding over, he put himself in the man's line of sight with a genuine smile. "Hi! It's good to see you out again, I was wondering if you were alright after the other day. Were you okay getting home?" He started to sit and then made a point of pausing as if absently realizing that he was breaking social norms. "Oh, is it alright if I take a seat?"

Sinclair gave him a surprisingly radiant smile. So, he had played this right. The validation of someone caring about his health was a boost to the poor little mouse.

"Oh wow, John, hi! I tried to find your office the next day, so I could send a thank you, but you weren't on the roster yet."

Kevin rolled his eyes in weary acknowledgment. "They're still processing my damn credentials. Can you believe it? I've been sitting in a hotel room twiddling my thumbs. Honestly, I'm bored out of my mind."

Sinclair grinned. "Well I can fix that. Come on, let me get you a drink to say thanks. So where are they putting you?"

He and Sinclair stood chatting away at the bar as easily as old friends, Kevin carefully maneuvering so that the smaller man was facing away from his table.

"Got it," Yvonne's voice whispered in his ear, nearly drowned by Sinclair's discussion of his boss's reaction to the sick day he'd taken.

By the time they took a seat at Sinclair's table, Tweak was long out of sight. Kevin chatted away happily with the techie, buying the next round. Really, this wasn't bad at all. Sinclair was a pleasant, intelligent and fairly educated man. He even got a joke about Diogenes. It would have been a nice evening if he hadn't had a constant stream of Tweak's grumbled commentary coming through one ear.

"Kay...in... password worked."

"Okay, main p-page...balls. He l-likes the visual setup. I hate the visual setup..."

"Kay, working on it."

"You fucker... suck a bag of ass..."

"Wait a sec... hah! Fucker."

"Okay attached..."

"Shit on a biscuit. Have to route around validation r-requirement.... Yeah, there."

"I got it! I got it. It just went out!"

Kevin's chest expanded. Since it wasn't completely out of sync with the conversation, he allowed himself to grin.

"Okay Kev get the guy out of his chair," Yvonne's voice muttered in his ear. "Tweak, wait until I give the okay."

"Gotcha."

Kevin brought the conversation to a natural end. "You know I'd better get back to my room, I've got an eight a.m. meeting tomorrow," he remarked, feigning a suppressed yawn. "What a month. But hey, grab a shot at the bar with me for the road?"

"Sounds good, I'll buy." Sinclair agreed with a grin.

Out of the corner of his eye, he could just see Tweak drop by the seat and tie her boot, then grab her bag back up. Since it was identical in every respect to Sinclair's, even the careful camera watcher wouldn't spot much in a busy bar like this.

Perfect.

He downed the last of his shot and turned to give Sinclair a polite goodbye, when everything went to hell. There was a scuffle, a yelp, then a high scream and the sound of something heavy thumping into the ground. Turning, Kevin felt his gut flash freeze.

Tweak had just laid a guy out.

"Laz," he sub-vocalized. "Flashbangs. Now. Brace yourselves everybody."

"Roger," Lazarus's flat voice muttered through the resonating mic.

Kevin closed his eyes. The world flashed into whiteness.

Startled shrieks filled the room. Kevin let himself be swept up in the flow of the crowd and out into the chilly night. The ads outside went insane as people flooded into the street. The night filled with random color and clattering advertising jingles.

"Regroup in the southeast corner," he murmured.

"That m-m-m-mean turn r-right or l-l-left?" Tweak's voice stammered out. Kevin repressed a sigh.

"Left, Tweak. Come out the front door and turn left." *I will not kill her, it would be unethical.* He repeated the sentence like a mantra, using it as a focus. *I will not kill her, it would be unethical. I will not kill her, it would be unethical.*

Coughing and waving at the smoke with everyone else, he made a show of stumbling over to the building corner, where Sarah and a very shamefaced Tweak stood, sugar plum faeries floating around them. "R-run?" Tweak whispered.

Kevin shook his head. "Walk. We *walk* away, quickly and casually, while everyone else is walking about in confusion. And then we get the hell out. Running people are chased, Tweak."

"We'll cover your back." Lazarus remarked. Kevin nodded as Yvonne joined them. "I've got point."

"Hunh?" Tweak turned her head as if it were on a spring. She jumped as a giant snowflake floated down on her left. "Stay beside me, between the guys." Sarah stated.

They turned the corner just as EagleCorp drones descended into the welter of people and holograms, speakers blaring, 'Please stay calm and remain in place!'

"So, what the hell?" Sarah asked as they feverishly packed what little they'd brought. Tweak pulled her coat tighter around herself. Finally, she sighed.

"S-some g-g-guy grabbed m-my ass. S-s-surprised m-me. S-s-sorry."

"Sorry doesn't get us out of here," Kevin remarked shortly. Yvonne caught his eye and shook her head. He reined himself in with an effort. "But for what it's worth you did fairly well up to that point on the covert front. Your coding, of course, is impeccable as usual. That goes without saying," he tacked on grudgingly. He even dredged a smile from somewhere. To his surprise, Tweak returned it.

"C-can we g-g-go b-b-back n-now?"

Kevin nodded. "Yes, we can go home. But let's change our clothes and head out separately. Tweak, with me. Yve, run with Laz. Sarah? You all right running alone?"

"No worries." Sarah bobbed her head.

They shoved Tweak into a heavy blue hoodie and gave Sarah her black jacket for the ride home. Kevin sent Topher a pickup message the second they were outside the Tech Center's gates.

He could be wrong, but he was fairly sure that he could already see signs of their work on their walk to the train station. Too many people were staring at their tabs with expressions of shock for pure coincidence to be in play. One woman froze nearly in front of them, shaking her head with her hand over her mouth. They had to step around her, which put them in the range of an advert that made Tweak jump a mile.

"Stick close, Tweak," he murmured as they boarded the train along with the rest of the nondescript crowd. He wasn't about to lose the little hellion now.

"'Kay," Tweak whispered. Surprised by the docile answer, Kevin glanced down. He realized that she was trembling.

His anger melted in that realization much like winter ice in the sun: unevenly diminishing but shrinking all the same.

Tweak had been terrified this entire time. She hadn't acted out, had she?

She'd cracked.

Reaching into his pocket once they'd found seats, he rattled a bottle just out of touching range. Over their heads, holographic snow fell from the ceiling. The ubiquitous music played incessantly.

"Brought these for you, just in case."

Tweak shot him a half-hearted glare, but she took the bottle and slipped an anti-anxiety pill under her tongue. Slowly, her little body relaxed. She risked a glance at him.

"T-thanks."

He managed the tiniest of smiles.

"Think nothing of it. But next time, do us all a favor. Carry your own supply and take the things beforehand. Not afterwards."

Looking away, Tweak nodded. "Yeah. I w-will."

A smiley face ad bloomed out of the wall to leer at them, and Kevin closed his eyes. He would be so glad to get home.

A bleary-eyed Topher was there to pick them up when they climbed out of the tunnel, the truck idling behind him. He grabbed Kevin in a bone-crushing hug the minute the older man was in reach. Grinning, Kevin returned the hug, slapping the other man on the back.

"It already showing up?"

"You broke the fucking 'net! Come on, we gotta get Sarah, but holy shit! Holy shit!"

"Holy shit indeed," Kevin chuckled, following the junior transport specialist to the truck with half an eye on Tweak behind him. Lazarus punched him softly in the shoulder when he took his seat, and Yvonne grinned on his far side. Tweak squeezed into her corner of the back seat, and Yvonne turned to high-five the air. "Kid, that kicked some serious ass!"

Tweak shrugged, but a smile was playing on her lips. "Yeah, I guess. Wait till we see the n-news. Not a kid." Then she blinked as if a thought had struck her and raised her eyes. "Um... t-thanks. A lot."

Sarah was leaning against a sumac tree when they pulled up, and Kevin hopped out and bowed her into the truck. "My lady, your carriage awaits."

Sarah laughed. "You jackass." Crossing the space, she grabbed him in a hug.

"We did it."

"We did," Kevin agreed.

Stepping back, Sarah pointed a finger at the sky. "Check it out."

Looking up, Kevin blinked as cold wetness dabbled his face. He laughed. "Snow. It's starting to snow."

In that moment, he couldn't have asked for more.

It was nearly six in the morning when they pulled into their own garage, and Kevin's eyelids felt like they had lead weights attached to them. But his blood was fizzing. He leaned over and shook Sarah's shoulder. "Sarah, we're home. Come on."

The woman curled a little deeper into her wife's lap. Kevin smiled tiredly. Yvonne stroked Sarah's black hair. "C'mon hon. Up and at 'em."

Lazarus glanced into the back seat. "Uh, guys? How're we gonna wake Tweak up without touching—"

"Immawake," Tweak mumbled blearily in the back.

"You guys gotta see the news," Topher interjected. Kevin gave him a weary smile.

"Record it for us Toph, everybody's knackered. We need some sleep."

"No—" Tweak managed, yawning wide enough to crack her jaw, "I w-want to see how it's going down."

"I'm in." Sarah added blearily. "C'mon guys."

Half-awake, the team wandered down the hall. Yvonne flopped down the moment she reached the rec room, lying across half the couch. Sarah curled up against her. Kevin pillowed his head on Sarah's thigh, letting his long legs hang over the arm of the couch. Lazarus took a seat on the floor by the girls' heads, flicking on the screen. Tweak leaned against the wall.

They didn't have to look long to find a broadcast. The news anchor who was usually so clean and neat looked haggard in this shot. Behind him, an AgCo factory was burning. Running people cut black silhouettes into the firelight and the pre-dawn sky. Drones sent swords of bright light scything through the dark.

"—social media, clearly faked by anarchist elements, nevertheless has convinced a number of—"

Lazarus changed the channel. Another stark commentator's face. A march in the streets of The Pearl.

"—disgruntled employees are accusing ArgusCo of mistreating human remains in unacceptable ways based on a viral set of videos that appeared last night. Since the unverified films appeared, there has been—"

"Fuck yes," Tweak muttered.

"I'll second that," Kevin agreed, fighting to keep his eyes open.

Another channel. Another shot of the burning pet food factory. Kevin heard Sarah start to snore.

Through half-closed eyes, the fire on the screen was beautiful.

The flame followed him into dreams, unwavering.

Aidan's tab woke him at five in the morning with a buzz that nearly sent him through the roof. He sat up with a jolt and winced as his entire body let him know that it didn't appreciate being asleep in a desk chair. Shit. He'd fallen asleep in his office waiting for the team to signal their return. How the hell had he fallen asleep? He scrambled for the buzzing tab.

Message Incoming. Sector Commander. Message Incoming

Aidan accepted the message.

Message Handle: Sector40COM

Message: I want to see you in person by 1100 for a full debrief. Congratulate your team, then get up here.

Aidan jumped to his feet and headed for his room at a jog, brain on autopilot. Wash up. Get changed. Get clean. Get ready. Officer wants your attendance.

The words sank in as he went through the motions. *Congratulate your crew.* Thank God. They'd pulled it off.

Stopping at the canteen, he grabbed two pieces of bread, spread them with peanut butter and jammed them into a makeshift sandwich, stuffing them into his mouth as he moved.

The only thing that stopped him was the sound of the TV in the rec room. Who the hell was up this early?

He glanced in as he passed. His feet stilled.

Sarah and Yvonne were cuddled on the couch, Kevin lying with his head pillowed on their legs. Lazarus sat on the floor with his head resting on Sarah's thigh. The four of them lay like little kids at naptime, dead to the world.

For a moment Aidan stood and watched his people sleep. He realized that he was smiling.

"Good job, guys," he whispered in the breathing quiet.

Giving himself a shake, he turned and headed for the garage, pulling up the news on his tab as he walked.

"Headly, this officer requested a meeting with you. Take a seat."

Aidan studied the stringy woman sitting beside his Commander as he took his seat. Two in-person meetings in two days. That had to mean this woman was important. Had he seen her before? Not that he could remember. She studied him with unreadable eyes. Was this good? Bad?

"Yes sir?"

Magnum inclined his head to the woman, who flipped her jacket's lapel back to show her rank badge. Aidan's brain froze.

"Co-Wy Regional Commander Hall, Headly. Heard good things about your work."

"Y-yes ma'am. Thank you, ma'am," Aidan stuttered. The woman smiled tightly, weathered face pulling into a web of lines around an old scar in her right cheek.

"At ease, son. I've been watching the news. A series of vids that are unquestionably real going out to everybody in this country. Magnum said it could work, but I had my doubts. Thanks for proving them wrong."

Aidan bobbed his head. "Yes ma'am. Thank you, ma'am."

Holy shit. The Commander who oversaw all of the Co-Wy region and every base in it. Was talking to him. Holy shit.

He didn't know whether he wanted to grin or turn and run, but so far, the odds were in favor of grinning. She was *smiling* at him.

"You been watching the news, Headly?"

"Yes ma'am... well, my subordinates have. They've been really enthusiastic about it."

Enthusiastic didn't even begin to cover it. Between the beginning of the Winter Holiday and the stunt they'd pulled off, the last day at base had been one long party. When the team wasn't watching the news with their tabs in one hand, they were leaning over Tweak's shoulders in the coding room to see the Social Feed in more detail. From what they could see, they'd pretty much broken the Net. The feeds were exploding with calls to fight back against every Corporation. AgCo had shut its feed down by midnight.

The regional commander nodded. "They've got something to be enthusiastic about. You've seen the news about the protest marches?"

"Six across the country at last count ma'am," Aidan agreed.

"Seven today," Magnum corrected gravely. "And given that there hasn't been a civilian protest march in thirty years, that's something to pay attention to. Of course, the Corps have labeled them paid actors, disgruntled employees fired for poor productivity, unfit social elements, even anarcho-terrorists. Whatever suits their narrative. That anarcho-terrorist bit was AgCo. Color me surprised." He smirked grimly.

"Unfortunately, there have already been deaths," Commander Hall added quietly. "EagleCorp has cracked down hard on every physical sign of protest. But what they're doing is just stoking the fire.

TechoCo has tried to take the Feeds down twice for 'maintenance,' but they're not able to eradicate the Folder. It simply propagates from a new source and starts spreading virally again each time they try. It even made it past the firewalls and out of the country, which means it's here to stay. That said, we're expecting that security will come down like a hammer for the next six months. You'll want to bear that in mind, Base Commander."

"Yes ma'am," Aidan agreed, his brain numb.

The woman stood. "And now for what I came here to do. Stand up Headly."

Feeling like his body was being directed by someone else, Aidan stood. This entire situation was surreal beyond belief.

Picking up the box sitting on the desk, Regional Commander Hall opened it. Seven medals gleamed in the office light.

"Commander Aidan Headly, you and your operational team are regionally commended for work that tangibly aids the Force." Taking one medal, she pinned it to Aidan's lapel and shook his hand.

"A file has been sent to your tab with a holo of my formal speech of thanks for your crew. But I wanted to meet you in person. Next time I've got something big in mind, I know which base to call."

Well shit. That's not good, his panicky mind whispered. He told it to shut up and smiled.

"It's an honor, ma'am. Thank you, ma'am."

It was nearly sunset by the time he got home again. The garage door rattled up, and Aidan started to pull the truck in on reflex. Then he stomped on the brake.

"What the... holy shit already?"

Six stockbots lay splayed out inside the garage, tended by Yvonne, Kevin, Dozer and Topher. Janice was already half buried in one, Blake taking notes beside her.

Aidan grinned. Pulling the truck to the side of the garage under the slick-tarp, he pulled its charge cable to an external plug, grabbed the box from the passenger seat and walked inside.

"Holy shit, you guys got them here already?"

"For the amount of money we spent they should have arrived *yesterday*." Blake replied irritably, tapping at his tab. "Okay, next VIN." Sticking her head in the next machine in line, Janice rattled off a series of numbers. "Last one, all got what Tip said they got." "They'd better," Blake remarked sourly, "because I'm *feeding* the next Grapevine operative who tries to rip us off into his own threshing machine."

Kevin glanced up from his own inspection of one of the machines and smirked. "You know this is the season of forgiveness, right?"

"Bite me, little boy."

"I respectfully decline, o' sage master of the ages."

Stepping across the room, Kevin pecked Aidan's cheek. "Welcome home. You're just in time for the festivities."

Aidan blinked. "What? I thought we'd already had the party."

Kevin pressed a finger to his lips in a 'shush' gesture, smirking. "You'll find out."

Janice guffawed, dusted her hands off and crossed the garage. "We'll have these up an' redesigned for seed plantin' soon. What you got there?"

Aidan glanced down and smiled, tucking the box under his arm. "You'll see at dinner. I can keep secrets too."

Janice eyed him. "Uh-huh. Anyway, c'mon. Need to run you through some things."

Aidan followed her inside. He blinked as high singing came ricocheting down the hall.

"Deck the halls with balls of holly, fa la la la la!"

"It's the season to be jolly, fa la la la la!"

Aidan blinked. "The hell?"

At first glance it looked like a misshapen animal with a red head and green body. After a moment of squinting, he picked out rudimentary leaves. The kids must have free-hand drawn the design into the 3-D printer's input. Up and down the hall, a straggling line of equally weird figures had been stuck to the wall with putty.

Janice burst out laughing. "Oh sweet Jesus screwing the donkey he rode in on, you two's scrubbin' these walls later right?"

"Sure Janice!" Dilly's high voice agreed happily. "Just like before!"

Janice shook her head, the biggest grin Aidan had ever seen her wear on her lips. "Okay, okay, only ask next time you use my putty, you got that? I'm gonna need more after this. Go on, finish up."

Janice caught him looking and rolled her eyes, smirking. "They always get like this 'bout this time. C'mon, your office or mine?"

"Let's do mine," Aidan suggested.

"Jus' wanted to remind you 'bout the big shutdown an' defrag of the system, kicks in tonight," Janice remarked easily, dropping into a chair once they'd reached Aidan's office. "All the safety an' life support programs'll keep runnin', the usual drill. But we got an older mainframe. You ain't gonna be able to log into the work computers for anything else for 'bout two days startin' tonight. You did clear it," she added, watching his face.

Aidan winced with the reminder. He'd totally forgotten that was starting tonight in the middle of everything else. Two days of playing sitting ducks with their defenses up and nothing else running. It had to be done once a year on every base, but it was as bad as a moving day for everyone's nerves.

"Right... thanks for the reminder. Winter Holiday's a great time to do this, we don't have much of a workload."

"Yeah, 'bout that." Janice leaned back in her chair, crossing her legs over one of its arms. "We got a tradition on this base to keep everybody from goin' batshit durin' defrag. Used to take a full week, but with Tweak helpin' me we got it down to lessn' two days an' that's great. All the same, the tradition's worth keepin'. We didn't go all out 'cause of Taylor bein' sick last year, but I'm thinkin' this year is gonna be big. If you wanna get in on it... now, I didn't tell you any of this, you got me? It's s'posed to be a surprise."

Aidan looked at her, not bothering to hide his confusion. "Um. Sure? This have anything to do with the weirdness in the hall?"

"I ain't tellin' you shit," Janice declared, holding her arms out as if he'd just pointed a gun at her. "All I'm tellin' you is….well, Kevin's a sappy lil' bastard, an' I get the feelin' you an' him are gettin' serious. You want him to know that, make him somethin' like you would if it were his birthday. Somethin' that'll make him grin, you get it? That's all I'm sayin'.'"

Aidan's brow furrowed. "Uh... right. And you didn't tell me shit. And I guess pressing for more information would get me cussed out?"

Janice's lips quirked up in a wry smirk. "See, you're learnin'.'"

Aidan sighed, raking a hand through his hair.

"Janice, this isn't going to get us in trouble is it? Am I going to have to write anybody up?"

"Why, you lil' chickenshit. Chill!" Janice laughed. "No, we ain't in trouble. This ain't a prank. 'S just a morale thing. Just go with it will you?"

Aidan studied her face. After a moment, he smirked. "Is it too late to put in for a transfer?"

Janice rolled her eyes, grinning. "Just get somethin' together, dumbass. It ain't that hard, an' you'll be glad y'did later."

Aidan chuckled weakly. "Yeah, yeah. Thanks for the head's up."

Smirking, Janice flipped a lazy salute as she stood. "Oh, an' by the way, the decorations go right back in supply; don't get your boxers in a twist." Then she was out the door and down the hall, the sound of her chuckle dying away with the sound of her boots. Somewhere else in the drafty halls, someone was singing.

Shaking his head, Aidan found himself smiling. He lifted the box of medals, grabbed his tab, and stepped out into the hall.

He had commendations to give out.

Turn the page for a sneak peek at the Wildcard's next adventure

"Okay Aidan, I'm going to ask you to start counting down from a hundred out loud."

Aidan focused on the surgeon's eyes, crinkled in a smile above her mask. The cool weight of the micro-injector pressed against the skin of his throat. "A hundred..."

Holy crap, this is actually happening...still can't believe it...

"Ninety-nine..."

Almost two months late, but still...holy crap...

"Ninety-eight..."

Please. Please let this work out...

"Ninety-seven..."

Aidan could barely feel his lips moving. He seemed to be drifting away from his body, only just aware of it.

God I hope there's no drone passes while they're working...

"Ninety-six..."

The world around him lost reality, growing distant. Aidan closed his eyes.

Man I hope...

this…

works…

Aidan woke slowly, letting the world fade into focus around him. Sound came first. People talking far off. Med-bay machinery, giving cheery blips and quiet whirs. Rustling cloth.

It took work to peel his eyes open and blink at the ceiling. What he could see was, mostly, white. Based on the size of the corner where the ceiling met the wall, it was a small room. He let his eyes drift closed and swallowed, trying to wet his dry mouth.

"Hey." Long, slim fingers slipped between his, squeezing gently. Aidan's heart expanded.

"Hey Kev." The words sounded odd in his ears, fuzzy around the edges.

"The medic said you'd be thirsty. Could you use some water?" His boyfriend asked quietly.

It took Aidan a few seconds to process the question. He nodded against the pillow and opened his eyes, trying for a smile. Kevin gave one of his heartbreak-sweet little smiles in reply. In the light coming down from the overhead lamps, he looked like a statue made from copper and marble. Those outdated glasses he liked so much sat on his nose like graffiti on a painting.

Kevin lifted a covered mug with a straw sticking out of it, hitting the button that sat the bed up just a little.

"Here. Just sip it, don't get enthusiastic," he murmured, pressing the straw against Aidan's lips. Aidan took a sip of the lukewarm water. It tasted odd, but he didn't know if that was courtesy of different water-recycling techniques used up here at the big Regional base, or the last of the painkillers.

Funny what your brain decided to focus on when it was free-wheeling.

Eyes half-closed, he took in the room. Small, white, sparse. A cabinet and workstation setup extruded from the far wall. A private room. That was weird. It was warm—nice change, their base was cold right now—and quiet. The beeping of the bed's sensory panel was comforting.

He shifted. He was dressed in something soft, loose and cozy. *Robe*, he decided eventually.

A holo panel gently sizzled into being, displaying his condition and full body scan in pastel colors. The sites where the slick white auto-pads were at work over the operational incisions across his chest and between his legs were outlined in soft blue.

"Good morning," the speaker above the bed intoned softly. "Your procedures of simultaneous mammoplasty with reduction, full hysterectomy and colpocleisis were performed successfully." Aidan's ears caught the pause as the automated voice stumbled, taking time to pull up his surgery record from Regional Medical's information bank. But you couldn't expect too much from the third-hand surplus tech that their Force could get its hands on. It was better than nothing.

"Your projected recovery is optimal," the program interface continued, "your current care: post-operative rest. Nerve block treatment. Delivery method: short duration nanoid conglomerate. Tissue and nerve regeneration treatment. Delivery method: Automatic Tissue Reconstruction Pads. Pertinent issue detected: slightly elevated cortisol level. Pertinent issue detected: minor dehydration. Call aid?"

"No, thank you." Kevin stated, loudly and clearly. The screen image displayed the Force star symbol as it softly dissolved.

"Your Automatic Tissue Reconstruction Pads are currently doing their work," the automated voice whispered. "Your body is processing general anesthesia. Drowsiness is normal at this time. Please relax and allow healing to proceed."

Kevin smiled and pulled his chair a little closer to the bed, brushing Aidan's hair back from his eyes. His hand cupped Aidan's cheek. "Looks like everything's squared away," the redhead remarked. "How do you feel? Or is that a stupid question?"

Aidan pressed his cheek into Kevin's hand and closed his eyes, enjoying the moment of comfort. "Feel like'm floating…"

"You look like you're high as a kite," Kevin replied gently, his smile soft. "Does anything hurt at all? I can get the surgeon…"

Aidan shook his head against the pillow. "Nah. Can't…feel much. Sorta numb."

He tried to prop himself up and take another sip of water on his own. Well, that and get a look at himself. The readout said he was in good shape, but he wanted to *see*.

Kevin's hands pressed gently against his shoulders. "Ah, you might not want to try that. The internal tissue scaffolds and the ligatures need to be kept still if they're going to integrate with your tissues, and you shouldn't stress surgical auto-pads until they've laid down a few layers of tissue."

Aidan smiled weakly. "Guess you'd know. Help me out here?" Kevin held the straw until he'd drunk his fill. Aidan watched as his boyfriend glanced behind him to make sure the door was closed, his body moving with a grace that was half logistics training and half crazy-good genetic tailoring. Satisfied that they were alone, the pale redhead leaned over. Kevin's lips brushed his.

"The surgeon said you might need a little more sleep; your body's cleaning out quite the chemical cocktail."

Aidan thought about protesting, but the words jumbled in his mind. So he smiled and mumbled an agreement, fumbling for Kevin's hand as he slid back into sleep.

Join the Wildcards' next adventure wherever books are sold

A Note From the Commander:
If you're struggling, you're not alone. Reach out.

Hi. Aidan here. You guys know I'm dealing with some crap, and I bet I'm not the only one. But in your world, there's a lot of resources if you're dealing with anxiety, depression and/or LGBT issues in the USA.

Crisis Text Line

Text 741-741 anywhere, any time to talk to somebody for free when you're in a crisis. That doesn't just mean suicide: it's any painful emotion for which you need support. The first two responses are automated. They tell you that you're being connected with a Crisis Counselor and invite you to share a bit more. It usually takes less than five minutes to connect you with a Crisis Counselor.

Trevor Lifeline

If you are a young person in crisis, feeling suicidal, or in need of a safe and judgment-free place to talk, call the Trevor Lifeline at 1-866-488-7386. Or text START to678678.

Trevor Space

If you need to hang out, Trevor Space is a social networking site for lesbian, gay, bisexual, transgender, queer & questioning (LGBTQ) youth under 25 and their friends and allies.

Suicide Prevention Lifeline

1-800-273-TALK (8255)

TTY: 1-800-799-4889

Website: www. suicidepreventionlifeline. org

24- hour, toll-free, confidential suicide prevention hotline available to anyone in suicidal crisis or emotional distress. Your call is routed to the nearest crisis center in the national network of more than 150 crisis centers.

Everyone Is Gay

Everyone Is Gay is a collection of voices lending advice and support to Lesbian, Gay, Bisexual, Transgender, Questioning/Queer, Intersex, and Asexual (LGBTQIA) youth, and also offers comprehensive lists of nationwide LGBTQIA resources.

Website: http://everyoneisgay. com

SAMHSA's National Helpline

1-800-662-HELP (4357)

TTY: 1-800-487-4889

Website: www. samhsa. gov/find-help/national-helplineAlso known as the Treatment Referral Routing Service,

this helpline provides 24-hour free and confidential treatment referral and information about mental and/or substance use disorders, prevention, and recovery in English and Spanish.

Veteran's Crisis Line

1-800-273-TALK (8255)

TTY: 1-800-799-4889

Website: www. veteranscrisisline. net

Connects veterans in crisis (and their families and friends) with qualified, caring Department of Veterans Affairs responders through a confidential toll-free hotline, online chat, or text.

<u>**S. A. F. E. Alternatives**</u>

S. A. F. E. is a nationally recognized treatment approach, professional network, and educational resource base committed to helping you and others achieve an end to self- injurious behavior.

Website: https://selfinjury. com/

A Wildcards Playlist, Part 2

- R∞, "1.6.1111.1," *1111* (2013)
- Don Henley, 'Everybody Knows,' *Actual Miles: Henley's Greatest Hits (1995)*
- Smadj, "Isotrope", *Equilibriste (2000)*
- Scandroid, "Aphelion (Instrumental)," *Scandroid (Instrumentals) (2016)*
- Scandroid, "Shout," *Scandroid (Instrumentals) (2016)*
- R∞, "7T10," TTT (2018)
- Mischief Brew, 'The Lowly Carpenter,' *Smash the Windows (2005)*
- Flobots, 'Dancing in the Light of a Burning City,' *NOENEMIES (2017)*
- R.E.M., "Welcome to The Occupation," *Document (1987)*
- Flobots, "Stand Up," *Fight with Tools (2007)*
- Queen, "Another One Bites the Dust," *The Game (1980)*
- Creedence Clearwater Revival, "Fortunate Son," *Willy and the Poor Boys (1969)*
- Bon Jovi, "Have A Nice Day," *Have A Nice Day (Japan import) (2005)*

- Flogging Molly, "Requiem for A Dying Song," *Complete Control Sessions (2007)*

- The Gaslight Anthem, "Refugee," *iTunes Session (2011)*

- Mischief Brew, "The Reinvention of The Printing Press," *Smash the Windows (2005)*

- Rodrigo y Gabriela, "The Pirate Who Should Not Be," *Pirates of the Caribbean: On Stranger Tides (2011)*

- Tony Allen, "Get Together," *Black Voices (1990)*

- Peter Gabriel, "I Don't Remember," *And I'll Scratch Yours (2014)*

- Arcade Fire, "Normal Person," *Reflektor (2003)*

- Liquid Soul, "Righteous," *Liquid Soul (1996)*

- Scandroid, "Salvation Code," *Scandroid (Instrumentals) (2016)*

- R∞, "16:5:] [",][(2018)

- Oceanvs Orientalis, "Asfour," *https://soundcloud.com/oceanvsorientalis (2018)*

- Ingrid Michelson, "This is War," *Human Again (2012)*

- The Beatles, "Hey Jude," *Revolution (1968)* **Quoted On Page 74**

- Fun, "Carry On," *Some Nights* (2012) **Quoted On Page 26**

- Rick Springfield, "Walk Like A Man," *The Best of Rick Springfield (1985)*

- Joe 90, "And When I Die," *Racoon's Lunch (2000)*

- Argent, "Hold Your Head Up," *All Together Now (1972)*

- Journey, "Keep on Running," *Escape (1981)*

- Bon Jovi, "Sleep When I'm Dead," *Tokyo Road (2001)*

- R.E.M., "It's the End of The World as We Know It (And I Feel Fine)," *Document (1987)*

- Billy Joel, "Running on Ice," *The Bridge (1986)*
- The Gaslight Anthem, "Boxer," *American Slang (2010)*
- Arcade Fire, "Creature Comfort," *Everything Now (2017)*
- Anthony Rapp, "Out Out Damn Spot," *Look Around (2000)*
- Bon Jovi, "I Believe," *Keep the Faith (1992)*
- Bon Jovi, "Next 100 Years," *Tokyo Road (2001)* ***Referenced On Page 102***
- Nickelback, "If Everyone Cared," *All the Right Reasons (2005)*
- Bon Jovi, "Breathe," *Bounce (2000)*
- Poison, "Something to Believe In," *Flesh and Blood (1990)*
- Mischief Brew, "Love and Rage," *Songs From Under The Sink (2005)*
- The Gaslight Anthem, "Our Father's Sons," *Get Hurt (2014)*

<u>About The Author</u>

O. E. Tearmann lives in the shadow of the Rocky Mountains, in what may become the CO-WY Grid. They share the house with a brat in fur, a husband and a great many books. Their search engine history may garner them a call from the FBI one day. When they're not living on base 1407 they advocate for a more equitable society and more sustainable agricultural practices, participate in sundry geekdom and do their best to walk their characters' talk.

Read more and download an exclusive free short story at

aceshighjokerswild.com/read-for-free